A challenge . . . and a dream

It began with failure, loneliness, and coming face to face with extinction. Greed came to push weakness. Power came to shove pride. But a man called Coyote rose to the challenge to rediscover himself, rekindle the spark of a love nearly lost . . . and become a new kind of hero.

He would champion a cause that was both personal and universal—the battle of the seemingly insignificant individual against the invincible forces of big business and supreme government.

* * *

This is a novel of love and determination, passion and power . . . a story that races with excitement and suspense . . . a book that will have you cheering at the finale, and leaving you with a happy sense of exhilaration and joy. You'll not forget the man called Coyote!

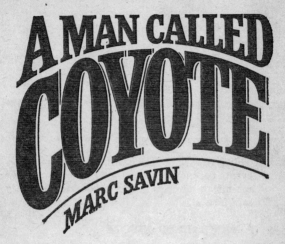

A MAN CALLED COYOTE

MARC SAVIN

PINNACLE BOOKS   LOS ANGELES

A MAN CALLED COYOTE

An original Pinnacle Books edition, published for
the first time anywhere.

First printing, July 1980

ISBN: 0-523-40500-6

Cover illustration by Bruce Minney

Printed in the United States of America

PINNACLE BOOKS, INC.
2029 Century Park East
Los Angeles, California 90067

Contents

COYOTE

Book I

Southern Colorado:

Penned

Coyote felt rooted in tradition.

The West stretched far in every direction, as it always had. The pioneers had come and gone. Now there were new people, but they still clung to the old ways. Then the old ways were gone. Only the old people remained.

And their children. Coyote was one of those. The fathers perished, the children took over the ranches. The children became ancient by fifty. They watched cable TV from Salt Lake and cursed the real world. They hummed hymns at halftime with the Tabernacle Choir, rejoined the Bronco game and died there.

Coyote was on his way back. The circuit would be his.

This was southern Colorado. The town was Trinidad. Coyote had been here only three months. He chuckled when he thought how glorious Trinidad once was. A hundred years earlier, on a bet, a mountain man named Beckwurth and fifty Crow Indians raided the Spanish settlements around Los Angeles of more than 10,000 horses, drove them across Raton Pass, across the desert, into Fort Bent, here in once glorious southern Colorado.

Today made three months.

Today, Coyote thought vividly about the outside. Some days everything remained dark, without light, but today when he woke he wandered outside and stayed there.

Outside. Coyote turned to the Rocky Mountains, pictured the Stonewall, a gigantic wall of stone outcropping from the Rockies, which vanished and reappeared with the range from Alaska to South America. In Walsenburg, where he lived, the wall was a smooth perfect face of white stone, standing straight up, nearly a football field high.

Inside thoughts invaded Coyote, like an barrage of insects. Thoughts of home. Home was Walsenburg, sixty miles to the north of Trinidad, on his father's ranch.

Coyote hated the ranch. Nothing on it was his. He grew up there, stayed way too long, and that was it. The finest land in southern Colorado and you couldn't make a dime off it. Coyote didn't want to return, but he knew he would have to. To get a truck, a trailer, and a horse. He'd approach Pa with a straight investment. Lend me the money, I'll send you my winnings. This would not be a loan.

Coyote stretched, tried to remember where the old aches were on his body. But the right knee had mended. The dull ache in his shoulder, he didn't recall where it hurt. The aches he couldn't pinpoint, the ones he lived with, were no longer stiff. Why would he be sore? Coyote hadn't ridden in three years.

4

Coyote began hitting his fist into his palm. There was so much to do. Coyote chose life. He was coming back. He switched fists, went over and over again how he got here, how he would stay out. Inside again. He had to escape.

To the west was Utah. Coyote was glad the mountains were there. They kept him isolated, made him feel rural.

Coyote felt spunky, on the rise. Handsome, wiry, energetic, thirty-seven years old, Coyote felt both experinced and curious, like a little boy.

Moving south, into New Mexico, was Raton Pass. Once booming with immense coal camps, Raton was starting up again, because of America's new need for coal.

Now Coyote practically twitched with energy.

To the east, rolling foothills formed the beginnings of America's great plains, plains full of farmers who used to pay to see him ride.

He was Coyote. He was the greatest. He was famous for being crazy, wild. Look at him now. He was coming back. He had to prove himself once more, he had to be the greatest again.

To the west were the magnificent great buttes between Walsenburg and Trinidad, which formed the majestic base of the Rocky Mountains. The West stretched all around him.

Amidst all this sat one small jail, and Coyote was in it.

Thomas was a Sioux Indian from South Dakota. He had been here when they brought Coyote in three months ago. Thomas didn't mind jail. It was all right. The weather was cold. Thomas needed a rest from life. He made an excellent cellmate. For an Indian, there were worse ways to spend the winter.

It had been Coyote's second bar brawl in as many weeks, so the judge decided to put the menace behind bars. Coyote guessed it was his only way of getting away from that ranch. Now, it was summer and both prisoners were itchy to get out. Only one was.

Sadly, Thomas sat on his lower bunk, watched Coyote packing his possessions into a potato sack. Coyote felt guilty. He felt Thomas staring at him. Coyote looked sincerely at the Indian.

"Should be you getting out, 'stead of me." Coyote chuckled in contradiction. He peered out the bars looking for the guard, then stuffed the pillow and blanket from the top bunk into his potato sack. The petty thievery lit his eyes.

Thomas leaned against the wall dreaming of the outside.

A door slammed. They heard the jailer's boots coming their way. Finally, it was Coyote's turn.

"Do me a favor," Thomas spoke. Coyote had forgotten Thomas was even there. "Sure," Coyote said.

"First woman you're with on the outside. Man, I want to be there, too."

Coyote understood. "I'll think of you. I promise."

The guard's heavy steps stopped at the door to the cell. Coyote was ready to dash.

The guard came in, immediately dug into

Coyote's sack, pulled out the pillow and blanket, tossed them back onto the upper bunk. Thomas cooed at the luxury of two pillows.

The guard walked out first. Thomas tugged Coyote's arm. Coyote looked back. "Hey," Thomas told him. "You can call me up without no telephone."

<u>Out</u>

Outside the county jail, Coyote began walking north. He inhaled, sighed, let his breath out a little too quickly. He didn't feel so cocky anymore. Little rocks, sandhills under his feet, formations in the Stonewall, all began taking shapes, forms from events in his life. They touched him deep inside, made him remember. He heard the late afternoon wind sweep through the canyons. Coyote braced his knees as the wind swept the foothills. Coyote reached up. The wind stopped in his hand. He let the wind go.

There was no one to meet him. His wife didn't know he was out and his pa was too sick to pick him up. Anyway, Coyote wasn't ready to be with his wife. First, he had something to prove!

Coyote decided to walk the sixty miles to Walsenburg. He needed time to think. Could he get a roping pony? A trailer? And a truck? He would have to borrow the money from his pa. Coyote knew Pa would have cash lying around because it was getting near time to make the bank payment on the ranch. Pa was a gambler.

His ranch came closer to going under every year. Now developers were buying up all the land in southern Colorado. Since Pa refused to sell, they were trying to drive him off. If Coyote could talk Pa into parlaying a small investment into rodeo winnings, they would both come out ahead.

But not at that ranch. Coyote wouldn't work a day on it. He hated that life. After his injury, he had tried it. But it was ranching that made Coyote drunk and bitter. He could never go back to it. He had to ride.

Coyote ran up to the highway, stuck out his thumb. He had to be on his way. He would come back. He was Coyote. He had something very big to prove.

Pa Cantrell loaned Coyote the money. Coyote didn't even have to get to the why of the story, why he couldn't stay and work the ranch. Pa accepted the terms of an investment because he knew it would be his only chance to save his beloved cattle ranch.

Pa dealt on Coyote's terms because he had been a world champion and because they were the only terms laid out.

Pa dealt. Now he would have to wait for the results.

Coyote felt charged all over. He swerved wildly in and out of lanes, passing cars every chance he could. There were lots of tourists in Colorado this time of year, from New York, New Jersey, Pennsylvania. Coyote passed them all.

The battered white pickup Coyote bought was old, but it was an "8". Behind it, Coyote pulled a horse trailer. Inside the trailer rode a young, thick-thighed, over-developed quarter horse, a beautiful pony, the kind used in rodeo exclusively for calf roping.

Coyote rubbed his lips together. They were dry, the way they used to feel when he was on the circuit. He smiled for the first time in months. The memory of competition, of victory, pumped him up again. He wildly waved his fist as he passed a Winnebago. The passengers cringed, convinced he was crazy.

No more dreams. Something dramatic was happening inside his body. His mind took a new state of clarity. Clarity. While his body roared, somewhere inside, deep below his insane rush back to the top, Coyote ticked in slow motion.

Coyote remembered this feeling. It was the feeling of champions, the power to pause the rush, to slow the brain until every muscle moved the way he willed, until the muscles moved before his mind gave the command.

Behind him a sign said LEAVING WALSEN-BURG, GATEWAY TO THE SOUTHERN ROCKIES. Coyote never thought again about his father's ranch. He had been there. It had served its purpose.

She was blonde, twenty-eight, not young any more, hitching by the side of the road. Pasted to her guitar case was a placard saying DENVER.

Coyote's mind went blank. He wanted to pick her up, slowed to pick her up, then coasted twenty yards past the girl because he couldn't

11

think of a word to say when he did pick her up.

Coyote stopped, attempted to back up. Then the horse trailer scissored, so he stopped a second time, jerked the truck forward, untangling himself.

She ran up to the truck. Coyote rolled down the window, neglected to unlock the door. She tried it, assumed it was stuck.

"Hi," she said, as simple as that.

It was a tough one. Coyote couldn't think of a reply.

"Hello," he said back, hoping his voice was deep enough. Ashamed, he felt his throat quiver. They were both silent. Again she tried the handle. In the trailer, the horse moved, shaking the truck.

"Are you going to let me in?"

"Of course."

"Then open the door."

Coyote felt like a pie-eyed sheep. There was no button on the door. The truck was old. He must have looked like another dumb, tongue-tied cowboy.

He unlocked the door with the inside handle. She stepped onto the running board, hoisted herself in. Keeping her suitcase on her lap, she put her guitar case between them. The she noticed how handsome he was.

"There's not a thing back there," said Coyote, battling for confidence. "Where are you coming from?"

"Taos, New Mexico," she said.

Coyote pulled back on the highway. There was silence. She breathed a sigh of relief. They were rolling.

"You going to Denver?"

"Farther." Coyote turned to her. "To Cheyenne. You like Cheyenne?"

"I liked Sugarfoot better."

Coyote smiled a weird smile. She laughed. They both remembered the TV westerns. It was an odd joke in the middle of the prairie.

There was nothing left to do. The ice was broken. He nodded at her, she at him. Coyote goosed it from Granny to seventy-five in under ten seconds, jammed it into overdrive.

Coyote felt his confidence returning. He kept wanting to peek at himself in the rearview mirror. It had been so long since he had looked at his own face.

"Do you live around here?" she asked. In the mirror he was noticing how pale his skin was.

"Uh, yeah," he said, nodding. "I have for the last three months."

She settled in her seat, got comfortable. "Where?"

Coyote looked at her with a sardonic smile. "Trinidad County Jail."

She make a face as if she tasted bad fish. But how could she be fearful? The Spanish Peaks were disappearing behind them, to the left. Colors began appearing from everywhere as the sun began to sink. A late afternoon blue, cloudless, high-ceilinged sky stretched on to the end of her sightline, where she knew Colorado Springs would be. Big splotches of snow that never melted formed crystal islands in a sea of red clay, as the Rockies' jagged peaks turned into silhouettes.

It was impossible for them not to relax. She

smiled as this handsome cowboy took her flying north up the highway.

By the time they reached the roadside tavern, he knew a lot about her. Her car had been stolen, last time in Denver. She lived in Taos, sang in the few folk houses still around. She was hoping that this time, her stay would be extended in Denver, so she could buy another car. To Coyote, her life seemed to revolve around $200 cars.

Inside the tavern, locals were kicking and shaking on the floor. A boogie band named Hawgma was playing a humorous Jerry Jeff Walker tune. "I went to this bar, outside of Colorado Springs . . . gonna drink a case of cold Coors, hear ol' Merle Haggard sing . . . "

But the song was slowish, and every time the musicians lapsed off the beat, the locals would flounder on the dance floor. Then someone would scream, "Boogie!" at the top of his lungs, which would force the bass player, the guitarist, and the drummer to kick it up again. Obviously the band wasn't entirely schooled in local audience customs. It was great. Off to the side, two guys in from the ranches were up on stage playing Jew's harps. Nobody heard their tiny twangs, but they didn't mind.

Coyote took advantage of the slow song. He led the hitcher in, immediately took her into a corny stroll across the floor. The bartender raised his glass. He knew Coyote. So did some of the people inside.

Then somebody screamed, "Boogie, goddamn-it!" and the band started rocking and rolling

14

again, with Marshall Tucker southern rock, and Coyote was lost.

But he didn't mind. He faked it along with the rest of the locals. Nobody could dance, not disco like city people anyway, but they kicked out their cowboy boots and stomped the floor. They were young, they were from Colorado, and they knew how to get loose.

The motel room was cheesy. It made her feel sexy.

For heat there was an ancient cook stove tucked into the corner. Its pipe climbed out through the roof. Next to the stove, the proprietor placed a box of sawdust, with split pieces of wood next to it. A can of lighter fluid on the dresser top waited to ignite the sawdust.

Coyote drew the drapes, opened the window. Instead of the band, crickets now played. It was a warm summer night.

She stood close to him. He felt like an idol when she touched him first. She parted his shirt, the Western buttons clicking one by one as they snapped.

He began to stroke her back, moved his hands up and down, then over her shoulders, down to her breasts. They were tiny. They were the first breasts Coyote had felt in months. He pressed the nipples in gently with his thumbs.

She dropped her hands to his thighs. Coyote nearly jumped through the roof. Farther down, Coyote was fidgeting with his cowboy boots, trying to slip one off deftly using the other, but he was sorely out of practice.

For a second he remembered where he was.

In a small room. Her hands rubbed up and down both his thighs.

His mind darted back to jail, to that closed-in feeling.

She knew about cowboy belts, how the hook slipped in behind the buckle. She undid the metal button of his Wrangler jeans, parted the zipper. He pulled her sweatshirt over her head, managed it through her hair, let it drop back onto the motel bed. Coyote couldn't take his eyes off her.

She took him around, held him in an intense bear hug. She held him tightly, tightly. Coyote began shaking. He felt cold and sweaty at the same time. The motel walls moved closer until Coyote felt them closing in. They pushed inward around his shoulders. His head felt very, very light, then extremely heavy until he felt afraid. He began clawing for air. The ceiling began dropping. He panicked. His passion was gone. She didn't understand. He pulled away shaking. She wondered what was wrong.

Coyote was trembling with claustrophobia. "I can't stay in here."

The hitcher relaxed. She wasn't the cause. Smiling, she shook her blonde hair loose, took three tantalizing steps toward the door. She looked back. "I don't mind. Let's make love outside."

Coyote composed himself, followed. He stopped, yanked the blanket off the bed, swiped the pillow, followed her out of doors.

Coyote never quite caught up. He didn't want to. The girl wore no top, his belt was loose, his zipper apart. Coyote couldn't believe they were walking outside naked like this. He got into it. He studied the hitcher's petite body. He wanted to remember every moment of what was happening.

They stopped by a little stream, a brook practically. He spread the blanket, she lay down, beckoned him. Almost immediately they began making love, fitting together perfectly, molding into each other.

Then came jolts and jolts of sensuality, a building of sex until Coyote exploded and exploded in her and she came seconds after him. After they climaxed, Coyote stayed trembling in her for a long time.

The excitement of the stranger was over. Now they were friends, or tried to be. A slight emptiness was setting in. That lack of permanence that said, this isn't forever. Both realized their lovemaking for what it was. Both were grateful for their luck with a partner.

Coyote was thinking of something else, something funny. He leaned back on his elbows. She didn't try to intrude, stared down at his body, then at hers.

Suddenly Coyote began laughing very hard. Out of nowhere something hit him and he began cackling. He slapped the sand to the side of the blanket.

"What?" she asked in a curious, hesitant voice.

Coyote looked at her, but kept laughing. He stopped, looked at her, straightened up, then couldn't control himself and started laughing again. She waited.

Finally Coyote was able to pause. "I should tell you . . . "

Her bare breasts reflected the moonlight.

"You see, my cellmate, this Indian. I promised I'd think of him the first time I was with a woman."

She took this in, wondering. "What's so funny about that?"

Coyote responded with shortened breaths. "I'm thinking of him."

He began laughing again. She saw the humor, didn't really laugh in the same way.

Training

Coyote awakened the hitcher a lot earlier than she was used to. He got her up and on the road by sunrise. The only people on the highway this early were all-night truck drivers, still wired on three A.M. bennies, driving crazily, dominating the road. Avoiding them, Coyote drove until he found the piece of open land he was looking for. He parked on this remote corner of some rancher's land.

They got out of the truck. A raging wind tore across the prairie, whipping the buffalo grass straight up. The wind stopped, the stalks sagged, swayed undecidedly back and forth. Suddenly another wind swooped down off a canyon, stood the lush grass at attention.

Coyote led the pony from the trailer, let the horse walk, stretching his muscles. The hitcher found a comfortable spot against a fence post, watched Coyote silently saddle the horse.

Coyote mounted. It was on the horse that Coyote became a giant. He started the horse slowly, then took him into a gallop. He gently pulled back on the reins, then violently ground the pony to a stop. Coyote sprinted the pony, racing him over a distance, along a rutted road that cut through the land. Turning around, Coyote slowed the horse to a walk in some tall grass, then sprinted the pony back near the trailer, where again he cruelly ground the horse to a stop, jamming the bit back in the pony's mouth with the reins.

He started the horse, stopped him just as quickly. He started the horse, suddenly stopped him. The horse was learning its rhythm from Coyote. Coyote was the master.

The hitcher said nothing, mesmerized by it all. She noticed the horses's thigh muscles quivering. Then Coyote raced the horse again in a series of wind sprints, stopped him like a German sports car. He leaned down, talked right into the pony's ear.

Near the truck again, Coyote got off, let him graze. He barely nodded at the hitcher as he passed her on his way to the horse trailer. She had never imagined concentration so intense. He had forgotten everything else in the world.

Coyote came out with a rope, fixed one end into a lasso, the other into a slip knot. He mounted, looped the slip knot over the saddle horn, twirled the lasso.

Coyote held the horse in a tight rein, then kicked him into a start running parallel with the fence. Coyote roped a fence post, jammed the pony into a stop.

Coyote jumped off, took the pony's face in both his hands, pushed the horse ferociously backwards, putting a severe strain on the rope. That was what Coyote wanted the horse to do, hold the rope tight, pulling backwards. Coyote nodded the horse's head up and down, psyching the animal with tremendous intensity.

Coyote undid the lasso, remounted, re-roped the same fence post, screaming "Yeah, Yeah," at the horse, trying somehow to simulate crowd noise.

He did this over and over, roping the post twenty times until the horse knew instinctively to pull back on the rope the minute the post was roped.

Exhausted, Coyote climbed off, smiled at the hitcher, said, "He's good."

New York had a hum. So did Chicago. Minneapolis didn't, neither did Houston or Dallas. Now they were in Denver. Once Denver had been an overgrown cow town. Now its hum sounded like Los Angeles. Its smog belt ran along the mountains, sixty miles north of Fort Collins.

Coyote had been to all the cities. They were nice to see when you were on top. He planned to visit them all again.

The hitcher had meant a lot to him. She had pulled him back into the human race. He looked across at her, tried to get her attention, but she had her own dreams to follow.

He knew where to drop her off. He had offered three or four times to take her to the door where she was staying, but she said no, it wasn't far, she needed time to think, to be alone.

He stopped at the botton of the off-ramp. Another on-ramp faced him. She smiled fleetingly at Coyote. He leaned over, touched her cheek, kissed her forehead, then her eyelids.

"Thank you," he said. "You brought me back into this world." His face had a touch of mourning.

She touched his cheek. "No regrets, Coyote."

She got out. He watched her disappear into the city.

A Last Peace

Coyote spent the night alone, forty miles south of the Wyoming border. He worked the horse again and again. The horse was young, but his discipline was developing. After a first sadness, Coyote, like the hitcher, had no regrets. She would have been a distraction. He needed time to touch base with himself.

Coyote went over in his mind a hundred times how he would feel when they pulled the starting gate. He practiced little tricks he would need to keep him calm. He remembered the weight shift backwards he and his pony had practiced, the weight shift needed to hold a roped calf.

He was prepared in case he had to remind the horse to pull back by dismounting awkwardly, from the rear of the saddle. It would mean an extra second, but the horse was new to competition. Everything had to be prepared for.

Starting the engine, Coyote drove into the morning sun. A sleek brown antelope dashed across the road twenty yards ahead. She rubbed her belly in the tall grass, then arched her sway back, slid under the roadside fence onto the other side of the road.

Now nerves set in. His time of peace ended. Coyote began driving unevenly. The strain of impending competition was coming all at once, invading his body, shaking at his hands, making it difficult for him to steer.

Going into Wyoming was always like coming out the other side of a time warp. The rock formations at the border, statues from Mars, were light brown with shapes from outer space and holes in their hundred-foot Swiss cheese faces like photos from the moon.

A big brown cowboy riding a bucking horse was painted on a pale yellow sign. It said WEL-COME TO BIG WONDERFUL WYOMING. Things were simpler up here, more majestic, the scenery more pronounced, the ideas and concepts of the people more understandable.

When Coyote pulled into Little America for gas, the attendant was so big and powerful, he literally rocked the truck and horse trailer when he scraped the bugs off Coyote's front window.

Book II

The Arena

For Coyote, driving down Main Street, Cheyenne, was like stepping one hundred years back in time. Today was fair day. The parade had passed only a half hour before. Nobody worked except the vendors selling ice cream this hot July day. Everybody in view wore traditional Western costume. People were dressed like mountain men, gunfighters, old time prostitutes, dance hall girls, faro dealers, sheepherders, and of course, Indians.

Main Street was littered with trash. Empty beer cans had been piled in waist-high displays outside the major bars. People were proud of their consumption in Cheyenne. A banner hung high across Main Street, proclaiming WELCOME TO FRONTIER DAYS, NATION'S SECOND LARGEST RODEO. Cheyenne Frontier Days was named the "Granddaddy of 'em All." It wasn't the national championships, but the rodeo at Cheyenne was the most prestigious, the most traditional, the greatest rodeo on the circuit.

Coyote watched the spectacle, waiting, held up in the bumper-to-bumper traffic. A drunken rounder in from the ranches staggered into the hood of Coyote's battered white pickup truck. A mother, crossing the street, ignored the man, tightened her grip on her little boy's hand. So Coyote pulled his brake, led the rounder to the center divider, laid him to rest on the grass. Instinctively the drunk woke up long enough to put his hat underneath the back of his head. Then he dropped off like a log.

Once the traffic unsnarled, the Frontier Days arena was only five minutes away. A huge canopy protected the best seats from the sun. Coyote got out, took his horse from the trailer, let him stretch as he got used to the arena.

Though the seats were now empty, the younger cowboys gawked at the arena's spaciousness. Coyote wasn't fooled by their apparent greenness. Everybody who entered Frontier Days was good. As Coyote led his horse to the chutes, to practice, he paid no attention to the arena. He had been there before.

Not wanting to be recognized, Coyote pulled his hat low. He passed cowboys who were joking and jostling each other. He was tempted to stop, listen to their talk. But it was old talk. He had heard talk before.

Then someone recognized him. He heard his name come as a question from deep within a young rider's throat. Two young riders stepped aside when Coyote mounted his pony and led him into the chutes for a practice run.

Coyote sensed the other ropers watching him, seeing how his reflexes were. That was good. Coyote wanted them to be wary of him. It would take their minds off their own technique, at least for now. Because it wouldn't matter when the crowd was screaming for a record time and it was time to ride. Nobody thought of the other cowboy when the time came. Not the good riders. Not the ones who survived. They knew it was only you, your horse, and a powerful, slippery calf trying to bust down the wood slat chutes.

Over and over Coyote let his horse get used to the chutes, to busting out fast, like the quarter horse he was. The horse took well to the new environment, was soon picking up speed as he did back out on the prairie.

Then, as they trotted around the infield a final time, a nervousness set in, but not for the horse. Only Coyote felt panic. Coyote looked into the stands, imagined 10,000 people watching him. He only felt more alone, a more intense stage fright. Coyote tried not to transmit his unsure feelings into the reins.

But he couldn't help it. The fear grew worse. It was similar to claustrophobia, but there were no walls, only spaces. He was alone and very afraid. Coyote understood one thing. He needed somebody, a friend, someone to accompany him in the chutes.

He knew Wrestler would be in town for the rodeo. He knew that for a fact. He had to find Wrestler. But he had to avoid having that first drink. He couldn't break down. Not one drink. Nothing.

That night Coyote went from bar to bar, in and out, looking for Wrestler. Luckily, if Wrestler was in a bar, there would certainly be a crowd around him, so Coyote didn't have to stay long in any single bar. Coyote looked like a crazy man. He had to find Wrestler. Either find him or remain alone.

Wrestler was Pa Cantrell's oldest friend. Now sixty, Wrestler made his living following the rodeo in summer, hustling the young studs in each town, taking their money at arm wrestling. He had dozens of names, but to his friends he was simply Wrestler.

Wrestler was so smooth at winning that most of his young buck victims chalked up their loss to experience. Wrestler didn't make them look bad, he just beat everybody. Wrestler rarely lost, even to much larger men. Rarely was somebody quicker off the jump than Wrestler. He knew how and when to press an advantage. His right wrist had nerves as quiet as the nighttime. Wrestler knew when to loosen his grip or tighten it, when to make his bicep rigid in defense, or when to deceive his opponent with a limp wrist.

And when he was beaten, which was almost never, Wrestler knew the wisdom of taking his losses. He also knew how to come back for double the stakes and not get caught cheating, or how to pat a victor on the back, then whip his friends for the same stakes.

Wrestler beat many a stronger man by feigning tiredness with a limp wrist, then pounding his opponent's fist into the barroom table. He was a master. He made enough money each summer to last through the winter.

Inside Crazy Wilma's Nude Bar, Coyote found his man. Bills were piled all over a center bar table in a tiny green sea, all bet on big Davey Johnston.

Coyote called, "Hey, Wrestler!" and immediately blew Wrestler's cover.

Wrestler almost died. His right sleeve rolled up, sizing up Davey wrist to wrist, Wrestler tried to ignore the voice. But all of Davey's friends were looking at Coyote.

Annoyed, Wrestler rose, stomped across the bar to the stupid voice that called him "Wrestler" just as he was about to score. Then he saw Coyote. "Damn you fool" Wrestler said in a hushed voice. "I got every stud in this house hooked to my bait and you're calling me Wrestler! What're you doin' here, anyway? Goddamnit, I don't care."

Coyote felt horrible. Wrestler pawed with his boot, shook his head in disgust. He felt Davey's friends staring at him. "Now it looks like a choose, and I'm gonna have to let you pin me!"

Wrestler kept shaking his head, thinking of losing all that good money back at the table. He kicked at the sawdust, violently shook his head no. "Can't do it. I hates to get pinned!"

Wrestler stormed back to the action table, sat down. "Let's get to wrasslin'!"

Both men's wrists crossed. The screaming, the rooting started. Wrestler and Davey squeezed each other's hands, pumping up, until both hands swelled, turned blood red.

It began. Both exhaled. The grunting started. Wrestler could tell instantly that Davey Johnston was a holder, dependent on stamina. Wrestler decided to see if big Davey, the pride of Cheyenne, would tire. Wrestler held with

Davey for seven or eight seconds, an eternity in arm wrestling, until he could see Davey was wishing he were someplace else. Then Wrestler quietly pinned him, not making Davey look too bad.

Wrestler pocketed the bills, nodded graciously like a Chinese waiter to Davey's friends, left the table, joined Coyote in the darkness, away from the betting crowd.

Nobody followed. Davey's friends were lucky. In a bar brawl, there was nobody meaner than Coyote and Wrestler. Wrestler put his arm around Coyote, led him to a small corner table.

"O.K., boy. What you drinking?"

"Soda water."

"Soda water?" Wrestler looked Coyote up and down.

"It's like potato chips," Coyote explained. "I can't drink just one."

"You look shaky," Wrestler told him. "How long you been out?"

"Long enough to buy a roping pony and get up here."

"You're gonna ride Frontier Days?"

"You shocked?"

"You don't believe," Wrestler said, "in maybe workin' your way up? Naw, you don't believe in workin' at all."

Coyote took a dig at Wrestler. "I don't think I'm alone in that."

"O.K., but why aren't you down with your pa, at least helping him before those developers send him to his grave?"

"Wrestler, how long do I have to be responsible for my pa?"

"As long as he's alive, son."

"Working down there would be trading one prison for another."

Wrestler decided to drop his attack. He asked instead. "Does your pa know you're up here?"

"He loaned me the money for the horse."

"You took money from Pa? I don't believe you! No principles."

The barmaid came by. "Two beers," Wrestler said. "Don't worry. They're both for me." Wrestler snickered. "Only tip once that way."

No one said anything. Wrestler couldn't believe that Pa Cantrell gave the last of his money to his son for a rodeo.

"So you're entered. The first go-round's tomorrow night."

"I know."

"You gonna ease in, I hope?"

"No. I'm going for all of it."

"Why? A go-round's not the finals."

"I need the go-round purse . . . to pay back Pa."

"I figured as much. Listen to me. I'm your pa's oldest friend. I'm tellin' you it's only a go-round. Get reaccustomed, feel your way back in."

Coyote repeated. "I need the go-round purse."

Wrestler got perturbed. "What're you here for? Why'd you come and seek me out?"

"I'm shaky, Wrestler. I need you with me."

"You look real shaky."

"I'm reaching out, I need somebody with me tomorrow in the chutes. I can't go it alone."

Wrestler whistled between his teeth. "How's your horse?"

"Young, very fast. Never been in competition before. I worked him hard on the prairie."

"I'll bet you did."

"It's the best way." Coyote waited for Wrestler to say he'd be there.

"I still think it's only a go-round. You ought to play it close to the vest." The barmaid brought two beers and one soda water. Wrestler sized up Coyote. "Oh, that old man is dreaming."

"I'm a two-time world champion and I can still ride a lot better than you wrestle, you broken-down old rodeo bum. Will you be with me in the chutes tomorrow, Wrestler?"

Wrestler accusingly pointed his finger. "You fall, Coyote, you miss one rope, you are eliminated. You'll be one more nobody."

"Please, be there. To calm me."

"I'll be there. But Coyote, take my advice. Be conservative, for one time in your life."

Cheyenne

All the glory of rodeo was in Cheyenne this
warm night in late July. The arena was filled.
The most beautiful girls in Cheyenne were scattered through the crowd with their husbands.
Nobody in Wyoming stayed single past twenty.
Doctors, lawyers, bankers and stockbrokers, all
wore expensive Tony Lama cowboy boots, two-
toned, fresh-toed, unworn the rest of the working year. In the center infield, a rodeo princess,
really a vaudeville performer, performed trick
rides on her decorated pony.

The rodeo announcer also travelled the circuit, like the princess, like the clowns. He was
the best, from North Hollywood, California,
with the gravelly voice deeper than Curt Gow-
dy's. He sat high in his booth overlooking the
arena. He was ready. His voice boomed through
the public address system. "Here we go, ladies
and gentlemen, with the *granddaddy of them
all!*"

The proud crowd applauded itself, its town,
tradition, its world-famous rodeo: *"Cheyenne
Frontier Days!"*

Behind the chutes, Coyote was crazy, hyped

out of his mind. Pacing back and forth, he pounded his fist into his palm, driven by lunatic-tinged adrenalin. "I'm there, Wrestler. I can feel it. I want this go-round!" Wrestler didn't know how to calm him.

The arena applause died down. The announcer continued, "And now, opening with go-round number one, the most traditional event in rodeo. One man roping a wild calf!"

Wrestler held Coyote by the shoulders. "Don't be wild!"

"I won't be wild."

"Take it easy. Settle down!"

"I'm in the zone. I can take it. I want this go-round!" Coyote had crossed into that zone of unbearable hyperactivity coupled with deep, slow, inside clarity. Wrestler couldn't see it.

"Hey! Get a ride under your belt! Listen to me!"

"My horse! Get me my horse!"

Wrestler still tried to settle the desperate cowboy.

"Bring me my horse, goddamnit!"

Wrestler left, to lead Coyote's horse over to him.

The starter yelled down to Coyote. "Cantrell! Two in front of you!"

"Three strides!" Coyote screamed up to the starter. "I'll rope him in three strides!"

Wrestler returned. He looked up at the starter. Both men realized Coyote was insane, out of his mind with nervousness.

The first rider was propelled from the chutes by his horse. The crowd noise hushed, turned to a groan as the rider fell hard. You could tell by the new hush that the fall hurt.

The cowboy got up. Then the crowd began clapping.

"That's the way," said the announcer to the crowd. "Rodeo doesn't subsidize its cowboys. All he takes home is your appreciation." The crowd responded by clapping harder. Cheyenne had the most knowledgeable crowd in rodeo.

Coyote put his tie rope in his back pocket, tried to mount his saddled pony. But the horse wouldn't cooperate. Frightened by the crowd noise, the horse bucked unwillingly. Panicked with motion all around in front of his eyes, the horse kept bucking, then suddenly started turning in tight circles.

People backed away. Coyote fought to make the saddle.

Finally mounted, Coyote held on with his legs, fastened the slip knot of his lasso around the saddle horn. The horse paused, started bucking again. Wrestler tried to hold the pony down, but the horse kept getting away, scattering people.

"Blinders!" Wrestler yelled up. "Give him blinders!" Wrestler reached into a pile of loose equipment for blinders.

"No blinders," Coyote called down from the saddle.

Wrestler fastened the blinders anyway.

Coyote ripped them from the pony's eyes, threw them in the dust. He leaned down, talked right into the pony's ear.

The pony calmed, quieted. He heard no crowd

noise, only Coyote's soothing voice. Horse and rider were one.

Coyote steered the horse into the rear of the chute. He took his tie rope from his pocket, clenched it between his teeth.

The announcer asked the crowd, "Y'all remember the Coyote?"

Coyote waited in the chute.

The crowd began to buzz. In the chute next to him, a slippery young calf was bumping the wood slats, angrily trying to escape.

Coyote's eyes found Wrestler watching from the fence. Deliberately Coyote held three fingers in the air. Wrestler turned away.

"On the comeback, in his first event," the announcer continued. "Hasn't ridden competitively in over three years. Former two-time World Champion, from Walsenburg, Colorado, Jake, *Coyote* . . . "

The calf was let loose.

Coyote was leaning forward, anticipating, already twirling his lasso. Coyote's gate ripped open. Everything focused low. The chase was on.

For the crowd it was a blink of the eye. Coyote's horse took three magnificent strides. Coyote flung his rope. The noose caught clean around the calf's neck, dropped to its wide shoulders.

Coyote reined hard. The horse ground to a halt, held the calf stationary with its mighty thighs. Coyote leaped off, snaked along the rope, flipped the calf expertly to the ground, held it there with his body weight.

Hands flying, Coyote snatched his tie rope

from his teeth, made a half hitch around three of the calf's legs. Immediately he raised his arms to the crowd.

The electric timer said 4.1 seconds, halving the previous best time. The hushed crowd exploded with noise.

Hat in one hand, both arms raised straight, Coyote screamed *"Howwlll!"* to one side of the arena, ran to the other side of the arena, screaming *"Howwlll!"* ran around the arena giving his famous Coyote howl.

The crowd howled back. It was crazy. It was wonderful. Time stood still. His motion was blurred. Everybody was with him as Coyote climbed to the pinnacle of his world.

Coyote's second go-round ride the next day was dismal. The magic don't catch the calf, they say, and it didn't. After seventeen seconds out of the chute Coyote finally tied the sprinter. The electric scoreboard had him in third place.

For the finals, Coyote replaced flair with perfection. Wrestler noticed a different man. Coyote's concentration was intense. He didn't seemed hyped. His awareness was total.

In the chutes, Coyote leaned forward, up on his toes in the stirrups. He gripped the saddle with his thighs. His rope was twirling, whistling by the pony's ear. The horse never flinched. The pony, too, had turned professional.

Wrestler watched from the top rung of the wood fence. "Six-eight, six-eight, c'mon baby, six-eight," he said to himself. Coyote needed that time to win the finals.

The calf was let loose. Coyote's horse took off at the same time. They caught the calf ten years from the chute. The pony pulled back and held firm.

Then Coyote did a right side dismount! Nobody had done one during this rodeo. Coyote leaped off the right side, snaked along the rope. For a moment, the calf tried to get up, to shake the rope like a barracuda trying to lose a hook. But the horse instinctively wrenched back, straining its thigh muscles like steel tension wire, and rodeo fans who watched horse instead of rider marvelled.

Coyote made a lightening-fast tie, stayed down making sure the tie held, then raised his arms in total victory.

The crowd began to howl. The knew it would be close. The electric scoreboard showed 5.7 seconds, then changed its digits to 6 seconds.

Coyote did it! He won.

His horse continued unnoticed to the end of the arena. Suddenly he pulled up lame, painfully walked two limp steps, fought it off, then exited the arena walking soundly.

Coyote stood in center arena, framed in victory. Humbly, he lowered his arms, then puzzled everybody by silently leaving the arena.

Wrestler wondered what was wrong with Coyote. He ran out of the arena after him. Wrestler saw Coyote walking solemnly in the opposite direction of the congratulatory flow of well wishers. It was as if he hadn't won. People stopped to admire Coyote, to wish him the best, but Coyote never once stopped even to nod. Confused by his reactions, the people filtered back into the stands talking among themselves.

But Wrestler felt jubilant, as though he had had a part in the winning. Running, chasing after Coyote, he finally caught up. "You did it! You did it!"

Coyote walked ahead. He was miles away.

Again Wrestler came up even with him. The words gushed with happiness. "C'mon, winner. Let's catch us some fun, find some women."

Coyote stared down at Wrestler. "I've been with a woman. Now I want to be with my wife."

Coyote's body filled the phone booth. All he had was a quarter. Nervously he tried to put it in the dime slot. In the dim light, it hit Wrestler that his role with Coyote was over. He was no longer needed. He walked back in the direction of the arena.

On the outskirts of Walsenburg, deep within the starlit skies of southern Colorado, Jolene Cantrell, an intelligent-looking, clear-faced ranch lady, was cleaning up inside her small rented mobile home. A place like this got dirty so easily. Everything looked transient. A small desk in the corner, filled mostly with paperbacks, leaned against the wall. The phone rang unexpectedly. She answered it.

"Hello," she said. "Hello." No one spoke.

In the phone booth Coyote said the only thing he could think of. "Honey, I'm out."

Jolene's breath sucked deep from inside. Her answer was long in coming. "Jake?" She paused. "Where are you?"

41

"Cheyenne."

"At the rodeo?" She exploded. "What for? Your father is sick! He needs you at the ranch. What are you doing up there?"

Then she stopped. She thought to ask, "Have you even called your father?"

Coyote felt like a young boy searching for approval. He spoke haltingly. "Jolene, I rode Frontier Days."

"You what? You entered the rodeo? Jake, you don't ride, you walk backwards."

She aroused Coyote's cockiness. "No, Jolene, not this time."

Something else hit her. "Jake? How did you buy a roping pony? Where did you get the money?"

"Pa loaned me the money."

"You sonofabitch! You took money from Pa?" But she should have expected as much. With her husband, the first surprise was an indication of more shocks to come. "Jake, how could you ask Pa to get you started? These developers are trying to break him. You know that!"

All her years of frustration with this man boiled over like stale water in day-old coffee grounds. She knew now she could never go back to him. He hadn't answered.

"Jake, goddamnit! Answer me!"

There was a pause. She waited. She thought she heard a chuckle at the other end.

"Jolene, I won."

"Oh my God," she muttered, then sunk back in the chair.

"I took the whole damn Frontier Days. I

won! I'll pay Pa back tomorrow. I took it all. We're on top of the world!"

"We've been there before. I didn't like it." Coyote's drunks were fresh on her mind.

"Jolene, I'm not drinking, and I'm not celebrating." In the phone booth, Coyote stood tall and proud. "Honey, I want you lying next to me."

Five minutes before she had been another single woman too old for the young men. Now her husband wanted her with him.

He asked, "Will you meet me? At the Denver Rodeo?"

"When?" She didn't mean to ask when. Not so soon. She needed time to think.

"Jake," she said. "I've got . . . "

Who was she kidding? He still had the magic. She fell for the dream once more. Still, she paused.

"Jolene. You got a man down there?"

Her trailor was so devoid of anything male that his question was humorous.

"No," she said.

"Well, you got one up here."

The Cantrell ranch house sat in a valley at the base of the mountains with an expanse of rolling green foothill land. It provided lush grazing in the spring, once the wind blew away the snowpack. During the summer, until fall when they were shipped to the packing houses in Chicago, the 600 Cantrell cattle grazed in the high meadows of the Rockies.

At either end of the valley, both north and south, the Cantrell land rose in ridges, both of which were boundary lines. The land was big. Pa wasn't sure how many acres but it was more than 1,000.

A railroad track passed the Cantrell ranch. Most ranchers weren't that lucky and had to truck their herd to a railhead, if there was one, at exorbitant prices.

But ranching, family ranching, was dying and Pa Cantrell knew no way to rejuvenate it. Prices on his level were set by the giants in Chicago, the meat packers. This year it was around forty cents a pound of beef. On the market shelf, averaged out between hamburger and steak, beef cost $1.50 a pound, over triple what Pa had to sell it for, and all that had been done was to transport the cows, kill them, and butcher them, which Pa Cantrell could do with a pint of whiskey and a dull knife.

The giants were content to keep their mouths closed and squeeze out the small rancher rather than complain and risk the chance of a wildcat trucker strike. For the truckers were powerful and charged whatever rates they wanted for shipping livestock. There was an old axiom that those in power stay in power unless there is a unified, opposing force. And the ranchers weren't it.

So the giants squeezed their profits from people like Pa Cantrell. And if he went under? There were other giants ready to steal the land and raise cattle their own way. They called it agribusiness.

But Pa Cantrell thought he had a way out and took it.

Nervously he listened to the transistor radio

for the results of Frontier Days, but the local news had nothing. Maybe the national news would broadcast the results. Pa switched stations, waiting for the nine o'clock news.

Pa Cantrell was an old groveller. He cut every corner to make a buck, but corners were wearing thin. Today he had to let his only ranch hand go. Until help came from his son, the cattle would have to graze unattended. That was O.K. The cows could graze until fall without supervision.

In fact Pa was glad in a way to let his help go. A ranch was a family business. It couldn't be run by hiring other people. But he couldn't understand why the life here turned his boy into a drunk. In a life full of things he understood, why his boy couldn't accept ranching hurt and baffled Pa. There were stripes on the back of a chipmunk, to remind the animal where he came from, who he was. Same with a man. A man can't forget his past. He just can't do it. So why did his boy keep trying to be a gypsy? A rodeo gypsy past his prime? Pa didn't know that either. But if Jake could keep the ranch alive with rodeo winnings, then he'd be worth something. Pa could work his understanding around that. At least he had raised a fighter. He'd take a fighter over anything.

So Pa settled into a country song on the radio, quit thinking about anything until the nine o'clock news. He was running out of patience. Pa had Parkinson's disease. He was also running out of life.

Then Jolene burst in. "Pa, what are you doing?"

"Screwin' Brigitte Bardot." Pa looked around

the room. Nothing was different. "What do you mean?"

Jolene put her hands on her hips. "You amaze me. Your banknote is overdue, they're pushing you off your ranch, you have no help, you can't afford help, yet you take your savings for winter feed and loan it to Jake for a horse!"

Pa was startled. "You heard from Jake?"

Jolene nodded coyly, turned to the sink. "You want coffee, Pa Cantrell?"

She decided to make him wait for the news. Pa growled. "I can't eat sugar, saccharin gives ya cancer, cream is bad for my heart and you know I hate black coffee. Now tell me what he said!"

"He's in love, Pa."

"Aw, c'mon. What?" Then Pa's heart felt for Jolene. "I'm sorry . . . aw, Jesus."

Jolene dropped a bomb. "With me, Pa. He wants me to meet him in Denver."

Pa was taken aback. "In Denver? What's in Denver?"

Jolene stirred instant coffee for herself. "A rodeo."

Pa asked, "You still love him, don't you? What're you talking about?" He pounded the table. "Another rodeo? You're dancin' with me, girl. You talked to him." Pa was sweating. "Tell me how he did. For Christ's sake! Did he win?"

"Everything in sight."

In his imagination Pa clicked his heels. He saw Jolene smile. He was pleased that she understood his gamble with the money.

"My God. You still love him, don't you?"

Jolene looked as if she probably did.

"Then grab him while he's on top, girl, 'n do your damndest to keep him there."

Being on the road was like a vacation for Jolene. Since Jake did the valves last year her station wagon ran worry free. She looked at the scenery along Interstate 25. What a sensation, to drive along the Rockies!

Then near Denver her anxieties returned. If Jake was drinking, if he had a bottle stashed anywhere, she would turn around and go home. She'd forget Pa, she'd forget her marriage, she would start all over again and live for herself. As she hit city traffic she made a pact with herself. If Coyote had changed then she'd stay with him. She'd nurse him through the circuit, listen to him complain, and tie his aching muscles with bandages. She would have a husband and Pa could keep his ranch. If he could beat those developers, Pa might live another twenty years. It meant that much to him. Jolene steered with her knee. O.K., she'd be the woman behind the man. The days on the circuit would be hard, but she would receive her credit when Jake knew he had a place to come home to. Now, she wondered, what would he do for her?

The hands on the front of her body woke her up, then sent her into shivers. They made her crazy. It had been so long since she'd had a man. When Coyote's hands pressed in on her nipples, she thought she was going to explode.

They let up, thank God. She started spinning.

47

She loved a man's virile instrument when it was hard like that. She pulled Coyote into her, and started coming right away. When her husband began grunting, pumping her, rubbing against her, powerfully holding her shoulders, she began spinning again. She didn't stop until she couldn't remember when.

Later that night, Jolene saw her husband watching her in the dim light of the neon sign outside the motel room. He looked so calm and peaceful, his eyes focused, watching, learning about his wife again.

She hugged him to make sure he was really there.

He was. She let him loose. Then she ruined the moment. "God, you were so vicious leading up to that bar brawl in Trinidad."

Why did she start up? She didn't know. So she repeated her question. "Why did you start it, Jake? You did start it."

"I started it. I meant to. It didn't even matter against who. But, Jolene, that wasn't me. It was the liquor, and that life. I can't retire." He touched her. "Jolene, I'm dried out now, so know this about me if you forget everything else. I can't live on that ranch. I'm not a rancher, I'm not a shitkicker. I hate it. It's all set out! Every day, the same!"

"But Jake, you're too old for rodeo."

"I can come back! I am back!"

"Jake, you know I need something to mold, and shape, and call my own. You know that. Not now . . . but when you're finished riding, I'll need that security."

Coyote moved his feet under the bedspread. "We'll worry about it then."

"I want, I need to always know that the ranch is there."

Coyote waved his arm. "That ranch'll always be there."

"No it won't. They're really trying to push Pa off it. They've bought up everything around him."

"He'll keep the ranch."

"You make sure of that, Jake Cantrell."

He nodded. She smiled at him. They had had this conversation before. He took her lightly by the shoulders.

"Look, I will continue to help Pa, in my own way."

"O.K."

"But don't ever expect me to work that land. Respect your husband's dream. That's all I ask."

He lay back. So did she. He thought of the big times.

"Damn, in rodeo we eat well."

"If we eat at all."

He grinned. She grinned. Two different people, in two different worlds, married to each other, loving each other, trying to co-exist.

The indoor arena in Denver was nicer than most of the other indoor arenas. As Jolene walked Coyote's pony, exercising him, acquainting him with the artificial sod, she watched the workmen leaning from the scaffolds, hanging banners and flags and setting up for the night events. Jolene thought ahead, looking forward to running into old friends, in Denver for the rodeo.

The pony walked uneasily. Jolene could tell the horse felt a difference in the indoor turf. He explored each step into the new-laid sod with his hooves. The dirt had been laid only the night before. It wasn't yet firm, was still soft and dippy.

Jolene looked around. She felt proud. Among all the others out with their horses, she was the only woman training her husband's horse. She rode bareback.

Coyote sat in the bleachers giving an interview to a magazine writer. The Denver rodeo officials were happy that he was competing. People bought tickets on his name alone.

Jolene decided the horse had walked enough. An open space lay before her. She took the pony into an easy trot.

The horse dipped a step, wobbled. Jolene immediately jumped off, crouched, examined the pony's foreleg. It felt fine, but the horse had dipped. A danger sign!

Jolene retraced the hoof prints in the infield, found no hole, no uneven places. She felt the sod with her hand. Coyote had finished, was alone. She ran to tell him, careful not to pull the horse too fast.

"Jake, your horse pulled up gimpy."

Coyote appeared unconcerned. He was caught up in the glory of being back on the circuit. "It's the indoor turf. He'll get used to it."

Then he saw somebody he wanted to speak with, ran off to catch him.

* * *

The motel room was dank with Coyote's sweat. He was in deep concentration, doing leg-stretching exercises.

"Jake, you should get that horse X-rayed."

Coyote wore the same clothes he would wear in the arena: long Wrangler jeans, old soft boots, a red shirt and a clean hat.

"Jake!"

Jolene interrupted his concentration a second time.

"I told you, he's fine."

"Jake, he's not fine."

Coyote ignored her, kept stretching. She scrutinized the man. Jesus, Jake, she thought. What if it's only a mild twist? Let the pony roll in the hay for two weeks. He's young. Not like you, Jake. But it was Denver.

What if it's nothing, Jake? What if the pony's all right? Do it, Jake. But no, she knew it wouldn't be nothing. Not with this man. Something always went wrong.

Jolene kept all this inside. She was a woman.

The chutes held nothing for a woman. Coyote paced back and forth behind the chutes, waiting for his ride. He was glad she kept away. He wished Wrestler were here. He needed somebody to be crazy in front of. You couldn't act crazy in front of your wife. A woman got embarrassed. But another man recognized craziness as preparation to meet a challenge.

The stable boy did not bring his horse. Instead, it was Jolene.

"Honey, please don't ride. Wait until the next rodeo. He might be hurt bad."

51

Others heard. He tried again to ignore her plea.

"Honey, I'm with you now. Please."

Staring coldly, he mounted. She exploded with the truth.

"Will you stop trying to prove yourself! We know you're a man!"

"Not before a ride," he muttered. But she had done it. His concentration was shot, gone. He would lose. Nevertheless, he went through the motions, led his horse into the chute.

Jolene couldn't watch. She turned her head when the chute gate opened.

Coyote saw it coming instantly. The calf was bad, a dodger, not a runner. His horse was built for power, not litheness. The rope never got tossed.

Coyote's pony crumbled ten feet out of the chutes. Coyote heard the horse's breath suck from his rib cage as the horse fell to the sod. The pony preferred the fall to standing, didn't resist. Anything to relieve the searing pain in his foreleg.

Coyote scratched for his life. He lifted his boots, pulled his heels backwards, sending all his weight forward into his groin. The pain was excruciating, but he had to see which side the horse would fall to. Then he safely pushed off the saddle horn on the left side, to safety.

The horse lay whining on its side, foreleg in the air. The crowd noice turned to stone silence. Most had never heard the death whine of a pony.

Coyote turned into a madman. He ran back

up, started screaming at the horse to get up. He slapped at its ears.

A rodeo official jumped into arena, bear hugged Coyote, lifted him away. Then he signalled for the doctor.

The doctor bent over the pony, signalled for more help.

Then rodeo cowboys responded. They had seen this before, knew what to do. They had heard the commotion between Coyote and his wife before. None of them looked at Coyote, and one cowboy spit as he ran past. They dragged the suffering horse to the side of the arena where some of the crowd couldn't see.

It was the doctor's job. Two shots into the horse's brain and the crowd heard no more whining.

Coyote watched his career end with two shots. There was nothing left to do. He didn't wait around. Not for anything.

By the time everything got taken care of, the sun had risen over the eastern plains. Denver. The name rang magic. And then Denver ended. As quickly as that. Open spaces began and the rolling hill country before Castle Rock rose and levelled like swells on a rolling ocean.

Two vehicles crawled into the morning light.

Slumped over the steering wheel, Coyote drove the battered white pickup truck. Behind him, he pulled an empty horse trailer. He watched the road through squinted, lifeless eyes. He looked very bad. This time the Rocky Mountains were to the right.

Jolene drove behind, her future plans forgotten. Her mind was empty. She had nothing more to plan. She thought only about how to survive.

Coyote was already feeling trapped. He turned on the radio.

Then he saw the hitcher. She saw him. She was heading back down to New Mexico. Her sign said Taos.

Coyote's eyes lit up. His body got hot and lusty.

She lifted her pack, waved. She moved into the road.

Coyote kept driving. This time he could not pick her up.

Book III

The Ranch

"Its the life, Jake."

Here was the great Coyote, immobilized, trapped, helpless in this deep-rooted lousy feeling. There was no way out, no money for a new horse. Not this late in the ranching season.

His eyes were locked into Jolene's eyes. He looked at her with venom. "Don't tell me about this stinking life!" He wanted to tear her apart into little pieces.

"I need you to work the ranch, Jake." Pa Cantrell pleaded. He spoke meekly from his bed, more and more sick these days. "I need you, Jake."

Nobody had any illusions. Jolene and Pa knew Coyote looked ready for a binder, a drunk.

"Face facts, Pa. Ranching never paid. It never will."

"Are you telling me to sell my land to developers?"

"If you make money, yes."

"What's an old man gonna do with money?"

Coyote clammed up. He was not prepared to go so deep into his soul.

Jolene continued on a practical level. "Jake, with what the developers are offering, nobody, not Pa or anybody, will come out better than even."

Coyote took an aimless step toward his pa. His face was that of a zombie, had been since he and Jolene arrived from Denver. He knew he was breaking his father's heart.

"Pa, your day is over. Ranchers everywhere are going under in droves! You can't make it anymore. None of you. Damnit Pa, face it!"

"Son, I can make it if you'll help me."

There were no chutes to ride into. Coyote turned his frustration into pacing. "No, Pa. No. You can't do it!"

Jolene opened the wound. "You rode that horse down. Nobody else. You."

"You've got to help me dig in, son. We can make it."

Coyote could almost taste it go down. He hadn't had a drink in four months. It didn't matter if everybody hated him. In fact it made it easier.

He felt relief when the screen door shut behind him. He shut it quietly, no slam, no displays. Just a leaving. That was the way he wanted it.

Coyote drank tequila hookers until the shaker ran out of salt. After that, he left the bars, began hard core public drinking with Walsenburg's score of bums. When the cheap wine hit, his memory went. That was what Coyote was after.

Like so many towns built in the late '20s,

Walsenburg's buildings were a deep red dirty brick. The streets flooded easily. The sidewalks were cracking. Coyote was huddled with five other drunks deep within an alcove in downtown Walsenburg. The hours had turned into days, then into a foggy night.

The squad car was making its nightly rounds. The alcove was stinking dank, but it afforded protection until the squad car passed.

Suddenly the squad car reappeared from another direction. The bright spotlight pinned the winos against the wall. Coyote's memory jolted back. The judge's words last time stung him. "Do your drinking at home, where you won't hurt anybody."

Coyote began to shiver. He had been so physically fit just a few weeks ago. Now his insides were like jelly.

"I need a dime. Anybody got a dime?" Coyote found himself mumbling. He wanted to call Jolene. She could help him. He needed Jolene.

They handcuffed Coyote. He couldn't take jail again. Already the claustrophobia was becoming unbearable. But maybe he needed jail. Oh no. Now he understood Thomas. It was too tough out here. Then the walls began closing in again, like before. He had to stay free.

One of the cops called for another squad car, but they were all busy. The voice coming over the radio said, "Release three of them." There wasn't room for everybody.

Oh my God. Coyote's heart raced.

"Not you, Cantrell," said the younger cop, then threw Coyote in the back seat with three winos, released the other three men. That was how it happened. His arms cramped, spasmed. The cuffs rubbed blisters into his wrists. The squad car pulled away. Soon he would be back in jail.

Maybe it was too tough out here.

The Walsenburg Bank was the most modern building in town. Built three years ago, it was one floor, with an overhang above the front entrance that made the bank frigid to enter during windy winter months.

Inside the lobby were four vinyl couches, a bright orange rug, and clean glass windows, all with a view toward the undeveloped mountains. Three tellers, two vice presidents, and a loan officer comprised the floor.

Off to the side, in the bank's conference room, four men sat around a conference table. On the wall hung a localized, very expensive relief map of the jutting mountains and receding valleys. In front of the map, on its own platform, was a large scale model development, slanting toward the conference table like the slope of the mountain it was built upon. Within the development were ski lifts galore, and long, wide ski runs cutting bare through former forests of pine. Down at the base was a glorious ski lodge with restaurants, bars, and health spa. Condominiums and seven different ski lifts spread from the lodge, finally ending on each side with a rise in the land which were Pa Cantrell's ridges.

This development in the virgin southern Rockies was to be called Gateways, in honor of Walsenburg's nickname. The developers, Gateways of Chicago, planned to build a recreation complex better than Vail, Aspen, or Steamboat.

Mr. Clinger, a fat, overeager banker, stood in front of the scale models with a pointer. He had not yet figured out that the Chicago developers were using his bank to avoid the illusion that outsiders were trying to make a colony of high yield estates out of southern Colorado. Nevertheless, the town was divided in its opinion of the economic feast that would happen with the development going up. People were bored. They wanted tourists, they wanted change, they wanted cash. Then there were those who wanted things to stay the way they always had.

Mr. Ricardo, the chief developer, was a dark, sunlamp-tan, perfectly tailored Italian. He stood, waiting for Clinger to begin his presentation on land acquisitions. Two other developers were seated. Unlike Ricardo, who wore a three-piece suit, they wore windbreakers, ideal for the field work they hoped to begin this week.

"O.K.," Clinger began, punctuating with his pointer. "Up to now, we have obtained most of the acreage you want to purchase through simple foreclosure; that means ranches going under, divorce in the family, folks simply losing interest in ranching."

Ricardo was impatient. "We know." What Ricardo was waiting to see, he wasn't seeing.

"What about that?"

"What?"

He grabbed the pointer from Clinger. "That!" Ricardo pointed to the prime area of valley. "What about the land for the condos and the ski lodge? How do we begin without that?"

Clinger knew what was coming. He had failed to secure the most valuable piece of land.

Ricardo exploded. "To make this development a reality we need the Cantrell parcel first, not the surrounding area. What is so difficult about comprehending that?"

"Cantrell won't sell," Clinger said.

"Make him sell!"

"How?"

One of the developers wearing a windbreaker spoke from down the table. "What's the problem with this Cantrell?"

Ricardo replied angrily, "He's an ignorant old rancher."

Clinger stood up for Pa Cantrell. "He's a proud old rancher."

Ricardo was stunned. "Whose side are you on?"

"This town's side," Clinger explained. "We need the development."

"Why don't we double his offer?" the fourth developer asked.

"What, are you stupid?" Ricardo flew off the handle. "Every rancher in the area would want to renegotiate."

Richard raised his arms high, reaching to the fluorescent lights above. "God! If this was ten years ago, we could have crucified him and nobody would have noticed!"

The other developer unzipped his windbreaker, cautioned Ricardo. "Remember, we want results, not revenge."

Ricardo came back. "What you ought to be worrying about is how to elect a new president, from a northern state, who knows how to ski!"

Ricardo pounded the table and all was silent. "I need the valley. Cantrell's valley. Now turn some screws."

Clinger reiterated his dilemma. "I can't foreclose unless he's delinquent on his payments."

"Is he prompt?"

"Always before the deadline."

"Does this ranch of his show a profit?" the developer asked from the table.

"Loses every year," Clinger informed him. "Like the rest of them."

Ricardo sat down, shook his head, complained, "It is getting impossible to make a buck."

"How does he work the ranch?" the same developer asked.

The phone rang. "He's got a son," Clinger answered, getting up to answer it. "The son worked the ranch . . . "

While Clinger spoke, Ricardo lamented the state of the developer. "Jesus, we've got titles to clear, brochures to print, environmental studies to get approved. Nothing, nothing is done quickly anymore!"

Clinger hung up the phone. No one understood why he was so happy. "That was my sheriff on the phone. The Cantrell boy's in jail. Another drunk." He touched Ricardo. "We got him!"

Coyote's cell looked as if a crazy man were inside. The air was thick. The cell had no window. The closeness of the walls came closer. Coyote trembled, shook, bounced himself into the walls. Anything to get his blood going.

He fought the claustrophobia with his eyes closed. He crouched on the steel corner of the box string, pretended he was outdoors, on a boulder. He pretended to be at Frontier Days, but that led to Denver and that led to jail.

Coyote's hangover was oppressive. He hadn't eaten.

He knew he was in jail, didn't try to fight it. Instead he got off the mattress, crouched on the floor of the cell and waited for something to happen. That was the hard part, not knowing when you would get out.

Rip, the sheriff of Walsenburg, couldn't be talked to, certainly not by his deputy, who happened to be Clinger's nephew. Rip saw no reason for holding Coyote past the morning, the same as any other drunk. "If there was something in the Bill of Rights against tying one on, I'd spend time behind those county bars myself," Rip reasoned, not knowing that the nephew had already phoned Clinger with a promise of longer, more serious consequences for Coyote.

But the sheriff did have a special message of his own for Coyote as he headed with keys for the cell.

In his cell, Coyote was just this side of crazy. He thought about sheepherders. When they finally slept with a woman, did they fantasize about sheep? Then he heard footsteps coming down the hall.

Rip opened the cell door. The man was huge. "You make me want to vomit," he told Coyote. Coyote prepared to get kicked around.

"Stand up!"

Coyote stood. Rip stalked him, walked behind Coyote.

"I idolized you as a rodeo cowboy. But I'm disgusted with you as a human being."

The cell door was open. Did the sheriff want Coyote to break for the door? What was he doing?

The sheriff kicked Coyote so hard in the butt that he sprawled five steps out the cell door into the wall beyond. The wall caught Coyote so he stayed on his feet.

"Grow up, boy! Stop hiding in a bottle."

With his burly arm, the sheriff motioned out.

Coyote was gone. If he could only remember where he had parked his truck.

That morning, Ricardo and Clinger drove out to the Cantrell ranch. With nothing more to do for now, the other two developers drove their rented car to Stapleton Airport in Denver and flew back to Chicago.

The anxiety of not knowing where Coyote was worsened Pa Cantrell's condition. He was weak all the time. His head felt light, then heavy. He was propped up in bed when Clinger and Ricardo knocked and were led into the bedroom by Jolene.

Jolene stayed in the doorway. Ricardo looked good to her. If he wasn't the enemy, she would have let him make a play for her. He was sure looking at her enough. He was smooth, she thought, not bullheaded like her husband.

Jolene put Coyote out of her mind. He wasn't there, never there when you needed him.

Clinger made the introduction. "Mr. Cantrell, I'd like you to meet Mr. Ricardo."

Pa scrutinized the sunlamp-tan man. "Ricardo? Hmm, don't look Mexican."

"Italian." Unruffled, Ricardo corrected Pa.

"Mr. Ricardo," said Clinger, "is vice president of Gateways Investment Corporation."

Pa understood. "Oh," he said to Clinger, "you mean he owns you."

This is getting nowhere, Ricardo thought to himself. It was time to move. He spoke sympathetically.

"I understand the plight of the small farmer, Mr. Cantrell."

He said the wrong thing. Neither Jolene nor Pa Cantrell were farmers. They were ranchers.

Ricardo continued. "In Chicago, which I'm sometimes ashamed to say is my city, I know the giant packers fix the price of beef, so you have to sell at the price they offer. No supply and demand, no competitive marketplace and you lose money on each cow you raise."

Jolene admired the way he summed up fifty years of ranching knowledge into two succinct sentences.

"Yet you must understand that these same packing houses are literally being robbed themselves, by the truckers who move your livestock from ranch to market. They have the upper hand because without their service, both ends of the cattle business are helpless. So of course the packers squeeze prices on you, Mr. Cantrell. You're the little guy."

By now Pa Cantrell was boiling. He told Ricardo, "Let's get one thing straight. I ain't no farmer. And I ain't no little guy!"

"I'm sorry, nothing personal, Mr. Cantrell. But unfortunately you are in a situation where the middleman has become costlier and more important than either you, the producer, or them, the sellers of beef. And that, sir, is sports in a cornflake."

Outside, Jolene heard a truck door slam. She mumbled *oh shit* to herself, knew it must be Jake. She wondered if Pa Cantrell also heard.

Outside, Coyote left his truck, a man born again, with a new lease on life. He saw Clinger's new Ford LTD, clapped his hands, marvelled at his timing. He softened his steps, hoping to catch an earful of what was going on inside.

Ricardo was concluding his summation. "So you see, Mr. Cantrell, Gateways really isn't so bad when compared with the system you're up against. We didn't invent weather conditions, nor did we triple the price of diesel fuel, nor do we cause your prices to be short. Sir, face it. The day of the small . . . excuse me . . . rancher, is over."

Pa Cantrell began to see the truth. "Diesel's so high a man can't afford to run a tractor, hay's so low, who'd want to?"

"That is right, sir." Ricardo stepped back, let it all sink in.

Then the front door closed softly. Jolene heard it. Why couldn't that drunk stay away? Coyote tiptoed through the living room.

Clinger spoke with attempted stature. "Mr. Cantrell this gentleman and his company is offering you the chance to retire free of any debts. And my bank will allow you to keep the revenues from this year's cattle sales."

Pa kept shaking his head. Ricardo sensed it was time for the kill. Jolene wondered if her ears were playing tricks. Where was Coyote? Richardo feigned sympathy. Then he broke the news.

"I'm sorry about your son. We're all sorry."

Pa's head jerked. "What about my boy?"

"He's in jail again on another drunk."

Ricardo looked to Clinger for confirmation. Clinger nodded.

"Awwww." This killed Pa Cantrell. He weakened and sank.

Ricardo poured it on. "You are a good man, Mr. Cantrell. The best kind."

Now Jolene knew she heard Coyote's boot step. Clinger heard it too. You could see fear in Clinger's face.

Ricardo only heard himself. "Life should reward you, Mr. Cantrell, not punish you in the end. My company would like to make things pleasant . . . "

Ricardo stopped. Coyote stood in the doorway. He winked at Jolene, like a little boy. She turned away.

He walked forward grinning at Pa Cantrell. He smelled horrible, reeked like a wino.

Clinger was forced to make the introduction to Ricardo. "This is the Cantrell boy." Ricardo eyed Clinger as if to say, what's he doing out of jail?

Jolene was even more confused. Coyote appeared almost cordial to Ricardo. He rubbed the stubble on his jaw, moved closer to the sleek developer.

"Appreciate your kind words to my pa." Coyote smiled at Pa Cantrell like the ideal son.

Ricardo nodded, suspiciously.

Coyote moved closer to Ricardo, let his stink permeate Ricardo's nostrils. "Boy, I'm filthy," Coyote observed. He came up to Ricardo, looked him right in the eye. "You got a shower in your house?"

"Of course." Ricardo was confused, about to retch.

"Nice shower, I bet. Tiled."

Coyote looked back at his pa. "You're a sweaty old buzzard, Pa. " He turned to Ricardo again. "My pa ought to use it too. Mind if my pa uses your shower?"

"What do you mean, use my shower? Why do you want to use my shower?

"Because if you're gonna kiss a cowboy's ass, you better make damn sure it's clean."

Pa Cantrell began cackling. Jolene suppressed a giggle, then broke up with Pa. Coyote kept staring hard into Ricardo's mind. Ricardo backed away.

Then Coyote turned to Jolene, a big boyish grin on his face. Like a spark, there was love again. As Clinger and Ricardo moved out the doorway in defeat, Coyote moved to his father's side, bent over, hugged him. Jolene did the same.

The Cantrell family came together. They were unified, happy. They looked like a family portrait.

Uplifted

Coyote slept off his booze for a day and a half, showered, shaved, got dressed, drank a gallon of coffee. The first thing that had to be done was to de-horn the bull. A sharp-horned bull could get excited during breeding season and puncture one of the breeder cows, which made very poor rump roast.

Outside the bull's private corral, Jolene filled a big syringe with tranquilizer serum and handed it to Coyote, who waited on top of the fence. Coyote held the syringe between his teeth, jumped onto the bull's back, rode him to a standstill. Then he stuck the neddle above the ribs, into the bull's neck.

Soon the serum hit the heart and the bull sunk to his knees, feeling a wonderful nothingness. Coyote smiled at Jolene as she handed him the hacksaw. "Reminds me of having a wisdom tooth pulled."

Coyote sat on the ground and began sawing away, first at the tip of one horn, then the other. He felt like a dumb lug, doing ranch work, but it was his second chance. He wouldn't complain.

* * *

After a day of cooling off, Ricardo and Clinger were back in the bank's conference room before the lavish scale model.

Ricardo was frustrated with schemes and counterschemes. He asked Clinger, "How does he ship his cattle?"

"He's lucky," Clinger replied. "Most ranchers have to truck. With Cantrell, a small train goes into the hills one time each fall."

"And picks up his cattle?"

"Uh huh."

"Any other way?"

"Way for what?"

"Way for him to get his cattle off his ranch?"

"Not to my knowledge."

"You sure? Tell me."

"Well, Cantrell doesn't have the cash to pay truckers. It's the railroad for him, or nothing."

"Good. How soon will the train be there?"

"Oh, say two weeks." Clinger wasn't sure.

"No later?"

"Never, it can't be. Snows too early around here."

Ricardo's mind was racing. "Who owns the freight line?"

"We do."

"What? You're kidding!"

"No, we own the freight line."

"You really do?"

Clinger nodded.

"I can't believe it." Ricardo started to hug Clinger, affectionately pushed him away. "You're the stupidest sonofabitch on two legs, but I love it. Why didn't you tell me before that you owned the freight line?"

"I don't know. We lease its services to the big packing houses." Clinger hadn't comprehended how ruthless Ricardo could be.

Ricardo threw up his hands. "I don't believe it will be this easy. I don't believe it will be this easy to freeze Cantrell out."

That afternoon, a summer wind funneled through the trees at the Cantrell ranch, knocking a bluejay nest to the ground. All but one of the babies were killed. Jolene found the baby jay screeching for food, its mouth open, huddled in the long grass. She cradled the bird, took it inside.

When Coyote came in that evening, exhausted from harvesting the last of the alfalfa, he saw a shoebox. Jolene had stuffed it with a pillowcase. The baby jay was inside. She was feeding it moist bread. Over the shoebox, there was a lamp turned sideways so that the bare bulb warmed the bird.

Coyote was touched. He joked, "I can see that bird when he grows up." He played he was blind. "I'm sorry. I can't go on any missions today. My mother was a forty-watt bulb."

Jolene looked up from the bird. "Pa wants to talk to you tonight."

After dinner, Coyote heard the wind finally stop outside. He was feeling the first pangs of cabin fever, the stir crazy disease. He needed a goal, a strategy. Anything would be better then mending fences and piling alfalfa to dry. He welcomed a talk with Pa.

As they sat in Pa's bedroom, Jolene, Coyote, and Pa, Coyote felt very helpless. It hurt him to see this robust man so weak, down, almost pathetic. Coyote hoped that because he was here, maybe the blood would once more rush through Pa's body, the way it used to be. Pa spoke.

"You two will have to pull a very heavy load. In fact, you'll have to pull all of it."

Jolene touched him, tried to comfort him. He scolded her hand away. This was serious. Pa continued. "We have enough money to buy some winter feed."

"Some?" Coyote asked.

"Our breeders have enough hay until March, maybe. After that, it's the great soup line on the prairie. Thawed grass by the creek."

Coyote found his humor a form of desperation. "Pa," he said. "We've got 600 head in high pasture. Now how do you expect to bring them down?"

Pa got angry. "A big damn outfit would truck 'em down, and shoot 'em with chemicals and steroids, wouldn't they? Well, this ranch won't do either."

Coyote wondered. "Then how do we get the cattle from high pasture to the loading corral? By ourselves?"

Pa's silence painted the picture.

"Pa, you expect Jolene and me to bring 600 head down that mountain by ourselves?"

"You've got a week and a half, easy, before the train gets here. Take your time. Besides, we'll be keeping 150 for breeders."

"We've still got to bring them down."

"You can do them last."

74

Jolene was already packing in her mind. Coyote couldn't believe this was happening. "C'mon, Pa, how're we gonna do it?"

Pa smiled his survival smile. "I figure you can do it seventy-five at a time."

The high country was a thing of beauty. Winter had already touched the tops of all the peaks with the first snow of the season. Coyote and Jolene rode bundled up, wearing hats, parka jackets, gloves, boots, with small packs and provisions tied to their backs and to their horses.

Beautiful at a distance, a mountain meadow became more than picturesque as they rode at somewhere over 9,000 feet. Over a gully the going got rougher, the horse's hooves kicking uncomfortably at the rocky debris. For them, the romance of the mountain had combined with reality.

Coyote pointed below. Jolene saw a large herd of Cantrell cattle nibbling in a clearing of quake aspen. Coyote grimaced, rode down into the rear of the herd, cutting off less than a hundred from the main body.

Jolene rode down the hill on the front side and kept any strays from running forward out of the clearing. Then they took their positions. Coyote rode to the rear and right, using a long lasso to whip a cow if it got out of line. Jolene rode to the front and left, keeping the cows bunched up.

Deliberately, slowly, tediously, they moved the cattle downhill back toward the Cantrell ranch. They rode as one, as a team.

The sun blazed at the ranch. Sweat rolled off Coyote's forehead into his eyes as he pitchforked loose hay to the cows in the wooden fenced loading corral.

Then Jolene turned an ankle, and they had to wait another day before riding back into the hills. By then the heat wave ended, and it wasn't until late afternoon that they found another bunch of cattle, so they settled in for the night.

It frosted that night. Coyote and Jolene were tucked deep within their sleeping bags when dawn awoke them. The horses were tied to a tree, blankets on their backs for warmth. Jolene had unconsciously rolled next to Coyote, seeking his heat through the sleeping bag.

Coyote woke up first and saw the icicles hanging from the frozen branches of the lodgepole pines. When Coyote moved, Jolene squirmed in her bag, moaned. Coyote sat up, exhaled ice, rubbed his hands together.

"Brrr," said Jolene as she opened her eyes.

Coyote was already sitting, pulling his clothes on. "Whew," he said. "It's so cold the jackrabbits are pushing the bunnies to get 'em started."

By late that day they had the second group of cows into the loading corral. The had pushed it, were both exhausted. But they had done it twice. Now they were veterans.

They slept at the ranch that night, but well before dawn, it was back into the foothills, then the high country.

During this ride, Jolene got very into herself.

She was feeling a certain pride that she couldn't describe. She was doing a man's work, keeping a man's hours, with a man's responsibilities on her shoulders, yet she was doing it all as a woman. Here, in the mountains, artificial distinctions between man and woman seemed so out of place. Each carried a load that was comfortable. A man's, of course, was bigger, but a woman could carry it. Jolene felt freer than any career woman in the city.

She watched her husband fill the canteen from a mountain stream. She chuckled at this great rodeo cowboy kneeling by a stream. Here's a man whose worst enemy was boredom, the boredom of ranch life. And here was this same man fighting for his life on a ranch. He didn't look the least bit bored.

He handed Jolene the canteen. She took a drink.

"You still miss rodeo?" she asked.

"I miss it."

"Keep missing it," she said. Then Jolene rode out in front.

Coyote rode a little taller in the saddle. He had become a man in his wife's eyes. He had to admit, the challenge was here. He was meeting it and for the first time in his life knew the meaning of the words self-respect.

He rode on behind her. They were in their own worlds. It was an introverted time.

Coyote was beginning to feel the exhaustion. Jolene knew that at the ranch, when he was supposed to be sleeping, he was up, forking loose hay into the mouths of the insatiable cattle, trying to keep their weight up for the train.

Coyote had a second wind around 10:30, lost it by noon. They found another bunch of cows at 12:30, but hesitated to ride into the herd. The cattle were restless. Coyote sensed a readiness to stampede. There was a tension in the herd. A stampede was nothing you could be certain of, but if it happened, you better be sure you had the energy for a long series of sprints and chases. The ground was still wet, slippery from the frost and dew. The horses found it difficult to get a footing. Mud had formed in shady patches. Neither Coyote nor Jolene had the energy to deal with a stampede. Yet they didn't have the time to stay the night and try it in the morning. They stayed on the ridge, looking down.

Coyote wanted Jolene to ride in first and she wanted him to do it. Both knew the other was uncertain. Then they heard horse hooves. The looked at each other. "Deer hunter?" Jolene asked.

"He'd be poaching," Coyote replied. "But why this high, anyway? Deer are moving down."

The rider became visible. First he was a shape, then a man riding closer. Then they saw who it was. He called, "Need another hand?" It was Wrestler.

Coyote and Jolene were overjoyed. Jolene had thought Wrestler was a broken old rodeo bum, but changed her opinion on the spot.

Wrestler was bundled up, carried supplies, rode a good horse. "Oh baby, all right!" Coyote rode up, leaned across, hugged Wrestler right there in the saddle.

Wrestler winked at Jolene. He slapped Coyote on the back. "How's this for ranching, goat roper? Just like ya expected?"

Now they were three.

Coyote, Jolene, and Wrestler formed a triangle around almost 200 cows, twice the number they were able to move before.

Coyote took the rear alone. It was his job to use the long disciplinary rope on any strays or cows that tried to stray. Jolene and Wrestler rode up front, on either side of the herd, keeping them bunched up. So, with a lot more speed, and with the herd instinct in their favor, they all moved downhill.

By now the Cantrell loading corral was filled to capacity. Except for a few more strays still up high, they had gathered nearly 600 head of cattle, almost five tons of beef.

Now Coyote had nothing to do. He climbed to the top of the viewing tower, above the loading corral, scanning the horizon for smoke, dust, any sign of the train. He would do this once an hour, often twice. Time after time he climbed the viewing tower, looked achingly for the train. He strained his ears listening through the foothill silence for any locomotive sounds coming his way.

He was driving everybody crazy. He didn't notice Jolene at the bottom of the ladder until he climbed down.

"Relax, honey. They're always late."

"You relax. They could be here any time."

Coyote clapped his hands together. There were cattle to feed. He was single-minded man.

* * *

Miles from the Cantrell ranch, a freight train, its cars filled with cattle, slowed by the outskirts of another rancher's loading corral.

There was a second herd waiting, outside the loading corral, apart from the large herd that was inside. The second herd belonged to a rancher named Mitchell, and his ranch hands surrounded the second herd.

Another rancher looked to be the owner. He stood atop his viewing tower, guiding the enginner to a perfect stop.

"Howdy," waved the engineer to the rancher who guided him in. Then the engineer saw a second body of cows and was confused. He saw the other rancher, recognized him.

"Mitchell," called the engineer, "what're you doing down here?"

But sounds from the opening boxcars drowned out the reply.

Coyote, Jolene, and Wrestler found their nine strays late that afternoon, made camp and were bedding down for the night,

"Don't worry about waking up early," Wrestler told them. "I got an alarm clock arrangement with those peaks. Anything I tell them'll echo back exactly eight hours later."

Coyote shook his head. "Wrestler's getting old."

"Varicose brains," Jolene quipped.

"Get up, you lazy cowboys! Get up!" Coyote smiled, played along. He knew the joke. Jolene drifted into sleep, ignoring Wrestler.

Up with the first sun, Wrestler snuck behind a boulder, hid from Jolene's sight. Coyote watched with one eye open.

Wrestler screamed at the top of his lungs, *"Get up, you lazy cowboys! Get up!"* Some echo.

Jolene levitated in her sleeping bag, she was so frightened, while Wrestler and Coyote cracked up.

Coyote couldn't stop worrying about the train. With the strays in, there was nothing to do but wait. Not even Pa realized how low their supply of hay was. Cows in the fall were fat. They ate a lot. If the train didn't come soon, these autumn cows would cut seriously into the winter supply of hay.

So Coyote separated the 150 cows to be used as breeders for the bull during the winter months. They looked as feminine as cattle could as they waited for the bull's private eight-month orgy. "You lucky mothers," Coyote said to them, then looked back at the bull. The bull wasn't choosy. He wanted all of them, and he would have them all.

Coyote had become a raving man. He climbed the viewing tower twice every hour, tormented everyone, was impossible to be around.

"You hear anything, Pa? Any train?"

Pa, of course, would shake his head no.

"Where is it, Pa? I don't know where it is!"

Coyote spent that night in the living room, not wanting any sounds to pass him by in the night. He hadn't heard from Clinger and something made him suspicious. But he didn't know what. In a tender moment, he left his vigil, crept into their bedroom, lightly kissed his wife on her face. "We did it, honey."

She woke slightly, her eyes blinked once, then fell back into sleep.

Before dawn, Coyote was already perched on the viewing tower. He fidgeted, was on nerve ends even this early. He picked on his sideburns, twitched with his lips. He saw no sight, smelled no smoke, heard no steel wheels.

Instead he heard the animals waking up. Squirrels were the loudest, then the bluejays. A skunk waddled by. Magpies cruised the air for carrion.

Coyote worried even more. If a train was in the area, the ground animals would feel its vibrations. They would be hiding. No animals were hiding. They were out. It was a normal day.

Now Coyote's questions were asked with hostility.

"Where's the train, Pa?"

By being derisive, Coyote hoped to force Pa's slow moving hand. He hoped that Pa had a trick up his sleeve, a way to predict the train's arrival.

But there were no tricks. Only the sounds of cattle chewing the supply of winter hay.

"Isn't there anything we can do?"

"We wait," Pa told him.

"They're late, Pa. Real late."

"I haven't heard a train, Jake."

"Damnit, Pa. Neither have I!"

Afternoon found Coyote still waiting, computing how much alfalfa was left, how much had been used for hay.

He passed Jolene on his way to the corral. She had hung a bamboo birdcage from an aspen branch. The bird had grown remarkably in a short time. It hopped perkily from branch to branch, staying close to the cage.

"She can't decide which to be, Jake."

The bird couldn't make up its mind whether to be wild or be a pet. She came back into the cage, took a sip of water, a nibble of moist pet chow that Jolene was now feeding her, then zipped back onto the tree. Jolene was trying to give the bird a choice, to be independent or to be a pet, and the bird insisted on a little bit of both.

Jolene forced a smile at Coyote. Coyote kept walking, never smiled back.

The train was late. There was no way not to admit this. A man of action, Coyote regarded his father as a man of inaction. Most of his contempt stemmed from that. He began to sound like a street punk whenever he confronted his pa.

"We are running out of hay! Hay, man! Hay!"

Pa finally suggested an alternative.

"Drive down to Mitchell's," he said. "See if they've been by there."

"Good, Pa. Good." Coyote mocked his father when the old man finally suggested something.

Coyote jumped into his battered pickup truck. He left prints in the dust where he walked. At least the isolation would be over. They would know something.

Mitchell's place was a good half-hour away.

Coyote looked around, saw no cattle. There was no cow shit on the ground. Only thing he saw was Mitchell, a strapping, dumb cowboy, smoking a pipe, looking into an empty loading corral.

"Mitchell, where's your cattle?"

"My cattle?" Mitchell didn't like Coyote at all, nor his pa, didn't care much what he was asking.

Coyote kept looking around as if Mitchell's herd might magically appear. "Your cattle, goddamnit! Don't tell me they're still in high pasture?"

"Now that'd be stupid with winter comin' on."

Coyote smiled. Stupid is right.

Mitchell barked, "Then why you tellin' me I'm stupid if what you have me doin' in your mind is stupid?"

"Mitchell, where's your cattle?"

"My cattle's gone. We shipped out a week and a half ago." Mitchell puffed his pipe, looked up into the sky. "That's right. Cattle's gone."

"How could you?" Coyote lost his wind for a second. "I didn't hear a train!"

"Same train as always."

"Didn't this train make noise?"

"No, boy. Silent train."

Coyote was ready to kill Mitchell. Mitchell sensed this. "Of course it made noise."

"Then why didn't I hear it from my place?"

"Simple. I didn't load from here."

"Mitchell!" Coyote screamed. "Will you

84

fuckin' make sense!" But Coyote's insides were crumbling. "Why didn't you load from here?"

"I loaded from McCallister's place."

"But that's ten miles from here!"

"I figured it was worth it."

"Worth what?"

"Clinger, at the bank, offered me a six-month delay on my payment if I'd walk my stock down to McCallister's place. I loaded from there. Like I said, train's gone."

Jolene heard the truck roaring down the dirt road and knew there was trouble. Like a madman, Coyote passed her, running into Pa's bedroom.

Then Coyote stopped. Pa was lying there, and Coyote got the feeling that Pa knew this would happen all along. Jolene caught up, took Coyote by the shoulders. "What happened? What happened?"

Coyote said simply. "They froze us out." But all the time he was staring at his father.

"What do you mean?" Jolene was confused.

"Tell her, Pa!"

The old man would say nothing.

Coyote screamed. "They isolated the ranch! We're all alone." He moved into the bedroom. "Right, Pa?"

"Coyote?" Jake stopped. She had never called him Coyote.

Jake turned back to her. "The train, honey. There is no goddamn train!"

Now Jolene moved toward the old man. "Pa?" She said it accusingly.

Pa weakly hit his damp palm with a limp fist. "I didn't think Clinger could sink that low."

"Pa?" Jolene said. "You knew."

"Of course he knew. Didn't you, Pa? We're trying to survive, and you're depending on some motherfucker's decency? Why didn't you tell me you were going to play a game of morals before we brought the goddamn cows down? You stupid fucking old man!"

Pa said nothing. Coyote leaned over him, screamed into his face. "We're finished! Do you understand? He beat you! It's over!"

There was silence but for Coyote's heavy enraged breathing.

"Goddamn you, old man!" Coyote slammed his fist into the wall.

Jolene touched Coyote, settled him. Coyote calmed right away. He was a different man. He bent over. "Pa, I'm gonna tell you something. It's called sense. Sell the place. We'll be O.K. You'll be out of debt. You'll get some peace. Please, Pa. Sell the place before they take it from you."

But Pa ignored Coyote. His mind was already somewhere else. He motioned Jolene to come closer. "Honey, c'mere."

Coyote straightened up and she bent over. Pa reached between the mattress and boxspring, handed her an envelope.

"Pay off the bank."

"That's my rodeo winnings!" Coyote became enraged when he saw the envelope. He moved to take it from Jolene.

"Leave her alone."

"Pa, that is cash. There won't be anything left for feed. You can't do it. You've got 600 head of cattle and you can't feed them. It's over."

"Pay off the man at the bank. It's the only move I have left."

Jolene cradled the envelope. Her loyalty suddenly shifted to Pa Cantrell. He looked calm, wise, reassuring.

Coyote screamed. "Will you sell this worthless piece of land before they destroy you!"

"No. I won't watch this land wither and die." Shaking his proud old head, he commanded softly to Jolene, "Make the payment."

Once he had loved his father, but the old man's pride and stupidity had driven Coyote to the brink. He had to mock his father horribly. "There's my pa. Going out with his boots on. Go out with your boots on, Pa. These are the seventies, baby. Nobody cares how you go out! You hear me, old man? Nobody cares!"

The Cantrells had little time left. The paint was running, the canvas parched and faded. They were another kind of family portrait now. They were dying.

In the small market checkout line, two well dressed town wives were taking care not to stand too close behind Jolene. With dirty jeans, boots, and checkered shirt, Jolene was clearly a ranch woman. The storekeeper eyed Jolene's cart of groceries.

"Will this be cash, Mrs. Cantrell?"

One of the women put down her *National*

Enquirer, looked at the other. Their eyes gossipped. So this was a Cantrell?

"We've always dealt in credit," answered Jolene.

The storekeeper jumped on her. "And what will you use this year?"

The town woman started in. "A lot of people want to see Walsenburg developed. Why is your family holding it up?"

"Well, I don't want to see it." Jolene was close to tears. "I live here because I want to. What about people like me?"

"Don't worry, dear," the second woman told the first. "It won't be for long."

"Will this be cash, Mrs. Cantrell?"

Jolene had no money.

"Could you pay for your groceries and leave?"

She couldn't pay. She was crying. She stepped past the register, then stopped at the door. "You bitches!" she called back.

The storekeeper and the two women were left staring at each other. He shook his head. "Damn ranch families." He looked at the groceries. "Now who's going to put these back on the shelf?"

The Wild Turkey burned as it went down, making his stomach hot like cheap Mexican food. The bottle was one-half gone, and at 150 proof, there wasn't much left of Coyote either.

Liquor made Coyote a bumbling, pathetic man. He used to love the attention. Today he drank because he needed to.

The horse walked slowly under him. A rifle lay across his lap. His right hand pulled a rope.

A 1,500 pound Hereford was walking to his execution. Coyote swayed in the saddle. He reached a pocket of trees. It was an effort to dismount. He tied the cow to a tree branch, let ten feet of slack develop in the rope.

The horse became squeamish, backed away. Coyote took another long swallow, cocked his rifle. The liquor really hit him, made him dizzy. He hadn't drunk since his last release.

The cow began to nibble. Coyote pointed his gun. The cow looked at Coyote from the corner of its eye. It had no idea that these were its last bites. The grass was good.

Coyote shot the cow deep within its brain. The animal's legs buckled. It had no feeling in its toes. Then it had no toes. The cow sunk to the ground, dead by the time it rolled over.

The poor horse went crazy. Coyote undid the rope from the cow, tied the horse to the tree. The horse was forced to watch. Coyote removed his butcher knife, made his first incision.

Hot blood from the cow spurted over his face, shirt, pants. It matted his hair. Coyote ripped the knife down, began to slice. More blood spurted as he tore an artery. But he was drunk. The blood was warm. It didn't feel that bad.

Jolene miserably washed a sinkload of dishes in ice-cold water. She regretted her marriage not being more stable earlier, or she would have planted a garden back in the spring. She could taste the vegetables that would be ready for picking now.

Then through the window she saw the spectacle of her husband. Coyote was drunk, weaving precariously back and forth on his horse, full of blood, dried blood on his face and hair.

He drunkenly screamed, "Get the freezer cleared out!"

Jolene forgot about her garden. Coyote changed directions, pointed the horse toward the pickup that he would drive back to load the butchered cow.

"Oh, my God," Jolene said, and held her face with both hands.

The horse took four steps, then Coyote fell off. He was so shitfaced that he fell off his horse.

Coyote staggered to his feet.

"Get the freezer cleared out!" He screamed again, braced himself against the truck. "Get the freezer cleared out! We're havin' steak tonight . . . and steak tomorrow night . . . "

Jolene's man was falling apart. She was a woman. All she could do was match.

Jolene saw the cattle broker pull up outside the Cantrell ranch. "The viper has arrived," she called to Pa Cantrell. A metallic sign on the side of both car doors said SIOUX CITY FEED LOTS.

Out of the agri-community had grown an alternative to the packing houses but it wasn't much. These were the feed lots. If a rancher couldn't cut it, he could always deal with feed lots like the big one in Sioux City, Iowa, just across the Missouri River.

A feed lot bought young cows, fed them in stalls, injected them with all kinds of fillers and steroids, then sold the "test tube" beef at inflated prices to mouths grown accustomed to tastelessness. Fast food chains were prime customers.

For a rancher the advantage was a dramatic slice in the year's overhead, and the feed lots operated their own trucking lines. For a feed lot, the advantage was a desperate rancher eager to sell for almost any price. The feed lot business boomed best after an especially bad winter.

The cattle broker knocked once, walked in when no one answered. When he saw Jolene in the bedroom, he walked in there. There was no use playing games. His values were cash and carry.

"Mr. Cantrell, is it? I represent Sioux City Feed Lot and I can solve all your problems before I leave your ranch."

"How much?" Pa asked from his bed.

"As you know, a great many ranchers nowadays are simply calving, then selling to us shortly after birth."

"How much?"

"But since your herd is mature, and since you have put in a considerable investment, my company's offer is fourteen cents a pound." He said it with a straight face.

"Fourteen cents?" Jolene reacted before Pa.

The broker reassured her. "Of course, you understand we pay for trucking and feed the cattle until slaughter."

Jolene replied, "I won't even eat the hamburger they sell on the shelf for $1.69! That's ten, over ten times your price!"

The broker replied snottily, "I didn't know

ranch families bought their meat off the shelf." To Pa Cantrell he turned. "Who, sir, am I dealing with?"

"You're dealing with me."

"Then, Mr. Cantrell, at some point, beef translates into dollars. Fourteen cents is your point. You have no means of moving your stock anywhere, so why discuss it? Do we deal?"

Pa motioned the man closer. He bent down. Weakly, Pa hit the broker across the face with a closed fist. It didn't hurt the broker any, though it stunned him backwards.

"Get out," Pa said to him. "Get out."

The broker left.

Outside, Coyote waited until the broker pulled away before he walked into the house. The meat had been butchered and loaded in the back of the truck. He still reeked of whiskey, but he had been weeping. Tears filled his eyes. His shirt was caked with dried blood, his hair was matted and red, his cheeks were smeared red, where tears had run down into clots of cow blood.

He saw Jolene, came to her, emotionally took her in his arms. She was like a baby. She was ready to crumble. She couldn't take anymore.

But Coyote was ready to fight. She could feel his energy. "You'll never see the day when we lay down," he said to her. He went into the bedroom, said, "We're gonna make it, Pa. Yes!"

He hugged Jolene again. "Honey, I don't want to ever hurt you again. You're the best thing that ever happened to me. I don't want to lose you. Honey, I love you so much."

He was like a teenager in his confession. He

pulled back, admired her. "I can't believe how much you stay beside me, put up with the things I do." He paused. He almost began weeping again. "I love you that much, too. I always will."

"Thank you, Jake." Jolene was now covered with dried blood, but she didn't care. She too began to cry. Nodding her tearful head, she whispered, "Thank you, Jake."

Husband and wife looked deeply into each other's eyes. They found the strength they needed to fight back.

Then there was silence.

"Pa Cantrell broke the silence.

"I've decided to sell the ranch."

Coyote was sitting atop a fence post, staring high into the Spanish Peaks. The sunset was throwing spectacular colors. First red, then orange, finally a purple hue took over the sky.

Jolene walked out to him. She leaned down, picked up a small, flat, brown rock. Imprinted on it were the paw and claws of a prehistoric mouse. She stuffed it in her pocket for memories.

Jolene leaned against Coyote's fence post.

"I'm gonna miss those mountains," Coyote said to her.

"I will too."

"Where are we gonna live?"

Jolene shrugged.

Neither of them knew what they were going to do.

"Jake, isn't there any way for us to survive?"

Coyote shook his head. "We're up against dreams. Too big dreams. Rich people's dreams."

There was nothing left to do but wait for the ranch to be sold. For Coyote, this time, waiting was like a sanctuary. He enjoyed the ranch for the first time in his life. He couldn't bear the thought of leaving.

The banker arrived not long after. Coyote stood on the front porch, then saw the sheriff, Rip, also get out of Clinger's automobile. Clinger saw Coyote standing there menacingly. He motioned the sheriff to walk between Coyote and himself.

Coyote didn't question the sheriff's presence. It was a job. It was over. Nothing would help now. Let it pass. Coyote gave Rip a half friendly nod as he passed. The sherriff nodded back. On the other hand, the by-play between Coyote and Clinger was intense, with Coyote doing his best to intimidate the banker.

Jolene was helping Pa Cantrell out of bed when Clinger arrived. Pa saw his rocking chair, wanted to maintain at least a little dignity. "My chair, bring my rocking chair closer to me." His voice was raspy, his order weak.

Jolene pulled the chair closer, tried to help Pa.

"I can do it." He brushed her hand away. Weakly, he pulled himself out of bed, into the chair. Jolene admired Pa. He appeared stately in his rocking chair. Jolene folded a blanket neatly over his lap.

Clinger entered, felt a pang of conscience. The sheriff nodded in respect. Coyote couldn't bear to watch, stayed outside on the porch. Clinger got down to business.

"You have made a wise decision, Mr. Cantrell."

"I've lived here 50 years." Pa's voice quivered. He spoke from his heart and his heart had broken.

Clinger nodded. Pa went on.

"I wanted you to know that."

The sheriff nodded sympathetically. Clinger was forced to listen.

"Take my little piece of Colorado . . . and spit on it!"

Coyote was now standing in the doorway. He felt as if he were attending his father's funeral.

Clinger wanted to get out. "I'll draw up the papers for you, and bring them by tomorrow morning. If that's all right." He nodded courteously, turned to leave.

"Clinger! I've lived here 57 years . . . "

Coyote was tearing apart inside. His father was going senile. Clinger had to turn back around.

"Clinger, I want to ask you a favor."

They all listened to the dying old man.

"I want to watch the season turn one last time. I want to see the aspens slowly turn to orange. I want to remember the leaves, the way they look, like thousands of dried apricots all orange and shining."

"I'm sorry, Mr. Cantrell. That won't be possible." Clinger cut him off abruptly.

"Jesus, let him stay." Coyote pleaded for his father.

"No, I cannot."

"Why, you can't build anyway until after winter!"

"I'm sorry. You'll have to move." For the first time, Clinger sounded snotty. Confidently Clinger walked by Coyote and out the door. Reluctantly, the sheriff followed.

Even Coyote was moved to tears. Jolene was crying, too.

Coyote moved in, sunk to his father, lightly took the old man's shoulders in his arms. "You just can't beat 'em, Pa. You just can't beat 'em."

Jolene kneeled at the base of Pa Cantrell's rocking chair, took the old man around the legs. Together they cried.

Pa Cantrell remained silent. He refused to weep.

Colorado's Even Prettier

The bar in downtown Walsenburg had every animal in the region nailed to the walls. There was an enormous rug made from a grizzly hide, not a dish-faced cinnamon which was common, but a grizzly. There was a buffalo head mounted above the bar, with horns dwarfing those on Coyote's bull. And there were three jackalopes, a cross between the antelope and jack rabbit, a species peculiar to this part of the country and to Wyoming.

Wrestler sat with two other guys drinking Colorado Kool-Aid, as Coors beer was called out here. One of the guys was a man, Food, who was forty, an overweight beast. As Food told Wrestler, "When I get depressed, there's one thing I do which works, guaranteed, every single time."

"What's that?" Wrestler asked.

"I compulsive-eat." Food looked as if he was down quite a bit. Two giant bags of potato chips were piled around his private pitcher of beer.

The other one at the table was a boy. Brains was nineteen, one of the few Walsenburg boys to go on to college. He was to be a sophomore come fall. The uneducated Food was fascinated and a bit sad envious of young Brains, and the opportunities education would provide him in life. But the book-learned Brains idolized Wrestler, and would do almost anything, even quit school, for the glorious chance to live out in the real world.

Wrestler had Brains transfixed with a hunting story, in which Wrestler brought down a grizzly from 150 yards. "Ya see, a grizzly's heart," Wrestler told the boy, "beats only once in nine seconds. And a bear like that one," Wrestler pointed to the grizzly rug on the bar wall, "can run 100 yards faster than that, once he gets started. So even if you plug a bear dead in the heart, he still has nine seconds of life in him, plenty of time to kill ya."

The effect on Brains was hypnotic. "So how did you kill it? Without being killed yourself?"

"Simple. I shot it in the paw, first."

"Hee haww!" Food cackled.

But Brains's mouth hung open. He held men like Wrestler in awe. "You are such a good storyteller."

Wrestler shrugged it off. "Hell, if your only entertainment was cable TV from Salt Lake City, you'd learn how to tell stories, too. I can't sit through a Bronco game without having to listen to the Tabernacle Choir at halftime."

They all drank. Wrestler noticed Brains looking sullen. "What's the matter? Girl trouble?"

Brains nodded.

"Hell," said Wrestler, "solve it the Colorado

way. Kick down her door, then ask her to marry ya."

Outside a hot van pulled into the parking lot. Gravel flew as the van spun to a stop. Fun Truckin' got out. That's what everybody called this kid, Fun Truckin'. He was also nineteen, with collar-length blonde hair. He liked older women. He was an extremely good looking but hard-assed kid, who in another era would have been Billy the Kid. Fun Truckin' had already dropped out of everything he could. The local girls loved him, especially the older waitresses. He worked construction with Food but the job was coming to an end. He had no prospects for the winter. Expecting another usual night, Fun Truckin' walked into the bar.

Food saw him first, said extra loud to Wrestler, "There's that lazy asshole I work with."

"Lazy?" The boy strutted to the table. "It's all I can do to get Food to roll down the window when he farts in the truck."

Food cackled, slapped Wrestler on the back. "See . . . I told you you'd like him."

Wrestler smiled.

Food asked, "What you drinking, boy?"

Fun Truckin' scowled. "Near beer."

"No, c'mon," Wrestler chided. "Have something."

"O.K." The barmaid came over. She was older. "I'll have a vodka, orange juice, and Folger's Coffee."

"What's that called?" she asked.

"A screw . . . Mrs. Olsen!" Fun Truckin' smiled up and down her body. Food cackled a

99

third time. Brains felt dwarfed by Fun Truckin's nerve.

Wrestler saw Coyote enter the bar. He looked down and crazy. Wrestler had seen that look before. He knew what was in store, already was anticipating the steps he'd have to take to stop the fight Coyote would surely start.

Coyote found a barstool, avoided the table. Next to him, a local roller with a big hat was buying for two ladies, carrying on with them as if they were chippies. The man was bigger than Coyote, but the way he was dressed reminded Coyote of the developer.

"Move over!" Coyote told the guy. "Tequila hookers," he told the bartender. "Four of 'em."

The man with the big hat moved a barstool over. He treated Coyote as a mere annoyance, reluctant to divert any attention from the ladies.

Coyote downed the four shots of tequila, one after the other, licking the salt, squeezing the lime. "Four more," he told the bartender. He waved off another lime.

At the table, Wrestler was leaning forward in his seat. A pretty young girl passed the table, said, "Hi, there," to Fun Truckin'. Fun Truckin' scoffed at her. "Two most overrated things I know: Coors beer and women under twenty-five." Insulted, the girl continued to the ladies' room.

"Goin' back to school this fall?" Food asked Brains.

"What's there to learn?" Fun Truckin' interrupted. Brains looked out of his league around the rough-and-tumble Fun Truckin'.

Food asked, "What're you studying?"

"Geology, with a minor in ecology."

"You gonna change the oil companies?" Fun Truckin' asked. "Work with them from the inside?" Fun Truckin' sized up Brains, hated him right away.

Wrestler kept his eye on Coyote who was finishing his sixth shot of tequila. He could see the meanness flushing into Coyote's face. Drunkenly Coyote again ordered the man with the big hat.

"Farther!" Coyote mumbled.

The man gave Coyote that look that people give winos or beggars, as if they were invisible. Anything, any reaction would have been easier for Coyote to take. He had to be noticed.

Coyote looked back, saw Wrestler staring at him. He called over his left shoulder. "Hey, Wrestler. 'Member how it was?"

"I remember," Wrestler called from the table. He knew he should stay seated.

"No fences. No people. Mountains for those who could climb 'em. Nobody crowdin' you."

"I remember."

"Four more," Coyote stumble-tongued to the bartender.

The two ladies tried pretending Coyote didn't exist.

The bartender refilled the glasses, didn't bother with new ones. Coyote finished his ninth and tenth tequilas. He'd had ten drinks in five or six minutes.

" 'Merica's a beautiful country. Colorado's even prettier."

Wrestler sensed the violence, could see it coming now.

"I hate your kind!" Coyote leaped across the two bar stools, began strangling the man, pummeling his neck, snapping it back and forth.

Wrestler was right behind.

Coyote lifted the man off his barstool, pulled him to the floor, started hitting him. But Wrestler ripped Coyote away before any damage was done.

"Don't go to the cops," Wrestler pleaded. "This guy, he just lost everything."

"All right." The man nodded, dusted himself off. To him, Coyote was one more crazy drunk, to be cleaned away like a stain on a coat. He escorted the women from the room.

If this was the story of these people's lives, for Brains, it was just a chapter. Soon he would be gone, away from southern Colorado, away from his girl, back in school. He watched, detached from the others, trying to understand everything about everyone.

It was near closing time. Most of the patrons had left. The bartender was washing glasses. Around the table, Wrestler, Fun Truckin' and Food shared the late night gloom. To Brains, Coyote was another story. Brains couldn't begin to fathom what this killer was about. How vain and desolate he seemed. He was a man of the earth in a changeable climate, from the mountains and high prairies where the weather was violent and everything swirled.

But none of this mattered. Brains was novocain-drunk. Soon he'd be away from these people. The others flashed glances at Brains from the corners of their eyes. Fun Truckin' despised him for slumming, Food envied the boy, and Wrestler never thought about it.

Coyote rustled in his seat. Something was stirring.

Brains eyed Fun Truckin'. "God," Brains thought, "if I only had those looks." But he didn't. He had to try harder, in everything.

Brains wanted a last beer. "Anybody want anything?"

"Not unless you got a sister," Fun Truckin' answered.

Brains longed for the day when he could talk back, when he wouldn't be afraid of people like Fun Truckin'. Maybe it was better he was enrolled in college, away from these people. Brains bought everybody the last beers anyway, bought a new plate of pretzels for Food.

"Anybody got jobs this winter?" Wrestler asked.

Nobody answered. Nobody had work. Winters were long and bleak down here. For a second, Coyote looked up. His eyes darted, as if he were deep in thought, or dreaming. Then he looked down again.

Food looked up. "I could use me a working wife."

"Lost your last one to a plate of custard," Fun Truckin' quipped.

"There ain't jokes in everything, kid," Wrestler reprimanded.

Food looked at Brains. " 'Least one of us is gettin' out."

Wrestler kept watching Coyote. Coyote was

coming to life. He seemed to be figuring something in his head. He looked like a mathematician without paper of pencil. Color was returning to his face.

Coyote looked like a celebration!

Suddenly he cackled. Wrestler waited. Coyote held up his hand. Not yet. He wasn't ready. Brains thought he had gone off the deep end.

Coyote cackled again. Now he was sure. He pounded the table with his fist. He stood up. He sat back down.

"What?" Wrestler wanted to know. Everyone at the table waited for more. The bartender sensed more trouble. The rest of the patrons got up and left.

"Ha!" Coyote laughed out loud. "Tell me!" Wrestler demanded.

Coyote slid up closer, then leaned back on two legs of his chair. "They don't own me!" Coyote proclaimed. "They don't own any of us!"

Coyote slammed the table with his forearms, jerking the bottles of beer. He stood up, announced, "I'm gonna drive those cattle to market myself!"

Wrestler sprung up away from the table, his eyes lit up. "You mean it? Think you can do it?"

"I *am* gonna do it!"

"Not alone you're not." Wrestler moved next to Coyote, slapped him on the shoulder. "I'm with ya!" Wrestler looked to the others. Fun Truckin' snapped his fingers. "Fuckin' A, a cattle drive!" He stood with Wrestler.

"A cattle drive?" Food looked confused, but stood with the others.

Only Brains showed any hesitation. Wrestler was jabbering away, pounding on everyone's shoulders, ranting about the excitement of a cattle drive. But Coyote, for some reason, was waiting for Brains's response. Skeptically, Brains raised a negative point of disagreement. "You can't do that."

"Why the hell not?" Coyote said.

"Because this nation is all land, fences, land, fences, land . . . " Brains drew the diagram with his hands.

Coyote patted him wisely on the shoulder. "Son, then the fences will have to come down."

Brains had one more question. He was grinning. Where to?"

Coyote was at the wheel. The pickup truck roared northeast out of Walsenburg, raced the pre-dawn rays of sun back to the ranch.

Coyote turned his excitement inside, pausing in his headlong rush. The open road was still his friend. His clarity returned. He slowed his mind, rehashed the plan again and again.

He knew the state. People in the state knew him. He was Coyote. He could drive the herd north, taking the back roads of Colorado, where the shoulders were fifty yards wide and the wild grass grew five feet high.

O.K.

Out of state. Then where? Cut diagonally across Nebraska. Sioux City, where the feed lot was, was right there. Though he didn't know the roads in Nebraska, they'd explore. How far? Not far. Five hundred miles? It couldn't be more than that. Big deal. That was nothing. Driving cattle at twenty miles a day. The arithmetic flowed. Coyote felt as if he were at the track. What was it? A month. How bad was that?

Coyote passed the first car he saw.

What else would he do? Sit around like Mitchell and watch his grass die, his fence rot, and his bull screw? For one month Coyote could not only beat trucking costs, but probably sell for three times what they were getting at the ranch. Even with an expected weight loss on the cows from travelling, they would be more than doubling their best year ever! My God, why didn't everybody drive their cattle this way?

Dawn was breaking but Coyote didn't feel close to tired. He remembered a shortcut back to the ranch. It was through another rancher's property. Coyote cut off the highway, busted through a barbed wire fence, whipped through an already harvested field of alfalfa.

Dust flew everywhere by the Cantrell ranch house.

Jolene was drinking her last cup of coffee in the kitchen when her wild-eyed husband pounded into the house looking like an insane inventor whose light bulb had just worked. Excitedly she followed Coyote into the bedroom. He shook his father out of sleep.

"Pa! Pa, wake up!"

Both eyes opened. Pa was up.

"Pa. How many head of cattle would we have to sell to come out ahead?"

"At what price?" Pa was shaking out the cobwebs.

"Top dollar, Sioux City Iowa." Coyote was grinning.

The confused Jolene waited for something to make sense.

"Retail price?" Pa figured. "I don't know, 200 head . . ."

"How about 450?" Coyote boasted.

"How about all 600 of 'em?" Both Pa and Coyote were laughing, both on the same wavelength, though Pa didn't yet know what Coyote proposed to do.

"Are you out of your mind?" Jolene asked.

"Yeah," Coyote said. "And it sure feels nice."

"What are you going to do?" she asked.

Before Coyote could answer, Clinger walked into the house. Nobody heard him knock. With a phony smile, he entered the bedroom. He stepped forward, papers in one hand, check in the other. Clinger extended the papers to Pa Cantrell.

Coyote reached for the papers, tore them slowly up, letting the pieces drop by the dozens at Clinger's feet.

"My pa's changed his mind." Coyote dripped with confidence.

The timid Clinger became enraged.

"You stupid hillbilly!" he shouted to Pa Cantrell. "Your stock is frozen. You're finished. You've got nowhere to go!"

"Is that so?" Coyote stepped forward, stalking the banker. "Well, you can suck my dick! 'Cause I'm gonna drive the sonofabitches to market myself!"

Jolene was astonished. Pa Cantrell *whooped*, then eased back on his pillow and felt strong. Clinger stood there shivering like a dog trying to pass peach pits.

"Now get off my land!" Coyote ordered him. Clinger timidly backed away, then turned and left.

The family faced each other. They realized their fate hung on one man—Coyote. Reality set in immediately. The cattle were fat and ready. There was no turning back.

So they got ready to embark, to send him on his way. The Cantrells were a portrait of determination.

That was how the cattle drive began.

Book IV

The Cattle Drive

From the air they looked like a long traffic jam of brown and white cars, with ears, hooves, and flapping, tail-like exhaust pipes that rhythmically swatted flies. The men had lined up 450 head of the finest Cantrell cattle two by two, on the wide shoulder of the road leading up to the ranch. Heading away from the loading corral, the cattle prepared to walk 500 miles to their deaths. The irony escaped no one.

Everyone from the bar was in. None of them, including Wrestler, had ever been on a cattle drive. It was an opportunity no one could pass up. They all had one thing in common. They wanted to live history.

Fun Truckin's van was parked crosswise, in front of the herd, stopping any forward progress. Confident his job was accomplished, he began walking toward the ranch house to tell Coyote they were ready.

For Brains, school could wait. For the past few days he had been studying cattle drives. There hadn't been a real long distance drive in more than eighty years! The night before, Brains's girl said she would marry him. What

111

more could he want? He was on his way. To-day, up in that saddle, keeping the cows in line behind the van, Brains was feeling like a man.

Food circulated up and down the herd, on his horse. He had no job, no home that he cared about, only a pride that he rarely showed. Food saw the month-long cattle drive as a wonderful way to go on a diet. His saddlebags were packed with fruit, not pretzels. When he was thirty pounds lighter, Food hoped he could find what he had wanted for so so long: a wife.

Wrestler stood on the porch, next to his oldest friend. The elder statesman, Pa Cantrell, sat in his rocking chair, radiating optimism and pride. Wrestler rocked the old man gently back and forth.

More than anything, Jolene wanted to go, but she had to stay and take care of Pa. "Jake, I think you're crazy, but I love it."

Coyote was saying goodbye to his wife. He knew how badly she wanted to go, understood she was making conversation so she could feel a part of the drive a little bit longer. "Please," she said quietly, away from the others. "Don't drink."

Coyote opened his palms. "Nothing."

Everybody heard Fun Truckin' whistle. "Let's stick it to 'em, Coyote!"

Fun Truckin' arrived, was immediately struck by Jolene's presence. "Excuse me, ma'am." She thought he was blushing. "I didn't mean to anyone in particular."

"You stick it to all of 'em."

Fun Truckin' grinned. "I will, ma'am. For you."

He wheeled around, got back to his place at the front of the herd.

Coyote shrugged, opened his palms again. "He likes older women."

Jolene smiled flirtatiously. "Nothing wrong with that." She pointed a finger. "One day I might want to adopt a child."

"All right, all right." Neither spoke. Coyote began to fidget. Both knew their lives were in the balance. He had to go.

Her mood shifted. "Sioux City is 500 miles away."

"Honey, we'll be doin' seventy-five. I'll be there in eight hours."

"That wasn't funny."

He put his palms on her shoulders. "Look, count the days. It'll still be Indian summer when we get back."

"Really?" She wanted to go on the drive so badly.

"Jolene, I gotta go. We're wasting daylight."

They walked to the porch, got Wrestler. Coyote hugged his pa, hugged Jolene, was down the porch and gone.

Wrestler put a farewell hand on Pa Cantrell's shoulder. "Don't give him nothing to drink." It was a plea from Pa.

Wrestler smiled at both of them, then he was gone, too.

Everybody brought supplies. Food's saddlebags overflowed with fruit and his one concession to calories—peanut butter, jars of chunky peanut butter with plastic forks attached with rubber bands, bulged from the leather saddle-bags.

Knowledgeably, Wrestler packed thin strips of jerky, dried fruit, and two quart bottles of Ancient Age that he told nobody about.

Fun Truckin' carried the heavier stuff in his van. He had hastily converted the rear into a makeshift kitchen. He filled his freezer full of ice, and bottles of spring-fresh water. He had lunch meat and bread for sandwiches. He laid wood shelves across bricks, used the arrangement as counter space.

Fun Truckin' led the way as the drive moved away from the ranch. With his van dragging in low gear at two miles an hour, Fun Truckin' made a mental note to rig a jammer on his gas pedal, so he'd have his right leg free. He packed his gas siphon, but with the mileage he would get at two miles per hour he might make Iowa in one tank of regular.

Coyote rode a short distance behind the van, keeping the cows from the road, near the front. His saddlebags also bulged. He carried a rifle in a sheath by his right leg.

Behind Coyote, performing the same function, rode Wrestler. He was calm, prepared, serious about this mission, but the little boy in Wrestler was also along for the ride. Contrary to what everyone might think, cattle drives were before his time, so he was caught up in the excitement like everyone else. Conscious of Coyote, he waited for a hill in the road before sipping the first of the Ancient Age.

The drive had moved to an uneventful half mile from the ranch. The cows were still two by two and holding steady on the grassy road. A bare patch of dried dirt stretched ahead.

Food struggled not to open the peanut butter. He tried everything he could not to think about it. Finally, he bit into a peach. It wasn't the same, but he tried not to think about it.

All the way in back, behind the last cow, poor Brains sucked dust from the entire Cantrell herd. He cursed himself for not bringing a scarf to wear across his mouth. He hoped nobody noticed how sickly he looked. If any cattle strayed, it would be his job to put them back in line. No one had to tell him this. It would be his responsibility. He would take it on himself.

They had travelled their first mile from the ranch. Fun Truckin' called back the mileage from his van. Now grass started up again. Coyote wondered if the cattle wanted to graze. "Slow 'em up, let 'em graze if they want to." Coyote issued his first command. He began to feel like a leader. But none of the cattle bothered to graze. Coyote wondered if they were too excited. Then he decided he didn't care about the moods of cattle, so he had everybody pick up the pace.

They were coming to the edge of Walsenburg, a mile downhill, to the right. Coyote was looking forward to being out of here. He loved the mountains rising abruptly to his left, but longed for them to be different mountains, not the ones he was used to. He needed to feel strange, untouched by familiarity. He smiled to himself. He guessed he wasn't all rancher. Not yet, anyway.

The grass picked back up to a tall stalk. The

breeze danced the grass, then stopped, letting the grass sag. First the hitcher, then Pa, then Jolene crossed Coyote's mind.

He looked around him. There was no mood as yet to the cattle drive. It was too new, uncertain. Coyote could tell that everyone there felt the void. Even Wrestler rode unsurely. Nobody knew yet how to pace himself. Coyote knew that would come in time, on another day.

Coyote grunted. He dug it all.

Walsenburg was now a mile behind them, back there on the right. They were climbing the hill which Coyote knew would officially take them out of the city limits.

Then it came.

They were on the top of the hill when they saw the squad cars waiting. On the outskirts of town waited the sheriff, Rip, with four other deputies. Rip was standing in front of his car, leaning on the grille. As he came closer, Coyote saw Clinger in another car, with Ricardo sitting next to him. Now he knew who was behind this blockade.

Coyote rode out in front of Fun Truckin'. How far in Clinger's pocket was Rip? First he set Coyote free, but then he accompanied Clinger to the ranch. Was he like the spring wind, blowing this way one minute, then the other? Coyote decided it was about time he found out.

Coyote withdrew his rifle from the sheath, rode into the blockade.

Rip agonized over what to do. When he watched Coyote pull his rifle, he too undid his pistol, pulled it from his holster, tightened his

116

hat, walked forward directly into Coyote's path.

The mood turned ominous. The deputies bunched together. It was the sheriff's show. Rip tried yelling at Coyote, but the cattle noises drowned his voice.

The cattle and everything else stopped when Coyote raised his arm. He moved his lips so Rip could not mistake the message.

"I'm comin' through, Rip."

Rip wanted it repeated. By now the silence made Coyote audible. "I'm comin' through, Rip!" Now everybody heard.

"You can't go no further, Jake. I've got to stop you!"

The sheriff was holding fast.

With a sweeping arm, Coyote motioned to his herd. "You stop my stock, you kill my pa. It's beyond both of us, Rip. I'm comin' through!"

The standoff stood. Everyone waited for Rip to turn Coyote back. Rip could see the intensity on Clinger's and Ricardo's faces. But Rip seemed to be hesitating. Then, suddenly, the sheriff made his decision. Rip put his pistol back into his holster. There was no fear in his move. The sheriff walked over, reached up, shook Coyote's hand. "If there was ever a man in the right, I'm lookin' at him. God hopes you make it."

Coyote pumped the sheriff's hand in gratitude.

Clinger hit his head as he burst out the door. Ricardo evacuated the vehicle too. Coyote noticed another lone man in another car, also getting out. He was holding a large camera with a flash attachment.

The cattle drive started up.

"I want him cut off!" Ricardo screamed to Clinger.

Clinger was screaming at Rip.

"Are you listening to me?" The sheriff ignored them both.

Ricardo turned to Clinger, screamed his instructions.

"Nobody lets him through. Nobody feeds him. Nothing!"

But the moment belonged to Coyote, to Rip, to integrity. Coyote smirked at Clinger, spit when he passed Ricardo.

The last thing Coyote saw was the photographer when the light from the flashbulb blinded him. His picture was being taken leaving the Walsenburg City limits. The blindness was bothersome, but it didn't matter. Coyote knew where he was going.

They were off. Nothing could stop them.

Is a Frog Waterproof?

Everyone else brought supplies, but Brains brought books. He brought maps, an atlas, law books, and topographical maps of Colorado and Nebraska. His plan was to be an encyclopedia on horseback. He spent hours looking up statutes dealing with driving cattle on roads, on shoulders of roads, across states, counties, and boundary lines in general. Brains was anxious to prove himself to Coyote and this would be his way.

It was the time of day flies like the best. They swarmed around you. They buzzed your face. Not even cow shit could change their high opinion of human flesh.

The drive had moved north, away from the Walsenburg area. They were still in the foothills, at the base of the Rockies. Coyote decided to ride away from the front, to make his first survey of the cattle.

Coyote nodded to Wrestler as he passed. He nodded to an unsure-looking Food. Food offered water from his canteen, but Coyote declined, imagining a backwash of peanut butter

119

around the spout. The cattle looked fine, in good shape, walking easily.

Finally he reached poor Brains at the rear. With no kerchief, Brains was still getting the dust from 450 head of cattle. But now, with Coyote there, he pretended not to be affected.

"Jesus, kid!"

Immediately, Coyote motioned Brains to switch positions with him. Coyote took his red kerchief and tied it around his mouth.

They rode that way for a while, Coyote letting Brains breathe his first real air of the trip. Coyote kept looking at Brains because it looked as though Brains kept wanting to say something. He reminded Coyote of Jolene, with something to say always on the tip of her tongue. And you knew it. If you were with her, you found yourself always waiting for her next burst of vocal energy, and that's how it was for Coyote now, around Brains.

"He was wrong, you know."

Coyote breathed a sigh of relief. Finally the kid spoke. Coyote knew Rip was wrong, but he had had a change of heart. "Yeah, well . . . "

Brains cut him off. "I mean legally wrong."

Now Coyote was interested.

"Look!" Brains told him, motioning to his saddlebags. Coyote saw the books, maps, and atlas. Brains pulled out the lawbook.

"You brought books, on a cattle drive?"

Brains got a boyish, inferior look on his face.

"No, no, it's a hell of an idea." Coyote tried to reassure him.

"It's a lawbook." Brains took the bookmark out, turned to a page. "I was looking up statutes." Brains fingered a place on the page. "See this?" Brains held it open, but Coyote didn't know what it meant. So Brains simply summarized from the book. "Not one single law against what we're doing!"

"It says that in there? You're kidding." Coyote took the law book.

"It's not what it says," Brains said seriously. "It's what it doesn't say. Either there's a law against driving cattle or there isn't. And there isn't. So it's O.K. See? Now there's all sorts of health ordinances, but nothing, repeat, *nothing* against driving healthy cattle on the shoulder of a public road. In other words, he—nobody has the right to detain us!"

"No right at all?"

"Not a single one!"

"Why didn't you tell me back there?" Coyote asked.

"I don't know. You didn't look like you needed to be told a thing."

"*Woohoo!*" Coyote couldn't believe how fortune smiled on him. A kid with law books. "Here." He removed his red kerchief, gave it to the boy. "Wear this, you'll choke on the dust."

Coyote rode excitedly off to tell Wrestler of the new legal developments.

Now Brains rode, dust-free, with a new position of legal adviser to the cattle drive, wearing the red kerchief of a two-time world champion over his mouth. He rode so proud, you could see the smile a mile away, even under the kerchief. He looked like a happy half moon with teeth, the indention of a grin permanently affixed on Coyote's bandana.

121

Coyote couldn't contain himself. He galloped up to Wrestler, embellished on the story as if it were his own.

"How'd you find this out?" Wrestler asked, when he heard.

"It's common sense. I mean, who ever would have thought to pass a law against cattle drives? Like nobody had to. They simply evolved out of existence."

Wrestler cut him off. "Evolved?"

"Sure, evolved. Like evolution. Horses to trucks. Monkeys to, well, guys like you, Wrestler."

"I see. Evolved."

"Yeah, evolved. So, we're gonna make it. The law's on our side. We got the law on our side."

Wrestler thought. "I don't think I've ever had the law on my side."

"I can tell you for a fact, you haven't."

They were both getting excited like a couple of big kids. Wrestler was semi-lit from the Ancient Age. "You mean we're gonna make it?"

"We're gonna make it." Coyote was convinced.

"You really think so?"

"Is a frog waterproof?"

"Yes he is," they both said together. "Yes he is."

They were such old buddies.

Wrestler winked at Coyote. Then he turned, looked all the way back at Brains, nodded his head. "That's a nice kerchief that kid is wearing. That's the one you wore in Oklahoma City for the second championship, wasn't it?"

"Well, it's just a kerchief."

"Pretty smart kid, that college student. Knows about law and everything."

"I'm sure he does."

"And words like evolved, and statutes."

"Wrestler, are you trying to tell me something?"

"Like the only statue you ever came in contact with had pigeon shit on it."

"Wrestler, my friend, every great leader surrounded himself with people smarter than he was."

"How the hell do you account for me being here?"

"Simple." Coyote trotted off. "You're the brawn. I do the organizing. You do the heavy work." Coyote called the last part back.

The warning lights were blinking from the front and rear of Fun Truckin's van. Coyote rode behind, his eyes never stopping, noticing everything. Well behind, Wrestler celebrated the good news of Brains's legal discovery by sipping on the Ancient Age. It was his very own, grown-up nipple. Between swigs, he cradled the bottle so Coyote wouldn't see.

Coyote kept trying to figure why the grass here was shorn, so close cropped. Up ahead, the road looked even more like a putting green. He worried for his herd. The cows already were slowing, looking for sweet grass to nibble.

Then they came upon bales and bales of tempting hay, to the right, beyond a rancher's barbed wire fence. In the distance, he saw two men seated in the back of a pickup truck, holding shotguns, guarding the hay from the cattle drive. Clinger's doing, Coyote suspected. He turned to confirm his suspicions with Wrestler, but saw him downing the Ancient Age. Coyote turned back. He feared for his herd. It wasn't so much the weight they would lose without grass, but what if one cow weakened and keeled to the ground? What would the other cows do? How would they react? They might stop walking altogether, especially if it was an important cow in the herd.

The road went on and on, until Coyote didn't recognize it at all. Unlike before, Coyote now craved familiarity. The wanderer got buried in a rancher's thirst for habit.

There were three constants in the journey. The Rockies rose consistently to the left, the great plains began on the right, and on the shoulder of the road, there wasn't enough grass to make a wig for a grape.

Now the road got hilly, long hills with no hint of tomorrow until you came to the top, saw it for yourself. The grass had been cut, shorn to the roots. Coyote began to fear starvation for his cattle if this kept up. So Clinger was going to bring them back through famine. Again he looked back at Wrestler to see if he noticed. Wrestler had put his bottle away, was shaking his head. Like Coyote, he sensed what was happening. How long would Clinger haunt them? How far would they have to go to escape his power?

As the long hill continued to rise, Coyote became a fearful man. All his paranoia returned, but this time without the clarity. There was nothing he could do, no one he could fight. He was helpless, at the mercy of other men, men he could not see. How could Coyote put up a fight? He didn't know how to combat an opponent he couldn't even find.

Finally they came to the top. Up ahead, parked on the left shoulder of the road, was a giant highway tractor/mower from the state of Colorado. Coyote knew why this road had no grass. The operator had sheared it before his coming. So this was the tactic. Coyote rode up past the van, not knowing what to expect.

The operator was a strapping Colorado youth. He had his feet up on the controls, was sipping a bottle of Coors. In the winter, these giants played football for Colorado U. In summer, they got the plush jobs for the state. Up high, the boy sipped his beer behind the Plexilass shield. He wore a T-shirt saying COLORADO FOOTBALL.

Then Coyote saw that the burly youth had piled the grass three and four feet high, along the route of the approaching cows. It was like a wonderland of grass, a green feast. The sweet smell of fresh-cut grass was almost sensual, like green mint in a humid climate.

The youth tipped his hat. Then he motioned Coyote to let his cattle feast on the grass. Still not sure, Coyote rode up to doublecheck what he thought was happening. The goodness of the boy overwhelmed him, more than the smell. The youth was smiling, red in the face from beer. Then he tipped his hat. Coyote tipped his hat right back. Coyote lifted his hat off, yelped in cowboy glee.

With Coyote and Wrestler showing the way,

they scattered the herd as best they could, formed an umbrella around them, then watched the cows make pigs of themselves as they wallowed in the knee-high feast of wet grass. It was nature's perfect food. For the cows it was breakfast, lunch and dinner, it was dessert. It was heaven, and it took fifteen minutes.

The cows began moving again. The highway shoulder had been shorn again. But as before, another tractor/mower, this time with an old man at the controls, had piled more grass. When the old man saw the cattle drive coming his way, he stopped the tractor/mower, leaned back, watched with pleasure.

Coyote realized that the word must have been out about the drive. Maybe it was the picture that reporter took, maybe it was word of mouth. He didn't know. But look at this. The cattle continued to feast for the second time. These were little people, doing the big deeds that you never heard about. These were Americans at their best, doing the things they used to be known worldwide for.

Brains didn't have a hat to tip, but he waved Coyote's red kerchief up at the old man as the last of the cattle passed under his giant piece of machinery.

"Ya gotta love it!" Brains screamed though it was doubtful whether anybody heard him. The whole scene was incredible.

They rolled on for a while until they saw that up ahead, another youth, a carbon copy of the first, had done the same thing. Grass was piled everywhere. The cows were almost too stuffed to eat, you would think. But when the umbrella formed, and by now Coyote and the boys just flanked into formation as though they'd been doing it all their lives, the cattle ate as if it were the first time in months they'd been fed.

Then the grass was gone. Locusts couldn't have done a more thorough job. Coyote was beaming as he passed. Fun Truckin' was waving, leaning out his van window, steering with no hands. Food was smiling and Wrestler was screaming at the top of his lungs. Brains tried to ham it up by riding sidesaddle, but he slipped off his horse. Luckily nobody but the tractor operator saw, so he slipped back in the saddle quickly.

The mood had turned into a celebration. Everyone had his arms off the reins, in the air. They were no longer alone. They were getting support. They rolled on, past the piles of grass. They were free of problems, in the foothills of the glorious Rockies, independent men, defying the system, rolling up the wide shoulder of a lush country road. What could be better?

A car crept into the vicinity, slowed. Its driver leaned out, snapped another picture, then gradually speeded up, continuing on its way.

A small green blue river fell from the Rockies, winding down through the rolling foothills maybe a half mile ahead. Its destination was east, perhaps the Platte, or the Missouri, eventually the Mississippi.

Coyote was the first to ride into the hip-high water. The others looked snappy under Coyote's command, as if they had drilled. The riders formed a diamond around the cattle, with

Wrestler and Food on each side, Brains still in the rear.

Up on the bridge, Fun Truckin' crossed cruising very slowly, looking down on the cattle. A carload of tourists from Pennsylvania had stopped. The people inside rolled down their windows, craned their necks to watch.

The father leaned out to say something to Fun Truckin'. Then his attention was distracted when his wife got out, started taking pictures. Fun Truckin' stopped his van, opened the door. Other people also stopped on the bridge, leaned over the side, watched below.

In the back seat with her brother, a cute fourteen-year-old girl watched Fun Truckin' get out of his van. He had left his warning lights still blinking. To her, he was a heart throb, a real life Western figure, carefree, daring, thin-lipped, a little bit mean.

Fun Truckin' immediately noticed her watching him. He ate up the attention, even though he looked totally aloof, concerned only for the cattle.

The girl couldn't keep her eyes off Fun Truckin'. She figured a way to meet him. "Daddy?" she asked.

Her father, in the front seat, didn't answer. He was too involved watching the cowboys cross the river.

"Daddy!" she repeated.

The father turned.

"Could I see the Colorado map?"

What she asked didn't register.

"The map, Daddy," she repeated. "The Colorado map."

"Oh, sure." Annoyed, the father shuffled papers, handed her the Colorado map. With her brother egging her on, she slipped out of the car, walked over to Fun Truckin', handed him the Colorado map and a pencil.

"You want me to sign this?" Fun Truckin' mustered all his charm, masked his surprise, easily slid the pencil across the map, writing "Fun Truckin' " across all of southern Colorado.

"He heh," the girl giggled. Fun Truckin' was tempted to ask her if she wanted to ride a while in the van, but was contented to admire her behind as she walked gratefully back to her father's car.

Waiting until she got back inside, he nodded, then touched his cowboy hat with his thumb and forefinger, pushed it ever so slightly back on his handsome blonde head.

The girl's eyes were riveted on him. Slowly he got back in the van, cruised to the far end of the bridge.

She would never forget him.

"Look, Pa. Look at this!"

Jolene came flying into Pa Cantrell's bedroom waving the Walsenburg afternoon paper. She handed it to Pa, who let his teabag rest inside his stained cup. Jolene stood over his shoulder while Pa gazed at the front page.

What he saw was Coyote's picture on the front page, leading the cattle drive out of Walsenburg. There was an explanatory caption and a full story.

"Your name's mentioned in the fourth paragraph," Jolene told Pa.

"*Woooo!*" Pa slapped the paper on his knee. "That's the thing about my boy," he boasted. "He never could do the normal things in life. He was cut out for doing something great. He always had to be great, or goddamn nothing at all!"

Coyote emerged first from the water. He howled to the skies. To the people watching from the bridge, he looked three sizes larger than life. The river had been crossed. The cows began climbing the banks. Then Coyote saw the people waving from the bridge. He spontaneously waved back.

Wrestler came out next, beaming, ecstatic. He felt twenty-five years old again, soaking wet, screaming, waving his hat.

The sun began to dry the men's clothes. The last of the cattle emerged, cool, safe, travelling. They looked eager to move after their swim.

The speedometer on Fun Truckin's van said they had done more than twenty miles that first day. It was enough. They stopped for the night.

Three small bonfires burned quietly around the perimeter of the herd of cattle. On an abandoned field, the herd nibbled on uncared for grass and alfalfa.

Wrestler pushed some brush and wood into his fire. Coyote stood, stretched, looked upward to a sky full of stars.

"God," he said. "Isn't that beautiful."

The next morning, right arm raised, Coyote sat on horseback, poised for the morning command. He mocked his own authority, winked at Wrestler. "How did John Wayne say it? Move 'em out?"

They passed Pueblo, Colorado on the mountain side. The stinking, polluted city lay to the east. The mountains were flatter here. The smog over Pueblo made everybody a little sick.

Past Pueblo, Colorado Springs waited ahead. Future miles dominated Coyote's thinking as he consulted with Wrestler.

"God, I wish we knew people in Nebraska. If we could find people who knew the way to take us through."

"There's got to be roads like these," added Wrestler.

"You know that for sure?"

"No, but it seems there would be."

Coyote was worried. "People are so unfriendly in that state. They're so odd, it's like the whole state's crossbred."

"You mean interbred," Wrestler corrected him.

"Yeah. I don't know." Coyote made a diagonal line in the air with his finger. "You know a simple diagonal across Nebraska puts us right into Sioux City. I mean right there."

Wrestler said, "I'll tell ya. First, we better be thinking about heading east so we can avoid Denver altogether."

"Where do you suggest we do that?"

"I don't know, do you?"

"I asked you," Coyote said.

They rode for a while.

Coyote had the answer. "I'll tell you what we all need. We need ourselves a scout."

They both heard it at the same time.

All of a sudden the horrible whine of a diesel truck came piercing through the air. They turned and looked. From the rear of the drive, a huge Peterbilt truck was bearing down on the cattle.

Brains was back there. Coyote screamed to him, "Watch out, kid!"

The truck punched up its speed. Coyote could see it was a cattle truck, making no effort to avoid the drive. From a quarter mile away and closing, the huge sixteen-wheeler seemed intent on rolling into the rear of the drive, burying Brains and any cattle that got in its way. It was going to be murder.

Young Brains saw the truck, but froze. He didn't know what to do. His mind raced but in all the wrong directions. He could ride across the road, try to escape. He could stay in the rear, protect the drive with his body. Brains's mind was coming up with choices but he was afraid of both alternatives.

He panicked. He jumped off his horse, ran to the barbed wire on the right, climbed and stumbled over it.

It was the worst thing he could have done.

The cows in the rear sensed his absence, began to break up. Here came the truck. He blared his air horn over and over. Cows stampeded the road shoulder, busting through the fence.

The trucker intentionally swerved into line with the rear of the herd. He kept coming. At the last instant, he swerved back onto the road, barely missing the cows, blaring his ear-splitting air horn the whole time. Wrestler got a good look at the trucker as he passed. On fifteen bennies, Wrestler thought. The man looked crazier than a wino with a ten-dollar bill.

The cows began scattering everywhere. Terrorized, at the rear of the drive, without Brains to calm them, some cows crossed the road. Others ran far into the fields beyond.

Coyote and Wrestler, on horseback, tore across the highway in pursuit. A speeding Buick coming from the other direction swerved, barely missed them.

Reacting with the most intelligence, Fun Truckin' immediately parked his van across the shoulder. This stopped the surge of cattle from moving forward, kept them comfortably bunched as a herd.

Trying not to panic the lead cows, Fun Truckin' slipped out the other side of his van without slamming the door, ran into the field on the right chasing loose cattle. When he saw Brains, he shouted furiously, "You could have stopped it! You let the herd go! You college punk!"

Brains was still standing there, shaken, not knowing what to do first. Books were no substitute for experience under fire.

So Fun Truckin' mounted Brains's horse, leaving the boy on foot. Fun Truckin' rode into the field, overtaking one cow, then another, redirecting them back toward the road.

By now, Coyote and Wrestler were doing the same thing. Food stayed near the road and did his best to intercept the returning cattle, re-forming them back into a herd.

Left without a task, Brains awkwardly ran back, tried to help Food organize the cattle. It was a long, stubborn job at best, leading cattle by their ears back into a line that had just been smashed by a truck. None of the cattle were especially interested in getting back into that sort of line.

Finally, after many hours, they got the herd back into shape, two by two, although they would never be the same orderly cattle they had once been.

Kerouac Country

Evening set in. Another vacant field provided grazing land for the cattle. They had begun to be peaceful again in the confines of the neglected field. Coyote had set small fires around the herd, to keep an imaginary boundary in the cattle's limited minds.

Ostracized by his shame, Brains rode picket position alone, on the far end of the herd. It was his job to keep the fires fueled and burning. He felt terrible, lower than a snake's belly, but as every moment passed, his craving for acceptance grew. He took out his maps and began initial planning for the moment that would be his. When they needed direction, only he would be prepared. Since his duties as legal advisor were limited, he would assume the responsibilities of navigator.

Behind Fun Truckin's van, the others sat in the evening. Coyote was smoking pipe tobacco, seemingly deep in serious thinking. A small campfire was burning. The pleasant aroma of woodsmoke and pipe tobacco hung in the air. Wrestler turned his head, trying to spot

Brains. He saw him in the distance. Wrestler felt concerned for the boy.

Reclining on his elbows, Fun Truckin' was a bit peeved by Wrestler's concern for Brains, but there was no way he could contradict Wrestler, so he dropped it.

Food was making sandwiches for everybody inside the van.

Coyote yelled, "Make one for the boy, will you, Food?"

Wrestler sensed how bad the boy must feel. He asked Coyote, "Did the kid settle down yet?"

Fun Truckin' interrupted. "That kid's a baby. He scares too easily."

"He'll be all right," Coyote told Fun Truckin'. But Fun Truckin' whined, "You ought to send him back to his nursery school before we get too far from home."

Just then Food handed out the sandwiches. Coyote took the extra one for Brains. "Haven't you ever been scared?" he asked Fun Truckin'.

"Not when other people were depending on me," Fun Truckin' replied.

Wrestler put his hands up. "Hey, he's a good kid. Lay off him."

Coyote had been doing some serious thinking. His face showed it when he spoke. He spoke reflectively.

"The truth is," Coyote explained, "we need everyone. That truck was no accident."

"No accident?" asked the fearful Food.

"That's right. Figure it out. Who does the real price gouging?" Everyone listened to Coyote's carefully chosen words. "Truckers! The meatpackers are scared shitless of them, so they gouge us. Who stands to lose if we win? Some people. Truckers are organized, we're not. They're powerful, they're the biggest union in the country. Hell, even the butchers are Teamsters."

Coyote felt detached from the person he had become, tried to sink back to the cowboy he had once been. But he had come too far, he knew too much. "But we're not supposed to understand that," he said. "Just be dumb, and fatten the beef."

Wrestler cursed them. "Goddamn chapstick fanatics." He was referring to trucker's greased lips for slick talking on a CB radio. He slid his lips from cheek to cheek. "Hello, Moon Dog, this is Big Baby, I may act seven but I'm really forty-three."

Coyote joked. "I threw away my walkie talkie when I was nine."

"Yeah, but that was just two tin cans," Wrestler quipped.

"It was still a toy." Coyote hit the meat of the matter.

"You know what pisses me off," said Fun Truckin. "They even copy the way we dress, hats, boots, Wrangler jeans. Shouldn't a grease monkey dress like a grease monkey?"

Coyote added, "We've been making their living for them. Here's my cattle, get rich, get me screwed." He paused, looked around. "So you all know what that was about? That near collision back there with the cattle truck?"

"What?" Food quavered.

Coyote talked to everybody. "They're afraid

137

some dumb shit cowboy like myself might figure out that for a month on the trail, he could sell directly to the buyer, and beat their inflated rates."

"How much is that?" Wrestler asked.

"Somewhere near a dollar," answered Coyote.

Wrestler added in the dirt. "We'll be selling at twice the price."

Coyote nodded. "We'll be close to tripling our money."

"Good," chided Wrestler. "Pay the damn help around here."

"I'll go with that, Wrestler. Pay you exactly what you're worth."

"Well, I'd want more than that."

"And you know," added Coyote, "with all my pa's years, it'll be the first time a Cantrell ever showed a profit off ranching."

Food could feel his knees quiver. "Do you think the truckers will come back?"

Coyote stood, looked down at Food. "Food, let me put it to you this way. I think the flavor has changed."

Brains fueled the small fires again, came back to his own, tied his horse to a tree, sat miserably in the grass next to his pile of maps.

He heard noises in the brush. They were coming closer to him. He got scared. Then he saw Coyote, breathed easily.

"I brought a sandwich for you, kid."

Brains was grateful, but he was already unfolding the maps, opening them in the light of the fire. "Look!" He motioned Coyote down.

Coyote bent over. In the flickering light he

saw a dark line drawn in magic marker. The area looked very familiar. Brains loked at him with a face full of the eagerness of youth.

"I traced a route for us all the way into Nebraska."

Coyote could only smile with complete appreciation at Brains.

They slept like babies. For everyone, it was their first good night's sleep on the road.

Fun Truckin's eyes were red from constantly looking into the sun. He was still in low gear, hadn't been out of it yet. He had rigged a jammer to his gas pedal, so both his feet were now free. All he had to do was steer. The slow pace was beginning to drive him crazy. He saw Coyote riding up in his side mirror. With the boredom he was feeling, this was like a major event. He leaned out the window.

"Fun Truckin'. How'd you like to be my scout?"

"Your scout? You bet!"

"Good. Here's some maps."

"Want me to autograph them?"

"Right." They chuckled. Coyote reached up, handed him the maps. Fun Truckin' took them.

"Uh, Brains drew them up."

"Yeah, well, fuck Brains." Fun Truckin' deflated instantly.

"I want you to work with him."

"Sure he's not too intelligent for me?" Fun Truckin' called down.

"Who did I ask to be my scout? You, or him?"

"Well, you asked me."

"That's right, Now look at those maps."

In the van, Fun Truckin' opened them. He seemed placated. Coyote took a deep breath as he rode beside the slow moving van. It was getting tough keeping everybody happy.

"O.K.?" he called up. "Now that's roughly the way to go."

Fun Truckin' turned his attention to Coyote.

Coyote told him what he wanted. "Find me a way northeast, so we avoid Denver, somewhere before Castle Rock. You see Castle Rock?"

Fun Truckin' looked down. Coyote called up. "It's circled. Just below Denver, there."

"Yeah, I see it."

"All right, we need to bypass Denver completely, cut underneath it."

Brains had drawn a dark line through the center of Colorado, then veered up and right, on the side roads, into the Nebraska corner.

Fun Truckin' was already anxious to go. "When do I start?"

Coyote held up his hand. "Not yet. We need roads like this one, up through Greeley, Colorado. I know a rancher there who'll let us graze and rest a few days. From there, we go right to the corner of Nebraska."

"I can do that."

"You do that. Find me nice grassy roads. With places to stop."

"Nice grassy roads." Fun Truckin' was smiling. "Right to the corner of Nebraska."

Fun Truckin' undid his jammer while driving. He was anxious to get going. But one thing was holding him up. Brains was in the rear of the van, making a sandwich. And he was taking his sweet time doing it.

Brains wasn't content simply to make his bologna sandwich. He had to spread his mayonnaise perfectly, on every air pocket of white bread. Fun Truckin' could see him in the rear-view mirror. Brains reminded him of his little sister, the way he spread the mayonnaise so perfectly.

Brains desperately wanted to make conversation. He knew Fun Truckin' was the scout only because of the maps he drew, and most importantly, because he owned the van. Fun Truckin' was the important scout, leaving Brains behind. Brains wanted to make conversation. He wanted to show Fun Truckin' he wasn't afraid of him. He was tired of being treated like a child.

Brains exhaled. "I'm glad we got the cows back." A friendly enough remark, he thought.

Fun Truckin' wouldn't answer. He ignored Brains.

"The maps give you a good idea of where you're going? Do you know where you're going?" Still there was no response. "Not yet, huh?"

Fun Truckin' wanted one thing, for that kid to shut up and eat his sandwich. But he knew his silence wasn't working.

"Heh, ever been up this far? Ever been this far from Walsenburg?" Of course he hadn't, thought Brains. He's probably never been anywhere.

"After Castle Rock, it's all New York to me," Fun Truckin' drawled.

Brains felt a wave of satisfaction, didn't realize Fun Truckin' was mocking him. Besides, magic rang between his ears, magic from the classic beatnik book, *On the Road*. Brains thought about the novel in his mind.

"Castle Rock," Brains sighed wistfully. "This is Kerouac country."

"Who's Kerouac?"

"Kerouac. Jack Kerouac. My God, he wrote *The Dharma Bums* and *On the Road*. He and Dean Moriarty used to stop in Castle Rock, in the '50s, on their way back and forth to Mexico."

The surly Fun Truckin' cut it short. "You mean, he was a book writer."

"What a writer! His publisher once flew him to New York just so he could kiss him after reading his mauscript."

Fun Truckin' reacted to that, turned around. "Well, I don't read books."

"Not even comics?" Thank God, thought Brains, he can't leave the wheel.

Fun Truckin' pointed his finger. "Don't be a smartass!"

"A smartass is someone who sits on an ice cream cone and can tell you what flavor it was."

Fun Truckin' had no answer for something as complicated as that. But his anger boiled over as he digested the remark. Brains was about to step off the back of the van.

"Just don't hold my education against me forever. O.K.? I'm just trying to better myself. I wasn't born with it like you!"

Fun Truckin' relaxed. Finally he was able to undo his jammer, follow the goddamn maps, pull off and scout the future of the cattle drive. He breathed easier now that Brains was away.

Rich Nebraska Farmland

With Fun Truckin' as a scout and Brains planning the route, they bypassed Denver, made it all the way up to Greeley. Both boys were taking more and more responsibility for the drive.

There were various but easily surmountable obstacles, like one small bridge with a warning sign saying 7,000 LB. LIMIT. So they sent the cows over single file and never had more than ten cows on the bridge at one time.

From Greeley, the mountains were only to be seen at a distance. Coyote daydreamed, imagined he was a mountain man seeing the mountains for the first time. He had traps on his pack horse and St. Louis in his past. He had tired of the settlement and civilized ways, had come West to trap beaver and live with Indians. Back then, there were no cattle, at least not cattle like these. There were only Texas longhorns, a cut above a jackal, really, in their temperaments, and hard, really hard to drive. If he was lucky, with a good nose and plenty of powder, a man lived by venison, or buffalo. The cattle were so bad that when the Indians were first exposed to the white man's delicacy, a beef steak, they fed it to their dogs. They couldn't stomach cow meat, even when better breeding methods developed cattle like those Coyote had. But the government encouraged buffalo hunting until the buffalo were gone and the Indians began to beg and claw at each other for the white man's rations of beef steak. They were like Thomas, who was glad to accept a jail sentence as a reprieve from life. Why was he thinking of Thomas? Thomas was gone.

At the Cantrell ranch, since Coyote was gone, Jolene never stopped working. "Take it easy, honey," Pa said to her.

Jolene pulled boots over her thick winter socks. "We can't assume he's gonna make it, Pa. We've got to try and keep going with what we have here."

Pa cursed. "I feel so helpless laying here."

"You get better, Pa. Without you, I wouldn't be doing this. Your being here is all the help I need."

"You're an amazing woman."

"When you're away from your man, Pa, there's a lot more hours in the day."

To save hay, Jolene took five or six breeder cows into the high country and let them graze there all day. She rode with the cows away from the ranch house, up the hilly terrain, until she was concealed by massive lodgepole pines and delicate quake aspens. The round green leaves of the frail bent aspens were turning shades of orange. She remembered how Pa put it. When the breeze blew, they did almost look like thousands of dried apricots shimmering in the breeze.

Leading her cows out of the shelter of the trees, she saw the meadow she wanted. It was wild with Indian paintbrush, bluebells, and sweetgrass. The cattle knew a good thing. They began to graze.

As they left Greeley, the mountains were practically invisible. After another couple of days, they were gone. Travelling east from Colorado, the land became extremely boring. Travelling from the East, this land would be the first magical terrain he would see. It rose and fell from great buttes into canyons. The flats were lush from the great Rocky river runoff. But there were fewer cattle to be seen. Soon they would disappear, yielding to corn, wheat, fences, and order.

Coyote and Wrestler, as was becoming the custom, rode next to each other. "It's gettin' flat," said Wrestler. "Mountains are gone."

Coyote nodded in agreement. "Must be near Nebraska." They rode on, then Coyote said, "No wonder these people are the way they are. In Colorado, you work, but you get to see the mountains, you know there's other worlds beyond your own. But here, everywhere, it's all Nebraska. Everywhere."

It was true. The land here became less and less rewarding to the senses. Oh, it gave crops by the bushel. If you planted a nail, a crowbar would grow. But it didn't excite a person. As a result, the people didn't excite an outsider. To a vistor, the land and the people were one and the same.

They rode on together, Wrestler, the wisened grizzled old cowpuncher with the enormous forearms, and Coyote, the bitter young fighter with with just enough vision in him to try to beat the system.

Up ahead was a sign, LEAVING COLORFUL COLORADO.

Everybody whooped! They were quiet whoops, for now they had left familiar territory and were riding into the unknown.

They came to the top of another hill, saw another sign, WELCOME TO NEBRASKA, THE CORNHUSKER STATE. Ahead was a bend in the road. It was there they heard the cocking of rifles and the loading of shotguns.

Fifty or sixty farmers waited in clusters at the Nebraska border. They looked vicious, unorganized, ready for random excitement.

To Coyote they looked like retards, men grown up on farms within the confines of custom and inbreeding. Coyote didn't know what to do, how to respond. He stopped the cattle drive while most of it was still in Colorado.

A farmer stepped forward. "No way you're bringing your cows across our rich Nebraska farmland!"

"But I won't—"

"No way!" The farmer had had his say. He was through speaking.

So Coyote thought. To the man they were guarding their farms. He looked around. All of them were pointing their rifles, at Coyote, at everything in the drive.

He decided to test them.

A crazy streak hit Coyote. He didn't know what to do, how to respond to this stupidity, so he began to ride through the rows and rows of clustered, armed Nebraska farmers. He didn't know why he was making this strange ride through the eerie silence of solemn men, but he continued.

The farmers wouldn't react. Instead, they watched Coyote with eyes as cold as the weather. They refused even to turn their heads when he rode by. They kept peering out of the corners of their darting, squinted eyes. Violence loomed a loose trigger finger away, but never erupted.

. Fun Truckin' couldn't stand the waiting. He climbed out of his van, walked toward one of the farmers. His steps were menacing. Immediately the farmer pointed his shotgun at Fun Truckin'.

"Hey you!" The farmer warned the boy to stop.

"Me?" Fun Truckin' replied.

"Don't see anybody else!"

Fun Truckin' turned around. "I see you! Hog dick dirt farmer!" Fun Truckin' stalked the farmer, testing him. He walked from twenty yards away into the barrel of the farmer's gun. "I'm gonna jam that up your asshole!" Fun Truckin' threatened.

Coyote saw what was happening, turned back, rode between the levelled gun and the boy. He latched onto Fun Truckin's collar, pulled him away from the farmer.

There was nothing left to do. They retreated

into a discussion, back near the Nebraska border. Fun Truckin's parked van and grazing grass by the side of the road kept the cattle in check.

"What're we gonna do?" asked Food. "We could starve to death out here. We gotta go back. It's into September. It's gonna snow!"

"Aw shit," Wrestler said. "It could snow once, then stay warm until October."

"Uh uh," complained Food. "Not this year. Feel that wind? It's gonna snow until it freezes, then stay that way." Food pulled his collar up to the north wind. It was true. The wind moved down from the North Pole like a sheet of ice across the open plains.

"Aw, Food, how do you know what it's gonna be like?" Fun Truckin' hated a coward.

"I know," Food replied. "What am I doing here?"

Wanting to calm Food, Coyote patted him on the shoulder. "Food, with what we're doing, you're gonna be famous. Ranchers everywhere are gonna look up to you." The thought of fame diminished Food's negativism. But they were still at a standstill.

Coyote resumed the discussion. "It's a cinch they won't let us cross anywhere in Nebraska. Every farmer on the border must be out. It's probably the biggest thing ever happened up here." He paused. "Anybody got any suggestions?"

Wrestler had one. "We could try South Dakota. Cross up there."

"South Dakota?" asked Coyote.

"Why not?" Wrestler replied.

"How far is that, Brains?" asked Coyote.

Brains consulted his map. "South Dakota? That's another hundred miles due north."

"Another hundred miles?" Food slipped back into his timidity.

"That's not bad," said Fun Truckin'.

"Seems to me," said Wrestler, "that's our only shot."

"Then what?" asked Food.

Brains pulled his head out of pages of state maps, had his scientific reply. "We cross to Sioux City, Iowa, same as before. It's on the same latitude. All we lose is our diagonal, which is minimal when you consider the alternative of turning back."

Fun Truckin' thinned his lips, looked at Brains as though he were all right after all. Momentarily, he accepted the importance of the college boy, big words and all. Brains noticed this, but both remained aloof.

Coyote asked Brains, "What's the food situation like for the cattle along the Wyoming/Nebraska border?"

Of course, Brains gave a speech. "Rolling grasslands like this most all the way. Alfalfa in Wyoming, corn in Nebraska. After a ways, in Wyoming, you have one county, one square on the map, with more coal than the next five coal-producing nations combined. Can you imagine? The next five nations combined? They can't even have a landfill dump because the bulldozers keep striking veins of coal."

"Shit," complained Fun Truckin' after the dissertation.

"We won't hit that coal?" Coyote asked.

"I don't think so," Brains replied.

"Then why'd ya bring it up?" Fun Truckin' asked.

Coyote raised his hand. "Never mind." He looked to Wrestler for assurance. "Sound like enough grass to keep weight on these beasts?"

Wrestler shrugged. He was unsure.

"For a hundred miles?" Brains measured his map. "Easily."

So the drive shifted direction, headed along the Nebraska border, directly into the north wind. Food reluctantly rode ahead, bundled up. He would feel ridiculous turning back. Besides, how could he travel across country, alone, on a horse? He might get arrested. Then who would bail him out?

Coyote rode next to Brains, both reading the map. The wind fought to split the paper. Brains saw a town, called it to Coyote's attention. "Do you believe there's a Maggie's Nipple, Wyoming?"

Coyote waved him off. "Just keep us straddling the border all the way up."

The cluster of farmers on the right thinned, but enough remained to keep the drive slightly to the left side of the Nebraska/Wyoming border, in Wyoming.

Coyote left Brains, rode back to join Wrestler. He saw Food was shivering even though he had two jackets on. Wrestler had his collar turned up, wore gloves. Coyote reached Wrestler, poked him with an elbow. "South Dakota, huh?"

"Why not?"

"Why not? It was your idea, remember?"

More farmers appeared up ahead, to the right. They rode past them. Up ahead waited another cluster of farmers. This group stretched on for quite a distance.

"You took a complete stab, didn't you," Coyote said to Wrestler.

Silently, Wrestler kept riding. Finally he spoke, poker-faced. "South Dakota, wonder what grows up there?"

"Nothing. Smile at the sonofabitches, Wrestler." Coyote turned, gave three farmers a big, wide, sarcastic grin as the cattle drive passed. Wrestler grinned at them, too.

Expressionless, the farmers kept up their vigil.

Inside a large office building in Chicago, Illinois, the president of Gateways sat calmly behind a massive teak desk, watched Ricardo angrily slam down the phone. He announced the news to the room.

"Shit!" Ricardo cursed. "He's going north."

They all reacted differently. Clinger, who had been flown here with Ricardo, turned to a large map of America that had been tacked to the paneled wall. A line in marker pen ran north from Walsenburg, turned east at Castle Rock, then ran to the southeast corner of Nebraska. The line was a copy of the one Brains had drawn. Only here there was a large X at Nebraska, indicating a stoppage.

Gateways had done its best, stirring up the local farmers with stories of a radical cowboy intent on trampling their corn and wheat fields with a large herd of renegade cattle. But they hadn't counted on Coyote going north. Already Clinger was extending the dark line north from the X toward the next state up, South Dakota.

Ricardo was pounding the table in frustration. He had staked his career on the success of this project. Privately, he was seriously beginning to wonder about that success. "What if we can't stop him?" Clinger asked aloud.

The president appeared completely calm. A handsome man of sixty-three, with razor-cut steel gray hair, he stood and moved toward the map. Clinger was impressed with the cut of his jib.

"There is no problem," the president said. He waited until the map was behind him before speaking again. "When he reaches South Dakota, we simply will hold him until help arrives from our most reliable ally."

He paused. No one knew who this was. "Who's that?" Clinger asked. The president smiled confidently. "Winter."

Ricardo's eyes focused better than ever before. He looked at the president closely. No wonder he was the president. How well prepared he was, with a backup plan for the plan.

The president waited for Ricardo to stop staring before he began his explanation. He extended his hand to Clinger who gave him the marker pencil.

"My friends at the Weather Bureau assure me that within two weeks, a series of storms will sock in the Rocky Mountain region." The president drew an inclusive circle around the snowstorm area. "That includes Wyoming, Nebraska, and South Dakota."

As yet, no one understood the president's meaning.

Then he circled an area out into the ocean, off the coast of upper Washington State.

"These storms are presently building off the Pacific Northwest. Gentlemen, understand this. Our third major stockholder is the head of the South Dakota National Guard."

Clinger almost burped as he inhaled. The president noticed.

"No, Mr. Clinger, we are not going to bomb the man. We are, however, going to detain him, for as long as it takes to turn him around."

"How?" Clinger asked. The president had to smile when the banker asked, "On what charge?"

The president leaned forward, put his elbows down on his massive teakwood desk. "Let's think of some, shall we?" he asked.

Down in southern Colorado, Jolene had her ear next to her transistor radio when the news came in. It was a big thing in Walsenburg. Everybody was talking about Coyote. The radio station was carrying reports on his dailly progress.

"They're going north, Pa. Up to South Dakota."

Jolene ran into Pa's bedroom with the news. The old man could hardly lift his head from the pillow. His disease had spread. The tension of worrying about the ranch, the complication of the farmers, then Coyote's going north had taken a toll on his already weak nervous system. He wasn't always in control. His bowels became irregular. He had a fever. His tea stayed cold in the cup these days.

"Damnit, Jolene. I'm not gonna die yet."

"No, Pa."

"But I keep feeling myself expire."

"Not yet, Pa. Hang on. Just until he makes it."

"You know I want to see him again. Tell him how proud I am."

"One step at a time, Pa. Wait until he gets across into Iowa. Then you tell him. Now I'm gonna bring more breeders up." She stood. "You'll be O.K.?"

"Damnit, Jolene! It's not that I'm not trying!"

"I know you're trying, Pa."

Jolene didn't bother with a fresh cup of tea. She knew he wouldn't drink it. She left for the cows. These days, cows were as important as your own kin.

The elements were beginning to dominate the cattle drive. You could hear the north wind coming. It would get creepy, silent, completely still. Larger creatures would hide. The smaller ones would cling to the ground.

Then it came at forty, fifty, often sixty miles per hour, a howl of icy wind that froze the marrow in a man's bones.

Coyote grazed the cattle early this dusk. Fun Truckin' had rejoined the guys, back from scouting. Everyone huddled inside the open back doors of his van. A fire on the outside kept the heat within a small perimeter, but the wind wouldn't stop blowing the coals around, so the warmth never stayed focused in one place.

They were fortunate to keep the fenced-in field for the cattle to graze. It was by the blessing of the wind that they kept it. No farmer ventured outside tonight.

Coyote and Wrestler watched the cattle carefully. They grazed not as a herd but in small bunches.

"It's almost as if they're unsure, like we are," Coyote said. "The way they're keeping in bunches like that."

Wrestler raised and lowered his eyes in agreement. It was too cold to nod, to move the head.

Brains recommended they stay with the road they were on. But Brains made his first mistake. He failed to see a town in tiny print, Henry, Nebraska.

So after crossing the North Platte on a deserted bridge they found themselves on the edge of a wind-bitten little town. Their procession halted. The sheriff stood there, holding up an outstretched arm, the town guardian.

Fun Truckin' denounced Brains. "Great map you drew, student."

Coyote rode up to meet the sheriff.

"O.K., cowboy. I ain't worried 'bout no wheatfields, no stories in the paper. I am worried about one thing, my steak for the winter. Seeing as how you got a bunch of cattle, and I got one town, I'll take a cow for my town, and you can go through my main street. Otherwise, I get help. Sound fair?"

"Aw, fuck it!" Coyote had no choice, so he

motioned to his herd, let the sheriff lead away a 1,500-pound Hereford, which even at the middle price of forty cents still cost Coyote $600.

As the drive passed through the town, the cow was already grazing in the sheriff's backyard. Coyote cursed the sheriff under his breath as they left the two-block town. One block was paved, the other wasn't.

That night, nobody heard Coyote ride through town, around the back to the sheriff's house. Coyote crept through the bushes, waiting for a dog to bark, but none did. Only the cow reacted to the slight rustling.

Then a rope lassoed the cow around the neck. Coyote gently pulled the cow to the fence.

A light went on inside the sheriff's house.

Quickly Coyote snipped the fence with wire clippers, pulled the cow out through the gap in the fence, and was gone.

Another light went on, but the sheriff had five acres between him and the crime, his dog was asleep inside, and neither would know until morning about the missing cow and the hole in the fence.

Another mood of somewhat milder celebration pervaded the drive that day. The wind finally let up. There were cornfields in full bloom to the right, in Nebraska. Rich grasslands for the cattle were to the left, in Wyoming. They had overcome the farmers. Only a few were to be seen any more. And they were well on their way to South Dakato, where all they had to do was turn right, move across the state, and presto, they would be in Sioux City. Everybody had learned to pace himself. Nobody expected instant rewards so expectations were lowered, and everybody was able to enjoy what he was doing moment by glorious moment.

The sky was overcast, the day was only a little chilly, and Coyote rode next to Wrestler. He felt like making conversation.

"How come you never got married, Wrestler?"

"I don't know. Always had more important things to do out here on the prairie than court a woman."

Coyote didn't know whether to laugh or not.

"You want to know the truth about women?" Wrestler asked Coyote. Coyote nodded. "If they didn't have cunts, there'd be a bounty on 'em."

Wrestler never changed his expression. Coyote couldn't laugh. Something about Wrestler looked so alone and desolate. His feelings, his opinions were so harsh.

"Now how am I gonna drive your cattle with a wife waitin' at home, waitin' for me to support her?"

Coyote wanted to answer, but Food rode by on his way to the van. Coyote noticed Food had lost a few pounds, knew it hadn't been easy.

Wrestler called, "How's yer diet, fat man?"

Pride wounded, Food turned back. "How's it look to you?"

"If someone told you to haul ass, you'd have to make two trips!"

Wrestler cackled. Again Coyote couldn't laugh. What was happening? Coyote felt himself changing.

Wrestler said loudly, "Baby doctor had to take him with a block and tackle."

Coyote hoped Food hadn't heard. He nodded at Wrestler, left. Was this what Jolene had saved him from becoming? Was this what happened to broken-down rodeo bums? Coyote was as mean as anybody, but now he couldn't stomach cruelty.

Coyote looked inside himself. Maybe he was becoming a rancher.

With Fun Truckin' gone scouting up ahead, Coyote rode lead horse. A cloud of dust coming from the north disturbed his thoughful, peaceful ride.

It was Fun Truckin' racing back at fifty miles an hour. He hoped the kid hadn't gotten caught siphoning gas. He parked on the opposite shoulder, ran up out of breath.

"They've blockaded a small town, maybe two miles ahead."

Brains rode up too. "What's wrong?"

"Just shut up, O.K.?" Fun Truckin' didn't want a word with Brains now.

"How big's the town?" Coyote asked.

"It's a three-block town. Neat as a pin."

"A blockade?" Brains caught on.

"Shit." Coyote kicked at the ground.

Fun Truckin' was walking alongside the moving horse as he talked. "They look serious. They've built a small fence. But nobody's out there yet."

"What's the countryside like?" Coyote asked.

"Kind of rolling hills all over."

"Any way we could sneak up on them?"

"No, they'd see us."

Brains asked, "How about on either side?" Brains had read that during the Cuban Revolution, a major army was waiting for Che Guevara in a town, so Che's men snuck around the town on both sides, continued to a more significant destination. The cattle could do that, too.

"Either side of what?" replied a surly Fun Truckin'.

"Of the town," said Brains. "What's the terrain like on either side of the town?"

"Aw shit!" Fun Truckin' tried ignoring him.

"C'mon, what's it like? Maybe I've got an idea here."

"Tell him," said Coyote.

"It's the same rolling hills. But it's all private, and what you'd call very well fenced, with barbed wire."

"These hills," Brains asked, "are they wooded?"

"Aw shut up, will you." Coyote was tired of trying to figure out Brains's riddles. He was figuring on his own. Coyote looked up at Fun Truckin'. Something the boy said stuck in his mind. He said to himself, "a three-block town," then he said aloud, "Neat as a pin huh?"

Fun Truckin' nodded. "Like a whistle."

Brains had to spill his idea. "There's a trick I learned—"

Coyote interrupted him fast.

"There's a trick I learned a long time ago." Both boys looked at Coyote.

"Stampede the motherfuckers!"

They stole the two-by-fours from a billboard

161

along the way, attached them to the front of Fun Truckin's bumper, so they jutted out from the van. The bumper smashed the small fence to pieces as the van powered through the town at thirty miles an hour, with 450 stampeding cattle right behind, surrounded on both sides by galloping cowboys.

The waiting townspeople scrambled for cover in their neat-as-a-pin town. The cars parked along the sides made a natural barrier to keep the cattle in the center of the street. They were mostly vintage 1950 vehicles. The people were the same, old and frightened.

Wrestler was whooping and yelling, "Hey, honey, you got a husband?" But nobody heard him over the horrendous roar of 450 head of stampeding cattle.

They made the town in about two minutes. It took three times that long to slow the beasts down to a walk again.

Coyote looked back in triumph at the people standing at the edge of their civilization, shaking their fists at him. Coyote smiled, did something he remembered well how to do. He flipped them all off.

Two-thirds of the way into Nebraska, the cold became more severe. Food couldn't take it anymore. Fun Truckin' offered to let him drive the van and Food gladly accepted. Fun Truckin' nudged him. "You know, you *have* lost weight."

Food looked very pleased. Fun Truckin' showed him how to wark the jammer on the gas pedal, then put his own belongings in Food's saddle bags, mounted the horse. The horse had to be happy about the lighter human who mounted him.

In the van, Food was happy and content. He rolled the windows up, turned the heater on until he began to sweat. Then he pulled it back to low and let it stay that way.

Coyote still rode lead horse. He chose to deny the cold by ignoring it. He wondered why the cattle companies hadn't ordered more of their truck drivers to sabotage the drive. Because of the danger he presented to the trucking companies' livelihood, he couldn't understand why they hadn't tried harder to break him.

Brains now rode behind Coyote, second horse from the lead. It was the first time during the trip that he had been out of the dust and despite the cold he was loving it.

Wrestler rode second from the rear, feeling loose and relaxed, his destiny up in the air, where he liked it.

On Food's horse, Fun Truckin' chose to ride the rear. He felt that since he had had it so easy until now, he should move Brains up and ride in the rear. Coyote respected the kid for that. He was tough, but fair.

This time everybody heard the trucks at the same time. There were two trucks. No warning, no horn, just the horrible whine of diesel engines, two sixteen-wheel cattle trucks, revving up for the vicious scatter and slaughter of the cattle drive.

A terrible fear crept into everybody's bones, already chilled to the limit. From behind the last cow, the two trucks rushed down a long downgrade of highway. Both trucks were full of cattle. They weighed enough to pulverize the rear of the drive and crush Fun Truckin'.

Fun Truckin' turned around once, from the rear where he had chosen to ride. He saw that the trucks were from the Sioux City Feed Lots, could tell by their color. Then he turned forward again, never once looked back.

He knew what he had to do. With his eyes glued forward, he rode ahead, well on the road's shoulder, between the truck's path and the cattle.

The first truck swerved clearly onto the shoulder, all its right side tires off the road, on the grass.

Still Fun Truckin' would not scare. He wouldn't move. It was simple, conquering fear. You pretend it wasn't there.

"Oh no," said Wrestler. He couldn't let the trucks hit the boy, couldn't let his youthful body be broken, splattered over the road because of a foolhardy notion of macho courage.

The trucks were closing the distance with incredible mass, weight, and speed. The first driver kept his tires on the road shoulder, playing chicken with Fun Truckin'. Fun Truckin' still refused to look back.

"Look out!" Wrestler broke away from his position second from the rear, rode full speed toward the rear of the cattle drive in a kamikaze ride. He called, "Look out kid! Get out of the way!"

Wrestler held his horse to the course. If Fun Truckin' wouldn't move maybe the truck driver would. Maybe he would see how insane this was and get back on the road. Somebody had to stop this game.

"Get out of the way, kid!"

Wrestler kept waving his arms.

The truck was now a hundred yards away and coming, its right tires aiming at Fun Truckin'.

Fun Truckin's horse began to bolt. Courageously, the boy braced the pony's head forward, stayed in position protecting the rear cattle. His horse resisted, panicked. Fun Truckin' leaned forward, held down the pony's neck.

"Here it comes! Move, kid!"

The boy had nerves of steel. He was too tough to scare.

The trucker had instructions to break up the drive, but the kid wouldn't move. His orders did not include murder. He came bearing down. At the last second he pulled his cattle truck back on the road, avoiding Fun Truckin' by not more than ten feet.

Wrestler saw this, tried to move back into the drive, into the line of cattle, but a cow moved over into the spot he was trying for. Now he was caught in the truck's path. He was hung out to dry on the road. Wrestler waved his arms again frantically for the driver to see.

The trucker saw him at the last moment, tried to swerve even farther. But it wasn't enough.

Wham!

The mirror on the truck's right side clipped Wrestler's right wrist, sent him flying off the left side of his terrified horse.

Wrestler threw out his hands, breaking the fall. Some of the small bones in his wrist broke and splintered. He landed at the hooves of the cattle.

The second truck continued bearing down. They had forgotten about it. Fun Truckin' still held his position. The first truck neared Brains, second from the front. It was blaring its horn, trying to frighten and stampede the cattle.

Wrestler lay there, writhing in pain, his horse gone. He was unable to move. Wrist smashed, wide-eyed, terrified, he lay on the ground, watching the cattle hooves flying by.

Brains saw this, knew he had to keep the cows in line or Wrestler would be trampled as he lay there. Acting courageously he did what Wrestler had done before him.

Here came the second truck! It swerved too, its right tires spitting grass churned from the shoulder of the road.

Brains bolted from his position, turned the pony around, rode at full speed toward the rear of the drive. He kept the cows in line as he rode, waving his arms, hoping to keep the second truck from coming too close to the line of cattle, or to Wrestler.

The truck had to swerve off the shoulder to miss Fun Truckin'. Then it had to stay in the road to keep from hitting Brains.

Brains's plan worked. By now, Coyote had also done the same thing, but he stayed near the front to keep the herd from stampeding that way.

"Oh, thank God," Brains said to himself.

Then he saw one poor cow wobbling in the middle of the road. It had been hit by the second truck, was fighting to stay on its feet. Then the cow sank to the ground. Nothing could be done. Brains rode closer. The cow was still alive, but crippled, and that was that.

Finally Brains reached Wrestler. He lifted Wrestler onto the back of his horse. Fun Truckin' got there at the same time, screaming, "You all right? You all right?"

Wrestler was able to nod. Brains nodded.

Fun Truckin' touched Brains on the shoulder, congratulated him. "That really took guts."

Brains was so shaken he could barely acknowledge.

Then Coyote arrived, assisted Wrestler to get down from Brains's horse. He tried to comfort the injured old man. Wrestler looked very old right now.

"There's a stream over there," Coyote said. "Let's take you to it."

As Coyote led Wrestler toward the stream, he saw all the cattle becoming restless around the one that was dying. Coyote pulled his rifle from the sheath on the side of his horse, handed the gun to Brains. "You're gonna have to shoot it."

With Food cross-parking the van, the herd held in position. By now the ponies were trained to stay by the line of cows. No cattle strayed onto the road. Fun Truckin' and Food were left to stay with the cattle.

Brains looked at the dying cow. He had his instructions. He tried not to think. He aimed at

the cow, but could not pull the trigger. Brains
had to see what he was doing. He opened his
eyes. He needed to experience the moment. He
looked closely at the cow's wounded face. It lay
flat, its chin against the road. Its body had totally crumpled from being broken inside and
from exhaustion. Brains aimed a second time,
still could not shoot. He felt ashamed all over
again, as he had before. He couldn't kill the
cow. There was no use pretending.

By now Fun Truckin' walked over. Gently he
took the rifle from Brains. "I can do it,"
Brains said. But Fun Truckin' nudged him
away. "Hey," Fun Truckin' told Brains, "you
don't want to be like me."

Without a blink, Fun Truckin' shot the cow
point blank in the head. The cow died immediately.

The other cattle now ceased to notice the
dead cow, ignored it as if it weren't there. Fun
Truckin' put his arm across Brians's shoulder,
walked the youth back to the horses. They made
a sling, did their best to drag the dead cow out
of the road. Their horses did the pulling while
the rest of the cattle grazed where they stood,
on the shoulder.

Over by the side of the stream, Coyote let
Wrestler sit down on the bank. Coyote took off
Wrestler's boots. His wrist was beginning to
throb badly, was starting to swell. Wrestler
sunk his ankles in the stream. Coyote felt the
break in two places.

"Wrestler, this is crazy."

"Hell, I know that."

Coyote reached into the bank, began forming

a cast for Wrestler out of wet mud. Wrestler knew what Coyote was doing. His own father had done it too, when Wrestler was very young. It was one of the old ways, from when there were no doctors on every corner.

Wrestler tried to relax while Coyote formed more slabs of wet mud around his wrist. The first mud was already caking, drying hard around the injured bones. It began to look like a cast.

Once the entire mud pack hardened, Coyote wrapped the cast with a roll of adhesive tape. Wrestler saw how nervous Coyote was.

"Relax," said Wrestler, trying to calm Coyote down. "It's O.K. It's only my wrist." Wrestler knew Coyote was wearing the guilt for his injury.

"Hey," Wrestler said. Coyote looked at the old man, listened as he spoke. "Whatever happens, we live free again. We live like cowboys."

The sentiment they both felt was overwhelming.

Coyote almost felt tears. He knew Wrestler was right. They were living the old way, out on the road, like cowboys. Wrestler felt the tears too. They looked at each other.

But somehow, they were both too tough to cry.

Dakota

They were getting close to South Dakota. The drive finally had arrived at the beginnings of the great wasteland. The badlands were to the right. The Black Hills were further north, straight up the map. Coyote, Wrestler, Fun Truckin', and Brains now looked calloused, intense, almost bitter as they pushed northward just so they could head east again. They held in their anger at the truckers, their frustration at being pushed out of their way. Little did they know about the stone wall they would face, which soon would be waiting for them at the South Dakota border.

One hundred yards ahead stood a lone roadside tavern and a filling station. A hippie was hitchhiking, frantically trying to wave down a car to get a ride. As they got closer, they saw in the parking lot the two cattle trucks from Sioux City Feed Lots, the same ones that had broken Wrestler's wrist.

Coyote and Fun Truckin' filled with rage at the sight of the trucks. Both looked at Wrestler riding with a limp right arm.

The hippie started to run away. Coyote saw that his face was cut and bruised, covered with dried blood. Coyote raised his hand in peace, asked, "What happened?"

"Those fuckers beat me up." The hippie's voice was quivering. He looked as though he wanted to be home, wherever that was.

Coyote looked at Fun Truckin', remembered his persoanl rage about how truckers imitated cowboys in their dress. "Lemme wear your head band," Coyote said to the hippie. Coyote gave him his hat to hold.

"Cover me," he said to Fun Truckin'. Coyote tied the headband. Its end dangled past his collar.

"I'll go in with you," offered Fun Truckin'.

"There's only two of 'em," Coyote scoffed. "Right, son?" The hippie nodded yes.

Inside the darkness of the tavern, the two truckers sat drinking cold beer. The bar was seedy-looking, with stuffed beaver and muskrat on the walls.

Coyote walked into the dim light around the doorway, looking just like the hippie, standing in the shadows.

"Look who's back," the first trucker said.

Coyote stepped into the light, made himself visible. The truckers were shocked to see Coyote. "He's dressed like the hippie," one said.

"Just didn't want anyone to take me for a goddamn trucker!"

Coyote waded into both truck drivers with 400 miles of fury. He demolished them with power punches to the kidneys, belly, and neck. Coyote wasn't crazy. He fought cold and brutal.

He punched hard, thudding punches, drawing no blood. He didn't care for glory. No one would see these men. He punched to break a man's insides, blows the victims would carry with them.

The truckers were crumbling. They hadn't the will for fighting. They liked it better in their trucks, where they were safe. *Bam!* Coyote backfired his elbow into the second trucker's kidneys. Cuts scabbed, then healed. A broken kidney would never be whole again. The bartender stayed on his knees behind the bar. Nothing of his was being broken. What was going on came from before, it wasn't his business. He stayed on his knees.

The men were like two aspen trees bent and mangled by wet snow. It was over. They were down, silent, broken up inside. There had been very little sound before, but for the grunting and the sounds of blows. Now there was no noise at all.

Outside another trucker pulled up, sensed trouble, left his truck. Coming around the front of his engine, Fun Truckin' slammed him in the belly, punched him flat on his nose. The trucker fell hard, head first, landing in his own pool of blood.

Fun Truckin' ran into the tavern. Coyote was just leaving. Fun Truckin' saw the fallen truckers. "We better get their keys, they'll come after us."

"No," Coyote replied. "I have a better idea."

Outside, Coyote unfastened the rear latch of the cattle trucks, set down the ramp. Forty or fifty cows barged out, eager to graze and get

out of the horrible closed-in trucks. Fun
Truckin' unlocked the other truck. Cows scattered every which way, thoroughly entertaining
the hippie.

The hippie gave Coyote back his hat for the
headband. Coyote asked which way the truckers were going. The hitchiker pointed northeast. "You better take him that way," Coyote
said to Fun Truckin', pointing in the opposite
direction.

Fun Truckin' took him a mile down the road,
came back, and the drive resumed.

More miles passed. The land became brown,
forbidding, parched. There was little for the
cows to graze on. But Nebraska was almost
over. South Dakota was only a few miles away.
Then they would be able to head east.

At a last chance roadhouse, a small boy had
been sneaking listens on his father's CB radio.
The air waves were bristling with news of the
National Guard waiting at the border to stop
the cattle drive. The only person who didn't
know what was about to happen was Coyote.

When the cattle drive passed, the boy ran out
and called, "They're waitin' for you, Coyote!"
Then he ran back inside before his father saw
what he did.

Coyote understood when he saw the thirty-
five members of the South Dakota National
Guard waiting for him, their jeeps parked well
behind them.

Coyote's face reflected extreme and helpless
frustration. "Jesus, fuckin'—come on!"

Coyote screamed this at the uniformed,

peach-faced bunch of young recruits he saw waiting for him. God help America, Coyote thought, if these were its troops.

Out in front was their lieutenant, waiting on the hood of his jeep. He was the only man over thirty in the entire force, and he was probably touching fifty.

Coyote galloped his horse forward, to confront the Guard, but he knew he was finished. His face, and the faces of the men with whom he had travelled so far, showed a limp faith in their high ideals. They felt utterly helpless.

"Why?" Coyote screamed. "Tell me why? You're defending a goddamn wasteland!"

Still riding, Coyote felt unable to do anything. This land was by far the worst of the plain states. Nothing was growing. Sage and topsoil sailed into his face any time a gust of wind blew. And now the National Guard.

"C'mon, talk to me. What the fuck do you care about my cattle?" Coyote was close, within speaking distance.

The lieutenant had no confidence. He tried summoning his most intense voice. "You're charged with transporting state cattle across stolen lines." Some of his troops snickered. He realized what he had said. "Charged with transporting stolen cattle across state lines."

Coyote dismounted, stormed at the man. "You're an idiot. A stupid fucking idiot!"

Then Coyote stopped. A calm ray of light turned on inside. He became a man of understanding. Coyote pulled back, lowered the intensity, played the game with logic. He needed to delve deeper, to comprehend why the Guard was really here, then compute his chances for success. Coyote had come a long way from that drunken, fighting fool.

"O.K." He snapped his fingers. "Show me the charges. Where's the court order saying you can stop me? C'mon, I want to see the piece of paper!"

But now he had confronted power.

"Don't need no piece of paper." The lieutenant looked cocky now.

Coyote was angry. Here he was, calmly playing the game and the guy comes back with a fuck you, don't need no piece of paper.

"All right," said Coyote. "What you'll do is take your men and check my herd. They're all the Cantrell brand. Go ahead, see for yourself!"

"Oh, we'll check you out all right, but not now."

"What do you mean, not now? When?"

"When our cattle inspector gets here. We don't know about cattle. All we do is hold you." The lieutenant turned back to his troops.

"Well, when'll that be? How soon?" Coyote got impatient, looked at his watch.

Nonchalantly the lieutenant replied. "Oh, a week, maybe ten days."

Coyote wanted to kick some ass right there. But he couldn't. This was the National Guard. They'd put him in federal prison.

"C'mon, a week, maybe ten days. What am I supposed to do with that?"

But that was it. The standoff began. The north wind conveniently reminded Coyote how close to winter they were in this part of the country. More sagebrush tumbled across the landscape. They could all feel the pressure front moving in. Coyote knew his herd would be decimated by any snowfall. A cow tried nibbling, came up with a face full of arid soil.

The lieutenant stayed next to his jeep. Coyote turned futilely to his men. Food seemed almost relieved. Fun Truckin' eyed one recruit. His lips kept saying, "Fuck you." The recruit turned his head, refusing to look. Wrestler waited patiently. He knew Coyote was going through a decision-making process. Brains took out his maps, but shook his head disconsolately. He too knew that there was nowhere to go but back, and back was too far. Back was out of the question.

And what, Coyote wondered, would he do when he returned? Most of the cattle wouldn't make it. Many of them would die. If he sold the ranch, he wouldn't get anything anyway. Not after this caper.

Coyote moved back, away from the lieutenant. He needed time to think.

Everybody saw the dust storm approaching from the east. It built up on the prairie, blew across the plains toward the standoff. Coyote walked behind the van. He welcomed the dust storm as a diversion, something to delay his moment of decision.

The dust kept coming closer, like a baby tornado.

Then Coyote thought, how peculiar! He looked back at Wrestler. Both of them realized that the wind was blowing down from the north, so why was dust swirling in from the east? Some of the kids in the Guard realized this too. They became uneasy.

Then the dust materialized into eight pickup trucks, all speeding this way. Now the Guardsmen began to twitch a little. Nobody knew what to expect.

Whoever they were, Coyote was glad to see them.

The pickup trucks all skidded to a stop, in a sloppy line. Each was uglier than the next, all old, like Coyote's, tattered, beat up. A few trucks even had running boards on their sides. Gears were shifted into neutral. Coyote could hear emergency brakes rudely cranked.

Everybody got out.

Coyote could see Indians driving each truck. Then other Indians got out. They were all Indians. Coyote counted fifteen.

They were tough, scarred, mean-looking characters. Coyote figured they had to be Sioux, descendants of the wild, buffalo-hunting Teton people. He remembered that most of South Dakota, in the south, was Sioux reservation land.

All the Indians except one older man moved away from their trucks. They were armed with .22 rifles. All had knives, pistols, clubs, and baseball bats.

The Guard spasmed with nervousness. They shuffled in place, not knowing what to expect. They were afraid, naked, wide open. They knew the Indians were unafraid.

Then the Sioux leader, the older Indian, moved behind his armed men. He walked past them, alone, toward the National Guard. When close enough, he spit at the feet of the Guard Leader.

The Indian moved away. With an arm, he motioned Coyote to come to him. Cautiously, Coyote ambled in the Indian's direction.

Then the Sioux leader called for all to hear. "Cowboy! You bring your cattle across this state, on Indian land!"

Which you could do! Coyote knew that! The event took Coyote by such surprise that his oxygen came in stunted breaths. Coyote paused to admire the Sioux leader, for he knew there was nothing more magnificent than an Indian who refused to be beaten, who refused to die.

Nobody in the Guard had dared to move.

The lieutenant was now the helpless one. He could do nothing more than watch. Indian land was sovereign. Only federal police like the FBI had authority on the reservations.

Coyote laughed as he saw a familiar Indian walk to one of the younger recruits and try to hand him a shovel. The Indian pantomimed that the boy should use it to clean up the cow shit.

Coyote saw that the Indian was Thomas. Thomas, his old cellmate! Thomas laughed at the young Guard "boy," mocked him, ridiculed his authority, motioning with the shovel.

Coyote nodded a deep respectful thank-you to the Sioux leader, who nodded back, raised his left hand, then silently got back into his truck.

By now, Thomas had run up, shovel and all, was hugging Coyote. When they pulled away from each other, Thomas said, "Been following you. Thought you might need a hand."

"I did. I did." Coyote felt very humble.

The good news filtered through to the back. Wrestler, Food, Brains and Fun Truckin' realized they had been given another chance. Their moods elevated to ecstasy.

Even the young men in the National Guard, who really didn't know why they were there, relaxed, glad the tension had eased off.

So Thomas and the other Indians escorted the drive across the first of many Indian-owned ranches, land that was the home of the Oglala Sioux, greatest of all Indians, who as a nation came to an end at Wounded Knee less than a hundred years ago.

As the drive moved away, the lieutenant and his kiddie corps heard a loud piercing howl. Anybody who followed rodeo knew it had to be the Coyote.

By now the radio station in Walsenburg was carrying twice daily reports on the cattle drive. The station owner, himself a rancher, like so many others, was rooting for Coyote.

In the Cantrell kitchen, Jolene gleefully turned off the radio. "They made it, Pa! They're going across South Dakota."

In the bedroom lay Pa. He had never recovered from the worsening of his disease. When he heard the news, he exhaled a long sigh of relief. Then he touched Jolene.

"Keep the ranch going."

"Pa, you'll be here." She noticed how weak his grip was.

He squeezed her wrist more firmly. "Please," he said. "Keep the ranch alive."

She wasn't sure what he was telling her. "We will, Pa. We all will." Then she left him alone. She would enjoy her husband's triumph in private.

Pa Cantrell waited until she left, then weakly sunk back into his two feather pillows. But the pillows were too warm. He turned on his right side. The pillow was damp. He turned back on his left side, facing the bedroom. The pillow burned wet heat. He tried to live with it. But the pillows only got warmer, on his cheeks, forehead, even on the front of his face. Everything, all over, was hot. Pa kicked off the sheets. The effort brought perspiration.

He had to get out. He knew not to rush. He peeled back the sheets until they were down by his knees. Then he swiveled his aged legs out of the bed, dropped his feet to the floor.

Pa braced himself until he could slip into his overalls. With some difficulty he fastened the bib top. Achingly he pulled first one boot, then the second over his feet.

He stood. His feet cooled in the soft leather.

Slowly, grabbing the bedpost for support, Pa counted the steps to his rocking chair. One, two, three, then four. Ahh, he made it.

Pa leaned onto the arm of the old rocker, waited until the swaying stopped. Then he lowered himself down into the chair. This was so nice. He sat, relaxed, and rocked and rocked and never once thought about his sweltering pillow.

From a table by his chair, Pa opened his wood box, took his pipe, filled it with tobacco. He patted down the pipe until it was ready to

smoke. He lit it, drew in and out until the tobacco boiled. Then he rocked back and forth,
began to daydream in the smoke. His lungs got
hot, his tongue tasty. Ah, how he loved smoking
a pipe. He rocked and smoked, rocked back and
smoked. The only thing wrong was, he was
sorry he couldn't see his son once more before
he died.

For the first time in so long she couldn't remember, Jolene walked aimlessly outside, with
no place important to go. She took it easy, like a
contented woman, confident her husband
would now make it. Her work with the breeder
cows could finally slack off. The fact that her
income would soon triple gave her dreams of
dresses she would like to sew this winter. She
created patterns in her mind. She counted over
and over again, figuring at a dollar a pound,
multiplying by the Cantrell herd. Like Coyote,
she had never been ahead in her life. So she
dreamed about the luxury of buying the finest
buttons to sew on her clothes. She might even
buy Vogue patterns. She might even allow herself to get plump. After all, plump was the
body's way of bragging. Those women in town,
those two at the grocery store, were fat. Anybody could get fat. All you needed was a little
success. But Jolene wouldn't get fat, just
plump.

Jolene reached the breeder corral. She
turned, admired the bull. He had one job and he
did it well. All winter long. Like a voyeur, she
gazed at the breeder cows. She had the power
of creation in her hand. "Who wants to make
babies? Who wants this gentle man?"

182

Speaking like a child, she looked back and forth. The bull sensed the attention he was getting. Alone in his pen, he pawed and panted. He wanted to breed.

Jolene undid the latch, let the bull into the breeder corral. The females began to shuffle. "Who wants this gentle man?" The bull circulated. He began to draw a crowd. "Oh, all of you do?"

The bull could have any one he wanted and he wanted them all. He began pushing one cow around in a kind of foreplay. Though she was dying to, Jolene didn't watch the rest. Letting nature take her course. she walked back to the ranch house.

Her mind shifted to Pa. He had gotten worse. But maybe the news of Coyote would bring him around. Pa was one of the old people, a self-healer. When he felt better, he would leave that bed and be himself again. She just wished he would drink his tea.

There was nothing outside but flies. She walked back inside the ranch house. She decided to check on Pa.

"Pa?"

Pa was sitting rocking back and forth. "Pa?" She couldn't understand it, walked closer. "What are you doing out of bed?"

He didn't answer. He was barely rocking now. He seemed at ease, his right hand rested on the arm of the chair. His left arm was in his lap, still cradling the pipe.

Jolene was confused, but pleased. He was asleep. He looked so happy. His boy had made it. Now it was his time for courage so he left his bed.

She leaned down to kiss him, noticed his eyelids were not blinking at all. She kissed him. His lips felt strangely cold. She panicked, leaned down, listened through his overalls for his heart. His body was cold even through his overalls.

Then his limp hand let go of his pipe. It hit the chair, rolled down to the floor. The ember was out.

Jolene started shaking, gasping for air. The pipe smoke felt heavy, oppressive. She pulled away, looked again at Pa Cantrell. She knew he had passed away.

Something inside her was angry. She felt taken, ripped off by his death. She couldn't believe it had ended like this. "Pa," she pleaded. "Pa, couldn't you hold on?"

She hung her head on his knees and tried to wish him back to life. After a futile moment her mind travelled out to the barn, to where she remembered the shovel lay.

Pa would lie forever in the shade of his favorite aspen, watching the leaves slowly turn to orange every autumn.

He Was Luckier
Than Most

The cattle drive passed a sign saying, ENTER-
ING PINE RIDGE INDIAN RESERVATION, OGLALA
SIOUX. They were on the badlands where the
most powerful Indian nation of them all, the
Oglala, the people of Crazy Horse, lived now.

Three Indians guided the cattle drive.
Thomas, with his two friends, switched a truck
for horseback as they took Coyote around the
edge of their land, which had enormous brown
wasted ruts hundreds of yards wide. Many
families used these ruts to hide in during the
desolate years following the Custer victory of
1876. Now their hiding place was their home.
Coyote thought, as he passed through this
wretched land, that the gophers here must have
noses made of steel.

Coyote learned of his father's death from Father Fagan, head of the St. Francis Indian Mission on the next reservation, fifty miles to the
east. Not knowing where to call, Jolene phoned
there. The Jesuit priest sent word with one of
his Indian teachers, across the Rosebud, into
Pine Ridge.

Coyote decided not to stop the drive, to let it go forward without him. Then he rode north, with Thomas, to pay his respects to his father at the Wounded Knee mass gravesite. It seemed the most appropriate thing to do.

The gravesite at Wounded Knee was no more than a hill, where more than two hundred Sioux men, women, and children had been persuaded to assemble by the promise of food and clothing. Then they were attacked on all sides by cannon fire and repeating rifles. Their bodies were dumped and covered with dirt in a common grave site known as Wounded Knee. Today, both a church and a sweat lodge stand on the site, symbolic of the two religions existing side by side. The white man killed their Jesus, but the Sioux hadn't yet killed their pipe.

Coyote stood solemnly over the gravesite, tears in his eyes. His hat was in his hand, over his heart. Six or seven tourists stood of the far side of the memorial, not daring to come closer, somehow afraid of the spirits that seemed to live in each blade of buffalo grass.

Thomas put his hand on Coyote's shoulder. "I'm sorry about your father."

Thomas took his hand away. Coyote saw him through tears. He nodded at Thomas. It was time to leave.

"Coyote," Thomas called. Coyote stopped, let Thomas come up to him. "He was luckier than most. He died with his land."

Coyote let out a deep breath of air. He felt closer to this Indian than to any other man on earth.

* * *

Pine Ridge came and went. The next stretch took them through a series of Indian ranches. Everything was in motion for Coyote. He had been on his horse for so long that a kind of land seasickness set in. It was a perpetual motion but with everything moving slowly enough so he could understand it. Comprehension came perfectly.

By now, Coyote comprehended the drama he was involved in. He understood the forces for and against him, and he privately marvelled that the drive hadn't been stopped. He especially enjoyed the irony of crossing this forbidden state on Indian land.

But above all, Coyote marvelled that he was spending so much time doing what he always thought people like Brains did: thinking, being deep in thought. With every step his pony took, Coyote found himself thinking. Thinking about himself, about others, about how he felt about others and how they might feel about him. He thought about himself as a person, as a single unit of nature on this planet. He even thought about other planets, something he certainly never thought about before, except as a kid. He wondered if some Martians, right now, might be looking down at this long string of cattle stretching across the plains. He imagined them checking their calendars, making sure it was truly the nineteen-seventies on Earth, not a century earlier, and wondering where their calculations had gone wrong.

In short, Coyote had never thought before, he just acted, and if the consequences hit hard, then they hit. But never had he let any thought start him or stop him. Now, that's all he was doing, thinking, analyzing, and, what was most startling, he found that after a little practice, he could travel great distances on the wings of an idea, free-flowing like a mountain stream down easy flat spaces, or down rumbling falls and rapids, churning his thoughts until he resolved them, and reached another peaceful flat spot, where he tried to rest; but that damn thinking wouldn't let him quit.

And that was how it went. He rode mostly alone now. The conversations with Wrestler had grown stale. He was enjoying more the conversations he was having with himself.

He wondered if city people were ever able to make the time to stop moving and figure things out. He reasoned they probably didn't, because it seemed impossible to simply set aside a space during the day and say, it's time to introvert. Anyway, it took so long, as Coyote was discovering, for a person's mind to calm enough to think things through, that by the time your mind calmed in the city, your allotted time was over, so what was the use in the first place? He assumed that city people didn't even try to think too much.

Coyote had been on the road so long he couldn't remember. It had to be nearing a month, though if you counted the time he and Jolene spent in the hills before the drive, it was probably well over a month.

Already he was dying for the next year to come around, so he could again spend time outdoors, reacquainting himself with this person he had met for the first time. His mind thought so smoothly now. Important thoughts came easily, slid through his mind like greased clouds in a buttered sky.

Then a sign stood out and reality reappeared. ENTERING ROSEBUD INDIAN RESERVATION, ROSE-BUD SIOUX. The word "reservation" had been shot umpteen times with bullet holes. What a word, Coyote thought. Like game "preserve," where people came to gawk and take pictures, and shoot the wildlife.

The Rosebud Sioux used to be known in the old times as the Burnt Thigh People, because of a great fire on the plains, which supposedly burnt the thighs of the fleeing population. For the last 150 years or so, they were known simply as those of the Rosebud.

The Rosebud land was hilly, windy, brown with early winter. The terrain and conditions stayed that way for sometime to come.

The farther the cattle drive moved from the Rockies, the more the weather changed. The storm predicted by the weather service never actually touched them, though all felt the tail end of it in the form of wind, and a drop in temperature.

But all in all, nothing was too severe. What was happening was that as they left the higher elevations, they moved away from winter into a pleasant, relatively comfortable, Midwestern autumn.

Then they came to the outskirts of a town. Coyote felt appalled when he saw the tarpaper shacks and rusted-out auto bodies in which so many Indians still lived.

The town was St. Francis, home of the Jesuit Indian school. School sessions had begun, but many of the 500 children had turned out to watch the drive pass their school. Many were smiling. Coyote was amazed, for even in poverty, these Indian kids had beautiful teeth.

Father Fagan stood in front of the children. Thomas had told Coyote much about this man. Here was a man of the cloth Coyote could love. A baldish man, of maybe fifty-five, Father Fagan once had been high in the Jesuit organization and could have worked anywhere. But he chose to run this Indian school, which had existed for many years. Coyote loved him instantly. He wasn't trying to convert the Indians to Christianity. He was trying to convert them to health, a far more difficult task. But Coyote identified with the pride he saw in the man's eyes more than anything else. It was same pride he used to see in his father's eyes. It was the way he would always remember his father.

Coyote raised his hand, stopped the drive.

Without words, Coyote selected five of his best cows from the front of the drive, led them to the priest.

"Here, Father. Shorten your winter."

Thomas stayed in the background. He had a daughter in this school, though he had never mentioned that to Coyote. Thomas had just spotted her among the large crowd of kids. She was waving to her daddy. Before, Thomas had urged other tribe members to help Coyote because of his own merits. Now Coyote had given the children 7,500 pounds of beef, and he had made the gift on his own. Yes, thought Thomas, their winter would surely be shortened.

Sioux City

They were almost there. By car, Sioux City was no more than two or three hours away. For the cattle, the distance grew to four days. All that was left was crossing the Missouri River.

Brains spread a map out, anchored it on the corners with rocks. Coyote and Thomas looked over his shoulder.

"Now where is Sioux City from here?"

Brains had it charted. Coyote followed his line across the rest of South Dakota until he reached Sioux City, on the west edge of Iowa.

"How the hell are we gonna cross that?" Coyote pointed to the river."

Thomas had the answer. "I know a flat spot."

So they travelled toward the river. Four hundred and fifty head were going to cross the Missouri River at Thomas's flat spot.

It was a melancholy time for Coyote. Soon four cowboys and a kid with a van would be on their way back to Colorado. Everybody would be handsomely paid, Coyote would keep a healthy profit. But there would be a winter to spend on the ranch. What would Coyote do during the winter?

There was always rodeo, the circuit. No excitement ran through Coyote at the thought of rodeo. With Pa gone there would be no one to leave the ranch with. But more than that, Coyote didn't think he could get it up for another try at the circuit. Then he realized winning a go-round was child's play compared to the competition of the bankers, developers, truckers, farmers, and recently, the Dakota National Guard. The sensations of winning this battle went far and above anything he found in rodeo. Coyote came to a decision. He would make this drive again next year. Not for the money alone, but for the experience of leading the life, for the pleasure of being alone. As Wrestler said, "No matter what happens, we live free. We live like cowboys."

They reached the river. Thomas and another Indian took a trial run on horseback across a shallow spot in the river that had opened the West, that ran from St. Louis into upper Montana. Coyote watched, nodded his approval, and the first of his cattle began crossing the shallow spot in the wide Missouri. As the first third of the cows were in, the lead cows were climbing onto the bank of the eastern side.

There was no send-off, just a final check of the maps and a farewell to Thomas and the two Indian guides. The cattle and cowboys waited while Coyote left in the van for Sioux City and the feed lots, to negotiate the sale of the beef.

Coyote felt funny on the freeway, a grown man driving this cherried-out, lowered van. He felt everyone was looking at him, and many people probably were.

He passed through Sioux City to the outskirts. The stench of the feed lot told Coyote he was there long before he arrived. A sign confirmed that this was the WORLD'S LARGEST FEED LOT. Coyote knew people liked to boast, but everything he saw made him a believer.

Wood fences held cattle farther than Coyote could see, probably even if he had had binoculars. As he got closer, close enough to see detail, he saw tens of thousands of cattle being systematically fed by a computerized feed system, carrying mixtures of corn, grass, and every chemical known to the industry into the endless cattle bins. Coyote knew these cows would be fattened until their jowl bulged with artificial weight, then put to sleep one by one, victims of electrical charges.

Coyote had never been to a feed lot before, never seen the way cattle were treated like an assembly line product. It disgusted him. It was so far from anything he had known in his youth. He had been taught the nobility of the hunt, had hunted all his life. Now it was all computerized and there was nothing left of the hunt. These feed lots, a creation of the fast food boom, were taking over. All Coyote wanted to do was get in with his herd, and out with his pay. He didn't want to deal with the rest of it. He didn't want his mind clouded.

They made Coyote wait quite a while outside the buyer's office before the buyer would see him.

Once inside, Coyote leaned across the buyer's

desk, and said truthfully, "I guess you know who I am."

The buyer looked so much like anybody else that when Coyote's eyes left him to explore the office, they returned not remembering what the buyer looked like.

"I know who you are, but I don't know why you're wasting your time in here with me."

"Hey! Market chains and fast food pay you $1.20. Stockyard prices on the ranch are forty cents. So let's talk somewhere in between." Coyote leaned over the desk.

"Mr. Cantrell, you don't seem to understand. We only buy cattle through our brokers. Company policy forbids me to undercut our brokers. I cannot offer you any more than he agreed to pay you at the ranch."

"Look, I got beef to sell and you buy beef. So let's drop the stonewall and settle on a price."

"Mr. Cantrell, I am not bargaining with you."

The buyer looked through Coyote as if he were clear glass.

"Then what is your offer?" Coyote asked.

"The same as my broker offered you at your ranch. Fourteen cents."

"Why?" Coyote dropped his guard. He really wanted to know the reason. "I beat your trucking, I beat your fuel, your maintainance, your time, what you pay your drivers, and your price comes down like I did none of these things. Why?"

"The point, Mr. Cantrell, is we only buy beef we can ship in our own company trucks. That way we can insure its quality."

"Quality? You call that force-fed lot of bullshit out there quality? They taste like fuckin' silly putty, that cancer-ridden crap."

It was time for the buyer to drop his façade. He had a motive. The cowboy needed to know the way things worked. Maybe he could be persuaded. "Mr. Cantrell, do you have any idea how many trucks this company owns and operates? Are you getting the picture? We would be fools to do it your way and cut our own throats. We do better on trucking than resale of beef!"

"You price-rigging sonofabitch!"

The buyer remained calm. "What are you accusing this company of?"

"Double dealing. Making money off both ends."

"I've already told you, of course that's what we do."

Coyote wasn't ready for this. No one had spoken so honestly to him before. "Why are you teling me all this?"

"Mr. Cantrell, it's no secret. We are not the only ones who know this. But a cattle drive is a filthy way of delivering beef. Our customers want quality, they want sanitation, and we give them both. I am trying to show you why your type of cattle drive can never, never work. I am trying, cowboy, to open your eyes!"

Coyote felt as if he were in the spin cycle of a washing machine. "But it has worked!" he claimed. "I made it, everybody can see that."

They buyer was unimpressed. "Who do you think is watching? Who do you think cares?" The buyer let this sink in. "And it hasn't worked, because I'm offering you the same fourteen cents you were offered a month ago at your ranch."

Coyote's mind raced with choices. The clarity returned. This guy was right. This deal was dead. What could he do? He couldn't go back. He could slaughter his cattle symbolically. Aha! The packing houses didn't own their own trucks. They contracted transportation, like the little train that serviced the Cantrell ranch. Picking up cattle was the packing houses' biggest expense. Coyote saw a way out, a long way, but a way.

That was all it took. He bubbled with inner confidence. "Hey." Coyote smiled cockily. "See this? Well, you can suck on it one more time. 'Cause I'm gonna drive these sonofabitches into Chicago."

Coyote was out of there, gone, out the door.

The buyer's spirits sunk like a loose second skin. He had failed to stop Coyote. The buyer became frightened. He knew Coyote had a chance, and how many other ranchers on the verge of bankruptcy would do the same thing? The buyer realized that this one man could crumble his company and with it bring down an entire system! It was pretty big stuff and the buyer didn't know how to stop it. He sat back down, but couldn't think.

Iowa

None of the guys were prepared for the news. Not even Brains had studied the possibilities of almost 400 more miles, across Iowa and Illinois. While no one was ready for another month on the road, when Coyote presented this alternative, nobody balked even the slightest bit. Brains predicted they would be easy miles.

There was one consolation. They had ridden back into summer.

Somewhere into South Dakota they had left the threats of winter. First the mountains, then the high plains and wind had come and gone. Then autumn touched them. Now it too had disappeared.

So, in a situation which should have riddled all their spirits with hopelessness and depression, their moods couldn't have been more optimistic. The drive to Chicago meant something big. Now they weren't pussyfooting with the feed lot. By taking the cattle directly to the packing houses, they were sticking it to them, really sticking it to them.

As Coyote told them, "Let them turn away 450 head of cattle at the packing house door.

Let 'em try. I'll butcher the beef myself with people starving in Chicago, I'll waste the cattle right on their front door. Give it away if I have to!"

As he rode into Iowa, Coyote's little cattle drive had turned into an issue larger than he could have understood originally. But that was before. Coyote was a different man now.

Before, he would have punched that buyer out. Now, he was going to beat him. Coyote felt like Mr. Little Man, and he aimed to be a force that wouldn't be denied.

Iowa was beautiful. Everybody loved it. The land had turned green again. The hills were lush and rolling. Food's sneezes could be heard from the van, as his allergies reacted to the new Midwestern pollen in the air.

There was even more traffic along the little road they were travelling on, and the people were nice. Almost everybody waved, and more than a few knew Coyote by face and by name. They called to him, waved at him.

Coyote knew something was building.

When the people along the way started waving, welcoming the five men from Colorado, Coyote knew he was getting the public on his side. Not all these people could be rodeo fans. Many of them, he was sure, only identified the name Coyote with this cattle drive across what were now four states.

Brains presented Coyote with two alternatives. One was staying on the road and going twenty miles out of the way. The other was to pass by some Iowa farms. Coyote decided to test his popularity. He chose the farms.

The cattle drive was at the moment waiting outside a picture-postcard farmhouse. On the mailbox was written HOLMES FARM, CORRECTION-VILLE, IOWA, RURAL ROUTE 153.

Coyote knocked without hesitation on the farmhouse door. A lady of around fifty-seven answered without showing fear of intruders.

"Hello, ma'am. My name is Coyote."

The lady was duly impressed. "Will," she called. "It's the cattle drive man."

Her husband showed up, extended his hand. "Pleased to meet you, sir. I used to ranch myself 'till I got into corn. Heh, got into corn. We all heard about you. You're doin' a fine thing for us little people. We admire you. We all do. I got the same problem you do, in farming, but different."

Coyote waited, made sure Will was finished. Then he said, "I need to pass over your farm, sir."

"You do?"

"Yes sir. We're taking them straight into Chicago."

"Chicago!" Will reacted. "Chicago, whew."

Coyote again nodded, waited for Will's decision. Will decided.

"Well, then, absolutely. Go ahead. And stay by the north fence. All my overripe corn is sitting there."

Coyote hesitated, then asked. "Uh, have you made a deal on your overripe corn yet?" Coyote had to feed his cattle.

Stepping forward, Will said in earnest. "Son, I'd rather *give* it to you, then sell it to the Russians."

*　*　*

Iowa was like that all the way through the western part of the state. Each time they neared a town, whether Holstein, Early, or Sac City, there were farms to go around, people to welcome them. Each person was nicer than the one before. Coyote felt as though he were running for Congress as he stood before each family of farmers, asking permission to pass through. One young boy held out a rodeo program for Coyote to sign. "Could you say from the World Rodeo Champion?" asked the boy.

Coyote grinned, held up two fingers. "Two times."

By the middle of Iowa something even more comforting happened. They crossed back into cattle country. The land was still green and rolling, but now cows grazed on it.

The Colorado boys marvelled at the beauty of these Iowa cows. They were corn-fed, with shiny coats, very healthy-looking beasts. They were all Angus or other bred cattle. There was something about corn-fed beef that made it a delicacy, at least to Colorado men used to beef raised on grass and alfalfa.

Wrestler pretty much stayed by himself these days. He felt a distance growing between him and Coyote. Coyote wasn't one of the boys anymore. He was making it. It always happened when someone made it. He left everybody behind. Wrestler saw Coyote talking like an equal to Fun Truckin'. That shouldn't happen. Fun Truckin' was just a kid. Wrestler concluded Coyote had just found the best way to get the most out of the kid, so he was treating

him like an equal. Wrestler watched Coyote
confiding to Brains, asking him for advice, appearing almost vulnerable to that snot-nosed
kid. Coyote could read a map. What did he have
to confide in that boy for? And Food. Telling
him he was looking better, that he was losing
weight. That old fart could gain weight just
standing next to a grocery store.

Wrestler's wrist hurt like hell. He didn't
complain. He didn't need any coddling to get a
performance out of him. But then he wasn't in
college. He wasn't good looking. He wasn't a
joke, like Food. He was the best damn cowboy on
this drive and he didn't need anybody to tell
him that.

Coyote saw a large van up ahead. Although it
was still a dot on the horizon, Coyote's initial
reaction was to fear the police. He rode up to
the van, looked through the binoculars.

Coyote saw a lady get out of the van, a tall
lady with carrot-red hair and loose-fitting
clothes. There were no lights on top of the van,
which ruled out the police.

Then two other men got out and began setting up electrical equipment, fooling with me-
ters and dials. He saw call letters on the van's
side. It registered with Coyote. There were TV
people. He gave the binoculars back to Fun
Truckin', took off his hat, started patting down
his hair.

All hell broke loose in Coyote's mind. He
caught a look at himself in Fun Truckin's side
mirror. Sheepishly he asked Fun Truckin' for a
comb. He stayed with the van, combing in the
side mirror, until he got his hair right. So the

drive really was becoming something. Ha. Coyote rode up ahead of the van, to be the first one the camera crew saw.

To the three people of the camera crew, the approaching drive was no longer a ribbon in the distance. The carrot-haired lady tested with the sound man, tested with the cameraman. Her name was Stephanie George, she was six feet one inch tall, she was from NBC, Chicago, and she burned energy like propane.

As he approached, Coyote saw a lanky woman with a beautiful, high-cheekboned, eager face. Coyote started to get off his horse.

"No, stay up there!" she called. Then they moved along at Coyote's slow pace. She signalled, and the machines started. Coyote saw the red light on the camera.

"Hello up there," she said.

Coyote went stupid, didn't know what to say.

"Hi," he said back.

The cameraman did a quick pan of the cattle, came back to Coyote.

"I'm from NBC," she said.

."I'm from Colorado." Coyote grinned at his remark.

She kept up with his pace.

"Amazing thing you're doing."

"Not really. Not when you think about it."

"Why are you doing this?"

"I was getting screwed!" Coyote looked directly into the camera, spoke with confidence. "I mean, we all were . . . getting screwed."

She changed the subject. "Aren't you afraid your beef will be too tough?"

204

"Uh uh. I use Accent." Coyote clowned, shook his wrist.

The reporter broke up. "From the plains of Iowa, back to you."

Stephanie had the cameraman stop the van at the first service station with a phone booth. She called her boss in Chicago.

Stephanie George had been a fashion model in New York. When she tired of the mindlessness, she returned to Chicago for a job in local television. She immediately became one of the most popular reporters in Chicago.

Her boss had been against covering the story. But with the drive halfway across Iowa and certain to enter Illinois, she convinced him he should.

Finally her boss came on the line. "Larry," she said. "Larry, he is great. A real throwback. He's even got lines."

There was no reply. Larry seemed unimpressed.

"I want to stay with him. Larry, this story is broader than we realized. Do you understand? This man is speaking for every food producer in the country!"

Larry conceded. "O.K. You can stay for a while."

"No, not for a while, Larry! I want to follow him into Chicago!"

The president of Gateways had politicians in his pocket who hadn't been elected yet. For him, bribery was a practical fact of life, a necessary part of his business.

The governor of Iowa was an honest man. Yet his curiosity about a world he had never entered caused him to see an old acquaintance, the Gateways president, when he proposed "an extremely tempting offer" over the telephone.

After dismissing his secretary, the governor waited nervously for the offer. He was well protected behind his desk. The president of Gateways seemed surprisingly at home, thought the governor. Then the corporate giant leaned forward.

"Cecil, on a personal level, we have a ten, possibly a twenty million dollar development on the boards for southern Colorado. Ski resort, condos, a whole winter playtown if it goes. Cecil, I am prepared to offer you five percent interest in this development in whatever form you would like. Your kid's name, relatives that don't exist. Anything. That can be camouflaged a hundred different ways."

The governor leaned forward. "What do I have to do, Roger?"

"Just one thing, Cecil, and it's well within your power. Stop that damn Coyote!"

The conversation paused. The two men had a long look at each other. Already the governor was figuring out what he could do, how he could stop the cattle drive and still remain popular for the next election.

Coyote's first interview was a huge success. It ran on the evening news, again that night, and also on the early morning local news. It seemed all of Chicago was buzzing about the cattle drive heading its way.

Their second interview was staged with a background of passing cattle. Coyote stood next to Stephanie with his hat off. Wrestler watched from a distance, disgusted with the whole thing. It amazed Coyote how Stephanie could set the whole thing up, then look perfectly spontaneous as she asked her first question.

"This is unbelievable," she yelled. "What have your cattle eaten?"

Coyote counted on his fingers. "They've been grass-fed, corn-fed, wheat-fed, alfalfa-fed, and even drank from three or four rivers."

As the crew smiled at the mention of the cattle's diet, Wrestler rode up, speechless, his finger pointing back in the other direction. Coyote looked, saw the battered white pickup truck stop. Jolene got out, saw Coyote, waved back and forth.

"There's my wife!" Coyote yelled. "Jolene!"

Coyote left Stephanie in mid-interview, ran the twenty yards to the pickup truck calling, "Jolene! Jolene!"

Stephanie signaled the cameraman to keep moving in on the couple. The truck started rolling backwards. Wrestler caught it, set the brake.

Coyote and Jolene hugged each other for dear life. Coyote began lifting Jolene into the air. He put her down, then lifted her again and again. When he finally put her down, she said, "You were easy to find."

He kissed her. There was so much to talk about.

* * *

The governor of Iowa was on his way home. He welcomed the time he spent in his limousine. It was his only time alone, to think, with no advisors hanging around. He turned the phone off, dreamed how nice it would be to leave Iowa for vacations in the mountains of Colorado. If he could purchase the condominium, then have Gateways reimburse him with cash, the deal could be set. But first, he had to discuss the matter with his wife and family.

Pompously, the governor left the limousine, walked up the steps through the columned front door of his mansion. There was no one to greet him.

"Hello," he called, walked into the living room, but nobody called back. Somebody always greeted him.

But parading across the twenty-five inch television screen was Coyote's cattle drive. The governor's three children were glued to the set, their attention undivided.

"Hello," the governor called once more.

"*Sshhhh!*" All three children hushed him.

The governor's wife pulled him toward the TV. "Have you seen this? Watch."

Just then a servant arrived with a telephone on a long cord. "The president of Gateways, sir."

His wife knew the name "Gateways" and gave him a nasty stare. The governor took the call. She moved back to the TV.

On the screen, Coyote was speaking with Stephanie. The cattle filed across the screen behind them. The children hung on every movement.

Stephanie asked, "Do you have a word for the president of the Gateways Corporation?"

The governor's wife whirled, faced her husband, who was still on the phone. She turned back to the TV.

"Like to feed the pigeons on his lawn prune juice," a grinning Coyote replied.

The children all laughed, carried on, poking each other.

The governor couldn't hear his call. "Roger," he said, "could you repeat that?"

As Stephanie asked her next question, the kids stopped laughing to hear. The governor's wife stood behind the children, kept her eye on the TV, her ears with her husband's conversation.

Coyote replied. "They've been grass-fed, corn-fed, wheat-fed, alfalfa-fed, even drank from three or four rivers." All the time he counted on his fingers.

The children made such a commotion that the governor couldn't hear anymore. "Roger, could you hold on a moment?"

The governor set down the receiver, joined his wife behind the children. They saw Coyote spot Jolene, say, "There's my wife!"

The governor's wife ran her arm around him, as the camera followed Coyote's run for Jolene, caught Wrestler stopping the truck, and witnessed Coyote embracing Jolene for dear life, then lifting her over and over.

The children applauded. The governor's wife had tears in her eyes. What could the governor do? He was an honest man. So it was a short vacation. His expressive face revealed a sincere revulsion at his own darker self. As he walked back to the phone, anger built in him. He picked up the receiver like a man who has barely escaped from the devil. "Roger," he said, "why don't you try the governor of Illinois? I'm sure he's much further in your pocket."

He waited for Roger's reaction to end, then concluded, "And Roger, sit on the curved end of a ski, won't you?"

In his exclusive office, the Gateways president smashed the phone down on his desk, shattering the top of his expensive glass blotter. He sent the debris flying with a vicious sweep of his arm.

Celebrity Beef

Jolene immediately switched with Wrestler. She was anxious to get on a horse, and he was dying to get off one. Once behind the wheel of the pickup truck, that constant, jarring pain that the saddle sent to his right arm subsided. Wrestler could feel the pain leaving his right arm the way you feel a slow sweat coming when you sit in a suana. He was in hog heaven. Now the caravan had two vehicles.

Jolene and Coyote spent the first day riding next to each other. "Jake," she explained. "I couldn't sit there alone any more after Pa died. I had to be here with you."

The cattle drive looked more and more like an event. The trail of cattle still stretched on like a ribbon, but now with more reporters, their crews, and various other hangers-on, the amount of people increased.

For Coyote, Jolene had come at the right time. His period of solitude had ended as soon as they made the move to cross Iowa. For some reason that was the catalyst. It became serious business once the decision was made to take the

211

cattle directly into Chicago, the meat packing capital of the world.

"Ah," said Coyote. "You just didn't think I could make it without you along."

"Well? Could you have?"

"You may be right, Jolene. We're not there yet."

They eased into their relationship again. Mostly they spent the day riding next to each other quietly as if they had never been apart. The cows needed less and less attention. They were used to their single file by now. Jolene commented, "They almost look like a drill team, they're so orderly."

The sun blazed down over the rolling Iowa landscape. Jolene thought she had never seen such beautiful soil.

"Jake," she said. "On the way back, I want to load up the back of the pickup with this soil, and bring it home for my garden."

"What garden?"

"The garden we're gonna have at the ranch. With black Iowa soil."

"Sure, why not? But no carrots. Don't shove carrots at me."

They rode on. "By the way," she asked. "Have you been drinking?"

"That's a shitty thing to ask. A typical wife question!"

Jolene shut up. Coyote was livid. But then he remembered what she probably saw.

"You mean that empty bottle of Ancient Age back there?"

Jolene nodded.

"That was Wrestler's. He's been half lit the

whole trip." Coyote raised his hands. "Not a drop."

"You realize, I never once thought . . . "

"No," Coyote said. "Of course not."

They stopped to let the cattle rest and graze. Wrestler drove next to Coyote and Jolene, parked under a spruce tree. "Come talk to me, Jolene." Wrestler motioned Coyote and Jolene to join him. The three of them sat in the truck bed.

One of the reporters had brought a case of beer, trying to ingratiate himself with everybody. He did with Wrestler. He popped open his can. Coyote was dying for one, but made no move.

"Oh, have one, for Christ's sake," Jolene said to him. "Gimme one, too."

Wrestler popped a beer for each. Coyote hiccupped, took care to sip, not gulp. He wanted to talk. Jolene anticipated his speaking. She could tell something was troubling him.

"You know," Coyote said. "I just cannot believe we are gonna just waltz into Chicago. It's been too easy so far."

"Easy?" Jolene exclaimed.

"Easy?" Wrestler followed. "What cattle drive have you been on?"

"They haven't stopped us is what I mean!" Coyote gulped his beer this time.

"Careful," chided Jolene.

"Oh, shit," said Coyote. "I'm not joking. I mean, we're not what you'd call enlightened. Why are we the first to try driving our cattle? Why isn't anybody else doing it?"

Jolene found it hard to believe that this was

her husband. His stubbornness and singlemindedness had been replaced by mindful, intelligent probing.

Speculated Wrestler, "Same reason most people don't do most things. Lazy, too scared to carry it off. Probably too dumb in the first place to think something like this up."

"Maybe," said Jolene. "They're not as tough as we are."

"Jolene, we're not that tough."

"We were pushed into a corner," she stated. "Very hard and very fast."

"O.K.," Coyote replied. "That was the kicker. But . . . " he stopped, thought, started to speak again. He paused. "I don't know."

Coyote sipped his beer, tried again. "We have been very lucky though. Every time something comes up, there's been another way to turn."

"So the gods are with you," prophesied Wrestler.

"What are you so unsure of?" asked Jolene.

"Jolene, it's too damn important that we be stopped. I know this. Now I don't know where, or who, or how, but I can feel them aiming at us."

"Who?" she wanted to know.

"I don't know who!" Coyote threw up his hands.

"I think you're gettin' backside loco," said Wrestler.

"Well, maybe I am. You see, if we just had the public on our side. Somehow we need them with us."

"We do!" Jolene said. "Look at all this media."

"I don't mean as a sideshow," answered Coyote.

Wrestler stared into the conversation, opened another beer, offered another to Coyote which he refused.

"We're beef producers," Coyote continued. "The public is beef eaters. Even those truckers have to buy beef. Now if we could do something for them!"

"Why?" Wrestler asked.

"Don't you see, they're just lining us up for a right cross. I can feel it coming, Wrestler. I'm tightening up, waiting for that punch. It's crazy. But I feel if enough people are watching us, they won't be able to get away with it."

"With what?" Jolene asked.

"I don't know that yet, either." Coyote was becoming more frustrated. He finished his beer, crushed the can.

Coyote turned to Wrestler. "If I'm gettin' so goddamn smart, how come all I keep saying is, 'I don't know'?"

Coyote turned to Jolene. "Do you understand what I mean?"

"Sort of."

"Well, I know there's something coming. Truckers, or something. I don't know what, damnit, I don't know."

Coyote stomped off the truck to the ground, untied his horse, returned to his position in the drive.

Jolene watched him.

"Got a lot on his mind." Wrestler tried to explain.

"He's changed," said Jolene. "Gotten so much

smarter." She lowered herself off the truck. "I think what we're seeing are growing pains."

She untied her horse, too. Her husband had changed. He had become concerned, sophisticated, almost worldly. He had a curiosity he never possessed before. Now he was working for an understanding both of himself and the world around him.

The afternoon continued with Coyote having fears, premonitions about how he might be stopped before reaching Chicago. This overwhelming fear strained Coyote, made him difficult to approach. Jolene was confused about whether he just wasn't glad to see her, or had too many other things on his mind. He only asked once where Pa was buried, and once about who had been hired to take care of the bull and breeders.

Coyote had realized that he was in a calm before the storm. He came to the conclusion that the presence of curious onlookers, while troublesome, had made it nearly impossible for truckdrivers to careen into the drive as they had before. The more people whose eyes were on the drive, the less trouble would come from corporations, or special interests who depended on this same public for their economic survival.

That night, one by one, Wrestler, Coyote, Jolene, Stephanie, and Fun Truckin' came to sit around the fire. Brains had volunteered to watch the herd, along with Food. While most of the reporters had gone to motels, three that stayed volunteered to park their recreational vehicles around the cattle, keeping them bunched as a herd.

Jolene watched amusedly at Fun Truckin' catering to the red-headed reporter. When she took out a cigarette he lit it for her cowboy style, with a flaming piece of kindling. He moved a log closer to her when he thought she might be getting chilly.

Across the fire, Jolene saw Wrestler getting more and more disgusted with the nature of the cattle drive. She heard him mutter "pussy-whipped" when Fun Truckin' moved the log over.

Yet Jolene was torn, but part of her felt like Wrestler. What was originally their little fight for survival, had grown bigger than they could have planned. It had blossomed out of their hands into an event many people, farm people, ranch people, city people, could relate to. For Jolene, and she was sure for Coyote too, this recognition brought with it a feeling that they, the participants, had no direct control over its outcome, over their own destiny. To hear Coyote wondering how they could get the public on their side had nothing to do with them, or their intent of getting a fair price for their cattle. But, she realized, and this was where she grew apart from Wrestler, this strategy had everything to do with succeeding. Without this kind of big picture planning Coyote was doing, their luck might run out. They couldn't depend on charm forever.

Jolene wished the silence would end. But nobody felt like talking. She was becoming more and more eager to contribute something to the effort, to the drive, but as yet didn't know what she could do. She was a woman. How could she help?

Finally, somebody talked. Wrestler was the first to say what was on his mind.

"Somebody better figure who's gonna buy that beef." It was simple, direct, and something no one had considered.

"Are you kidding?" answered Stephanie, who always had an answer. "That's celebrity beef!"

That ticked Wrestler off. "What the hell's celebrity beef? Those cows wear sunglasses or something?" The old cowboy turned to Coyote. "Tell you what, star, you better be the one to figure that out. Who's gonna sell the beef?"

"I'll sell it!" Jolene saw her chance to contribute.

"What?" Everybody turned, looked at Jolene. Coyote was about to speak again but shut up. He knew not to doubt his wife.

"I'll sell it," she repeated. "This isn't on the spur of the moment. You don't need me around here, I've been looking for a way I could help. It's my chance. I'll go to Chicago and sell the cattle."

"I'll be damned," said Wrestler.

"You shouldn't have much trouble," said Fun Truckin'. "Those cows are famous."

Everybody laughed, even Stephanie. Coyote felt a surge of relief. It was so like Jolene to come through when he needed her. Coyote moved closer to her.

Wrestler watched Fun Truckin' put his hand on Stephanie's leg. She moved closer. He began groping her. Wrestler shook his head, locked into his own private disgust. "I'm going to watch the cattle," he said, then got up and left.

Jolene sensed it was time for her and Coyote to leave also. She took Coyote's arm, led him away from the fire and the groping lovers.

"So it's settled," Coyote said when they were alone.

"Uh huh," Jolene nodded, and that was it.

"Jolene, I'm sorry I've been so distant."

"I didn't understand at first. I mean, the drive looked simple to me. I didn't realize there was so much for you to think about, so many decisions you had to consider."

"It's unbelievable," said Coyote. "You've got to stay on top of everything."

"A leader hardly has time for warmness, or intimacy."

"I hope I haven't gotten that bad."

Jolene said nothing. They kept walking. By now, the firelight was a flicker, a match flame, a distance away.

Jolene touched Coyote's chest with her finger. "You *have* changed, so much." She got his interest.

"How?"

"You want to know?" He did. "You used to, I mean, on cue, fuck up everything you got involved in. From your horse in Denver, I can start counting. But I won't. Because you have come so far. Look at you. You're a winner."

"Not yet. We're close, but not yet."

"That's what I'm getting at, Jake."

He wasn't sure what she was getting at.

"Jake, if something goes wrong, if there's

trouble, promise me you'll do your best. But if we're beat . . . "

"Jolene, what are you trying to tell me?"

"I couldn't stand waiting if they put you in jail again!"

"Jolene, why are you telling me this? Why now?"

"Because I know how much you're anticipating them stopping you, and I'm afraid you'll kill somebody or your temper will come up and you'll do something crazy!"

"I won't."

"I believe you. But that's all I think about. I mean it, Jake. I couldn't bear living with you in jail another time."

They walked further. She said nothing more. Maybe she had been too strong, but she had to let her fears sink deeply into her husband.

Finally she said, "I'm sorry."

"It's O.K." He raised his hand, lowered it. "You're right."

Jolene grinned at him. "Besides, I've never been to Chicago."

"You think I have?"

"You bet you have. You fell on your ass there in '72, got drunk for three days, missed the next rodeo in Peoria."

"I forgot." Coyote smiled.

"I can see where you would."

They walked further, veered another direction, circled back toward the fire. They both were glad the talk had lightened. Jolene hoped she could believe her husband's assurances.

"Did Pa feel any pain?"

Jolene shook her head. "It was the most natural death you could imagine. He fell asleep smoking his pipe, never woke up again."

Coyote said introspectively, "I'd like to go that way, too."

"You? You'd probably start a fire."

"Boy, you are feisty." He put his arms around her.

"Feisty kitten." She clawed his stomach.

"I got a fire in me."

"Do you?" She continued to tease him. "Well, let's get the business out of the way first. Chicago." Her voice trailed off.

"We're getting closer to Illinois. " He put his hand well below her stomach.

"That's not Illinois." She looked down at the longness in his pants. "Though that does resemble Florida. A smaller version of course."

"Business," he said. "You put business first."

"Business," she agreed. She squeezed Florida.

"Then we'll explore the states." He slapped her hand lightly. "Which reminds me. You need to consult my official mapmaker."

"You mean Brains?"

"Yes." he laughed. "Can you believe it? Everybody else brought supplies. Wrestler brought booze. You know what he brought? Maps, atlases, and a lawbook. He's been my most valuable man."

"As a matter of fact, he was showing me the route we were taking a little earlier. He said we'd be near enough to Chicago in four or five days for someone to go in. Who knows? Maybe I can find a buyer the first day!"

"Maybe you can." His voice trailed off. Something was coming. She could see it. Then, *boom*! A lightbulb went off. "That's it!" He snapped his fingers.

Jolene looked around. "Please, don't howl. Not here."

"No, I won't. Listen. That's where we can get the attention we need. We don't have to sell for market price. You, Jolene, are going to undercut everybody! We are going to sell for below retail!"

"How can we?"

"That's what is going to get us into Chicago. Do you understand? If the public is with us, if they're watching us, and rooting, whatever trap they're setting will not work. That's what we're going to do. If we can do our part in driving the cost of beef down, the public will buy for less, and that's what'll get 'em on our side."

"What about our profit?"

"We beat the middleman. We'll still double our best year ever."

"Wow." She was amazed. He slapped his hands. They realized they had found the way.

"That's what we're gonna do," he said. "We're gonna sell below retail."

"Below retail." She contemplated.

"That's it!" Coyote reiterated. He knew he had found the way. "Hey," he said. "Make love with me." He pulled her close to the fire inside.

"Just like that?"

"The boy offered me his van."

Jolene looked back to the empty fire. "I think the van might be in use by its owner."

Coyote saw her point.

"I have a better idea," she said. "Let's do it under the stars." As they lay down, the grass was soft and deep. She pulled her husband into her. They made love, then lay there undisturbed until the chill set in and the stars lost their appeal.

They dressed, walked quietly back, found their sleeping bags, crawled in, slept until 5 A.M., got up, then drove their cattle across the eastern half of Iowa.

Chicago

The meeting took place in the back seat of a limousine that belonged to the Teamsters Union, Chicago local. The glass was sealed; the chauffeur couldn't hear. Two men rode in the rear. One felt threatened, the other didn't.

The head of the railroad union was a stately, silver-haired man who had grown up around trains and loved them. Like so many other people who had followed the cattle drive, he was amused by Coyote's charisma. And since Coyote was attacking the truckers, not the railroad, there was no reason for the head of the railroad union to feel threatened.

The Teamster boss, on the other hand, felt that his union was about to be busted. The Teamster boss was a short, stocky, rough, pugilistic-looking man, exactly the man for the job he had. Although he had no great rank-and-file support against the cattle drive, he had to protect all his drivers, and that included the bad apples who worked for the cattle companies. He also had visions of his drivers forming lines in the unemployment office, put there by the repeating hooves of cattle drive after cattle drive, once other ranchers caught on. There was no way this cattle drive was coming into the stockyards. The Teamster boss looked not at the issue, but at the big picture, and like Coyote, this made him a formidable adversary.

For now, he needed a united front to stop the cattle drive. It couldn't look like a personal feud with the Teamsters. But the railroad boss was unconcerned. The Teamster was furious.

"Don't tell me cowboys, Indians, politics, or playing it safe with public opinion. Look! We're both union men all our lives. What doesn't come in on your railroads comes on my trucks. So here we are. The stockyards contract is Teamster. It stays Teamster! Got it? We set up a line. He tries to make what we call an unauthorized delivery, we deal with him, right then, at that time. My understanding stops there!"

"Well," asked the railroad boss, "why do you need me, then?"

"It's gotta come from both of us. Both unions, against him. That way, no press can focus on one of us, we both absorb the attention, and the public can concentrate on the legitimate issue at hand. It's our contract for the beef. Our trucks furnish health, safety, whatever. It's like that."

"I feel differently. I'm against having a showdown."

"That's what we got! A showdown! He brought it to us!"

The chauffeur continued driving down an obscure waterfront street.

"What are you going to do?" asked the railroad boss. "Shoot his cows?"

"He'll load onto our trucks," answered the Teamster boss assuredly.

"I doubt that very much," the railroad boss replied. "Look, you can't turn him away once he is at the stockyards. The public will howl. People are starving and we're throwing good beef away. I, for one, do not want consumer groups against us or we are both shit outta luck. That means maybe investigations against us for price gouging. Right? I want my trains to stay clean. Like your sanitary trucks."

"So do I." The Teamster boss was being led in a direction he didn't like, but he followed nevertheless. "I sense a wisdom here."

"I'll take you to it," the railroad boss explained. "We stop him quietly, way before the stockyards. He doesn't get into the city. Now, it's a union issue. That's good. But let's get the cops there, to lend the legal touch. My lawyers found a Cook County ordinance clearly forbidding hoofed animals from passing over an interstate highway."

"The interstate highway?"

"You haven't been reading your maps, have you? That's his only way into town. Over the interstate. He'll have to block traffic. It'll never work. So we stop him that way. It clouds the union issue, but right now we don't need power plays."

"All right," said the Teamster to his silver-haired counterpart. "Legitimacy . . . I'm sold."

"Good, now you can drop me off."

The Teamster boss switched the power window down, told his driver to return the railroad boss to his office.

The Teamsters boss went on. "So my men will man the line, but it's the police who'll really stop him."

"Exactly, which means the mayor will be our only problem." The railroad boss leaned back, remembering the past. "God, I wish Daley was still here."

"Don't worry." The Teamster talked tough regarding the new mayor of Chicago. "Labor put him there, labor tells him what to do."

They reached his office. The railroad boss got out. The Teamster said, "I'll take care of my men. We'll put up a nice blockade!"

The Teamster Hall was empty except for a few union staff workers. The Teamster boss walked in, happy, contented with the plan to stop the cattle drive before it reached the city of Chicago. He found his assistant, gave him the orders to carry out. It would mean a lot of phone time.

"I want you to line up thirty of the meanest, no questions asked rank-and-file we got. We're throwin' up a line against the cattle drive."

The assistant nodded, pulled the goon roster from his desk, began making the calls.

Coyote became conscious of his looks. Before crossing the river, he snuck into an open school locker room for a shower and shampoo. He put on a fresh shirt. Today was a big day. A man owning a fleet of ferry boats had volunteered to take the herd of cattle across the Mississippi River and Coyote wanted to look his best for the occasion.

Jolene could understand, but to Wrestler, Coyote had become a pain in the ass. All this vanity was getting to Wrestler. What the hell did cowboys do before they had locker rooms to change in? "You're becoming a pussy, Cantrell." Wrestler snuck in these words when a shaven, cologne-scented Coyote rode by. Coyote tried to ignore Wrestler, but the words hurt, they stung.

The ferry boat crossings were quite a spectacle. Hundreds of people lined the east bank north of Moline, Illinois. The crowd was looking for a reason to celebrate and they got it. The reporters were almost as much of an event as the cattle themselves. A banner was strung up between trees, saying MOLINE, ILLINOIS WELCOMES YOU. Everyone wanted to talk with Coyote, and he talked with them all.

Once the crossing was completed, the drive drifted into Illinois. It was hot and the land was flat and extremely boring. But to the cattle it was lush, full of rich grass that was fed by damp, wealthy, dark soil, watered by the Mississippi itself. None of the Colorado men had ever seen such fertile land as this, irrigated by the mighty river.

A rancher came down on horseback, a lone man wearing a dirty straw hat. He asked where Coyote was, found him.

"I want to join your drive." Just like that. Coyote took him in. Another rancher put his money on the line, "I don't have far to truck 'em," he told Coyote. "But one mile's too far for me."

"All right! You're in." Coyote was feeling ec-

229

static at the way things were building. He told both ranchers, "You understand, we're selling below retail."

The first rancher nodded, left to bring his herd into the drive. The second rancher said, "I'm still with you if you got room for one more. We'll clean up anyway beating the truckers."

"Great, friend, how many head?" Coyote asked.

"Two hundred eighty-five. All of 'em Black Angus!"

"All right! Black Angus! The Rolls Royce of beef! Give this drive a little class." He slapped the Black Angus rancher on the back as he left to bring up his herd.

Coyote raced to new heights.

More ranchers came in. So did some of their friends. By the time they had crossed the first third of Illinois, the herd had nearly tripled. All the ranchers saw the wisdom of beating the middleman, and like Coyote, all felt they were blazing a trail for years to come. It was a rancher rebellion.

Stephanie and her crew caught up to Coyote. "Hey, Coyote," she yelled as he passed her on horseback. "Is this catching on?"

He leaned down, grinned. "You betcha!"

A couple invited Coyote and Jolene to dinner that night at their ranch house. It was Coyote's first hot meal in well over a month, and afterwards, Coyote insisted on doing the dishes because he had a craving to feel hot soap and clean water running over his fingers.

After dinner, Coyote had the treat of seeing himself on television for the first time. He couldn't believe it, he loved it, and if the couple had invited him, he would have stayed for the ten o'clock news, too.

The Teamster and railroad bosses were riding up in the elevator to meet with the mayor.

"God, I wish the old guys were back in City Hall," griped the railroad boss again, as he held the elevator door for the Teamster boss.

Neither of them bothered with the secretary. They walked past her directly into the mayor's office, into the inner sanctum of city government. It was nothing new for either of them. They had been here many times before.

Both had the same reaction when they saw the new mayor. To the labor bosses, he looked almost meek, like a man who had been an assistant all his life. The mayor confirmed what the bosses were thinking with his first words.

"You are both asking me to take a very unpopular stand."

The Teamster boss put it more simply. "Hey! Either ban him from the city or don't!"

The mayor slanted an eye at this crude speech.

The railroad boss put it more subtly. "Mayor, the truck drivers do have a very legitimate grievance. And they are prepared to bear the brunt of public opinion. What they need from your good office is the presence of police to back up their legal blockade."

"Yes sir. We think that would work," said the Teamster politely.

"And who the hell eats the polls for the police

department? Who do you think eats that?" The mayor was worried.

"The police chief," affirmed the railroad boss, "not you. This way, if there is any trouble at the blockade, then the law can be enforced."

"What law are you speaking of?" asked the mayor.

"You have the ordinance on your desk, there." The railroad boss pointed.

The mayor picked up the piece of paper he had been sent earlier, put it down. "That law was written in 1915 to keep horses from shitting on the fenders of Model A's."

"But, sir, it's still a valid ordinance. And for good reason."

The Teamster boss kicked the floor. "Jesus, what a bunch of pansies we got now in this city."

"Mayor, if you're not satisfied with the law we gave you, have your health inspector examine the cattle."

"And then what?" asked the mayor.

The railroad boss blew up. "Hoof and mouth disease! I don't care!"

The Teamster boss threatened, "You don't back us with the cops, I promise you, you got a street fight out there!"

The railroad boss countered, "You were elected to keep the peace. Now do it."

But the mayor still wouldn't come to a decision. He wasn't reacting much at all. The Teamster boss had had enough. He leaned hard on the mayor.

"You waffle on this, you can forget the support of labor in '81! You hear me? We'll run you down. Forget labor. Forget it!"

Now the mayor was cowering.

"So make a choice!" screamed the Teamster boss.

"All right, gentlemen," answered the mayor, "you can relax."

"I will relax when you make a decision," replied the railroad boss.

"I will inform the police chief to be present at the blockade with his men, and to provide backup assistance to what will be termed a 'legal union issue.'" He paused, looked at both men. "Just keep him out of this city!"

The line of cattle stretched as far back as the eye could see. Here, in central Illinois, the land was flat, green, covered with alfalfa.

Ranchers along the way were volunteering alfalfa for the herd. And each new rancher who joined the drive brought hay, as a guest brings a bottle of wine when invited to dinner.

The roads continued to be wide-shouldered, often without fences. And alfalfa grew everywhere, often available for the cattle to eat.

Coyote found himself taking a consensus among the local reporters every time he wanted to try a new road. That soon became a pain in the butt. Coyote realized that his way was usually more accurate then some urban reporter's guess. So Brains purchased county maps, and he still guided the cattle drive the way he had done through the last four states. The original system worked fine.

Coyote was also worried that most of the reporters were finding it very dull covering a cattle drive. Their idea of a hot story was not moving across America's plains at two miles an hour. They began filtering away, sometimes not returning at all. Coyote was searching for an idea that would make the drive more attractive, more exciting for the travelling reporters. After all, they were the key to getting into Chicago. Coyote, the politician, was convinced of that. Yet he didn't know how to keep them around. He was working on it.

Fun Truckin' was keeping Stephanie around. They were spending a lot of time in his van, and it was funny to see the van way off the road somewhere, in the shade under a tree, bouncing up and down from the activity inside.

Coyote was most worried about Wrestler. Since their drive had become successful, Wrestler hadn't been the same. He decided to ride back and see what Wrestler was up to. On the ride, Coyote realized why Wrestler had been so depressed. He wasn't used to success. Wrestler was far more comfortable as the bitter loser. The attention that success brought Coyote overwhelmed Wrestler, as it once did Coyote on the rodeo circuit during his drinking years. He didn't know how to handle doing well. It was a ghetto mentality on the plains.

Coyote saw Wrestler on his knees, off to the side, checking the weight on one cow. Wrestler, a cowboy to the end.

When Wrestler saw Coyote approaching, he called very loudly, "Weight seems to be holding up! They ain't gonna butthole us again, those tight-assed motherfucking—"

Coyote cut him off. "Will you stop talking like that!" Coyote looked around to see if anybody was listening. Wrestler had to shoot off a foul mouth, had to act like a loser, even now.

Wrestler replied, almost sheepishly, "I didn't mean nuthin' by it."

"I know that," Coyote said. "I grew up with you." Coyote motioned to all the city people around, the media people. "But they don't know it." He could see Wrestler getting mad.

"You're sure gettin' concerned with what people think."

"Wrestler, goddamnit! We're depending on what people think!"

Coyote couldn't hack a loser anymore. He loved Wrestler, but couldn't stand being around him. Coyote rode away.

At the rear of the drive, Jolene was caring for a sick cow. The drive passed the poor cow by. The cow wanted to catch up, it tried to catch up. But it couldn't. The cow kept stumbling, getting up. Meekly, it tried to moo, to call for a friend, but none of the cows turned around. They just left it there to make it, or die.

When Jolene found it, she knew right away the cow was too exhausted to travel any further. She tried to comfort the cow, but what could she do? She kneeled by it, but didn't know where to start, where to touch the cow, to make it feel better. It was a pitiful sight, reminding her of a doe she found as a child, wounded by a hunter and left there to perish. She let the cow lie there on the shoulder of the road, alone. It was too weak to even nibble at the grass. For a second time the cow tried to get to its feet. Then it stumbled one last time and did nothing but blink its eyelashes.

Jolene found Coyote near the front of the drive. She told him about the cow. "Jake, that one cow isn't gonna make it."

"Is there anything wrong with it? That you can see?"

"It's just exhausted. That's all. What should we do?"

Coyote had a flash. What had to be done, had to be done. "Whose brand is it?" he asked.

"Our brand," Jolene told him.

Coyote reached into his sheath for his rifle. "Tell Food he's got some butchering to do. We're gonna have a barbecue."

"What?" Jolene asked.

"That's right," Coyote smiled. "A barbecue."

Rifle in hand, he left to put the cow out of its misery. Little did the reporters know what a treat, what a tasty delight they had in store.

By early evening, many of the reporters returned. Everybody was gathering around a large campfire. Many of the new ranchers on the drive were getting to know each other for the first time. One topic they had in common was that many of them lived in Illinois, yet they had never gotten together, never formed a plan or an alliance. It took a man from Colorado to bring them together.

Around a smaller fire, Food was roasting large hunks of meat over a makeshift spit. Food was a magician with his sharp knife, sampling the meat as it sizzled and spit. This was

Food's first opportunity at drawing attention, and he was dazzling. His face registered delight as he teased and tempted the waiting diners by turning the chunks of meat. The grease sizzled and popped loudly as it hit the coals.

Away from everything, Brains was having an intense conversation with Coyote. In his hands, Brains held a detailed map of Chicago and its outskirts. In dark pencil he had outlined all of Coyote's alternatives.

"Here are the stockyards, over here." Brains pointed them out.

Coyote peered at the involved map. Brains went on, "See, it's a whole damn industrial complex."

"Whew! That's big."

"Sure it's big. Look." Brains showed Coyote an aerial view of Chicago's stockyards. "That's what it looks like. We'll be coming in from here. But I've got some news for you. Are you sitting down?"

"C'mon, kid."

"Well, look. According to these maps, to get from where we'll be, the only way into the stockyards is to go up one of these on-ramps, and onto the interstate highway for two miles."

"What?" Coyote's voice squeaked into falsetto.

"That's right. I can't find any other way. Can you?"

Coyote looked down at the map, dark-penciled to perfection. "Well if you can't, I sure can't. But you mean all these cows on the interstate? Do you know how many cattle we now have?"

"I can't count that high."

"Brains. This is serious."

"A decision is only serious when there are alternatives. But this is our only way to go. So, we stop traffic and do it!"

"Why didn't any of these reporters, any of these other people say anything?"

"You think they give a shit? Most of those reporters are just along for the ride."

"You'd think they'd say something."

"They probably thought you had it figured."

"Lemme see that." Coyote grabbed the map. Brains had marked the spot where they climbed onto the interstate.

Coyote felt another flashbulb go off. "That's where they're gonna stop us. Right there." He touched the X on the map.

"Who?"

"It doesn't matter. That's where it'll happen!" Coyote said. "There can't be only one on-ramp like this map says. How many on-ramps are there right here?"

"Let me get my city of Chicago map." Brains didn't fumble. He knew right where to look. "There are, let's see, four or five on-ramps. Probably the easiest two would be these last ones. This one seems the best. The January Street on-ramp. It's right off a back road."

Coyote looked at the map. "You're right."

Then somebody came up with congratulations at how well they had done and the subject was abandoned for the moment. But the responsibility, the weight, never left Coyote.

A disgusted Wrestler sat off to the side, on a log. Nobody was talking to him, nobody was

238

around. He watched a group grow around Coyote as he travelled from rancher to rancher. A bit jealous, Wrestler watched Stephanie and Fun Truckin' drink wine from the same cup.

He saw Food acting like a clown, getting the steaks ready to eat. "Well," Wrestler said to himself. "There's always good beef steak if that fool doesn't overcook it."

Coyote refused a beer from a reporter. Instead he clarified to another rancher who had joined the drive, "We all sell at the same price." The rancher nodded in agreement. "Every one of us," Coyote repeated. The rancher again nodded. "Good," said Coyote. "Gimme your hand on it." The two ranchers shook.

"Here it is," Food called from the cooking fire. "Here it is, come and get it. Who's gonna be the first?"

Wrestler walked over. "Gimme some of that, you fat sonofabitch." Wrestler jammed his own knife into a juicy filet, pulled it off the skillet. One of the reporters brought paper plates, but Wrestler didn't bother. His teeth pulled tender bites of juicy filet right off the knife. He walked away from the crowd, to where the cattle were grazing. He caught Coyote's glare. He didn't want to embarrass anybody.

Jolene joined Coyote. Sadly they watched Wrestler, but there was nothing they could do. "Jake," Jolene said to her husband. "I know how you feel about Wrestler, but you can't let him pull you down."

"I feel like I'm watching my closest friend."

"Closer," she said. "You're watching yourself, Jake. That's you without the ranch, without me, without this drive. Without anything to live for. He could be any of us, but he's not. He's someone we know. He's Wrestler."

"Well, I love the guy," said Coyote. "I just can't mess with him."

The others began arriving at the cooking fire, holding paper plates. Fun Truckin' and Stephanie were first in line. The boy was eager and hungry. Coyote chided him. "Let the lady go first." She gave Coyote a long look. Coyote hoped Jolene wasn't watching. He looked. She wasn't.

Food waited, his cutting knife glistening, hot with grease. Stephanie was hesitant. She had never eaten this way before. A freshly killed cow, cut and butchered on the open plains? She would much rather have had it in a restaurant.

"Go on," Jolene told her. "It'll be the best steak you ever had."

Fun Truckin' handed her plate to Food. Food sliced her a filet. Stephanie took it, looked it over. "The meat looks so good and rich."

Coyote said, "I promise you. That's what meat is supposed to taste like. Go ahead."

Stephanie took her first bite. Her teeth were prepared for something tough. Instead they sank into the medium rare filet. The juices filled her mouth. Her eyes lit with pleasure as if she had eaten a great French delicacy. In fact she had tasted great American beef. "Mmmmm, you're not kidding." She took another bite, then another.

That broke the ice. The other city people now came up to take their own steaks. The looks on their satisfied faces told Food, the chef, that they would treasure these moments forever.

Coyote had become a backslapper among the reporters. "There ya go," he told one cameraman. "You want to ski, you go to Aspen. You want beef, you come to Colorado."

Later that night, Jolene and Coyote were sitting on a rock, away from the barbecue, saying goodbye. Early the next morning, she would leave for Chicago.

Coyote kissed her cheek. He kept thinking how young, how youthful her skin had become. He noticed freckles, freckles he hadn't seen for years. He loved those freckles, kissed each of them, then the entire cluster.

They looked at each other.

"I don't know what to tell you, baby," Coyote said. "I don't have any advice. Just good luck in Chicago."

"I feel so confident going in there. Luck is something I just don't feel I'll need."

"You act like it'll be so automatic."

"Who could resist buying so many cows at such a low price? I don't see how it could be difficult at all."

"I don't either," said Coyote. "But it will be."

"Difficult?"

"Yeah! Difficult." He nodded his head in emphasis.

The Auction

Everything began moving normally for Coyote again. Jolene had left on her way to Chicago. Coyote was back on his horse, minding his drive. Right away, Wrestler became more cordial, even said, "Hiya, buddy," as he passed on his way to the van for food. They were cowhands again, they were equals.

Then they got to Cook County and everything changed.

This was it, Cook County, stockyard county, beef central. It all happened here. Beef was bought, sold, traded, priced, labeled, slaughtered, sliced. Ranchers were given either a new life, or another year in debt. Supermarket chains all over America stocked their shelves from Cook County.

Stephanie and her crew were waiting for Coyote. The interview was all planned. Even the cow had been chosen. Coyote knew what he wanted to say, the message he had to convey to the public if they were to make it onto the interstate, into the heart of Cook County, and the stockyards. It was the last part of the drive, but the only part that mattered to Coyote.

For this, the all-important interview, Coyote was standing on the plains, with Stephanie, in front of the camera. Next to him, alone, apart from the herd, was a single cow. The cameraman began filming. Stephanie began speaking.

"I am standing here with a man from Colorado, who has ridden across America on a horse. His name is Coyote."

Coyote became very unsure of himself. All the other interviews had been spontaneous. But for days, he had been mulling over what to tell the public. Most of Chicago was watching. He stumbled as he began to speak.

"We are, all of us here, are asking for your help." Coyote looked down at the cow, put his hand on its shoulder. "This is the source of our meat. He is born, raised, and bred to be eaten, so take a look at him, or her, because it never really had a sex. What I want to tell you is that each of these beasts nowadays is costing me more to raise than I make from selling it. That is because our potential profit is going into transporting, that's trucking for the most part, these cows from my ranch to your market. So we take a loss, year after year. When I go under, how're you people gonna eat? We're tryin' to feed ya, but we're dying trying! We've come a long, long way. Farther than we imagined." Coyote stepped back like a speechmaker, motioned to the enormous herd behind him, then resumed. "We've grown to over 1,200 head! We've talked this over. We don't want to cheat the public. We don't want a windfall profit! It's not what this drive's about.

"We're going to undercut everybody in Chicago, driving the price of beef down on your supermarket shelves! That's what we're about. We want beef prices to be reasonable, affordable.

"We need you, the public, to turn out on the interstate and lead us into town. They'll try and turn us away, but if the public is there, nobody can stop us. So please, welcome us to your city, and don't settle for beef that's been shipped, and force-fed with fillers and crap like that."

Coyote stopped, finished. He simply stood there, drained of energy. Around him, motion resumed. Coyote became flushed, embarrassed at so much attention.

As he looked up from the tops of his boots, he saw Wrestler laughing. Coyote realized he was still standing next to a cow.

Coyote shooed the cow away.

The mayor of Chicago had plenty of time to mull his problem over as he rode away from the windy city down to smaller Springfield, the state capital. He needed to speak with the governor, who was an old hand at tough situations. The mayor was new in office, inexperienced in making hard decisions. He was torn between stopping the cattle drive or letting it into the stockyards. On one side of this obviously popular event were the votes of the public who elected him. On the other side was labor, and the people who financed his campaign. Who was stronger and how long was the public's memory if he halted the drive? These were practical political questions he could not answer.

At the governor's mansion in Springfield,

the mayor was left waiting for nearly an hour. He paced nervously, checking his watch. He felt that the veteran governor was mocking him by making him wait this long.

Finally the governor's secretary told the mayor, "The governor will see you now."

The mayor spilled his story, explaining more fully than he previously had over the phone. When he finished explaining the convergent elements twisting around in his mind, he noticed that the governor was practically smirking as he talked. The governor looked distinctly superior. The mayor became immediately aware of the difference in altitude between them.

"Yes, Mayor," began the governor, "I do agree with you. You are caught in a hell of a bind."

"The mayor's cheeks twitched in tension.

"On one hand, you lose labor's support in the next election if you let this cattle drive in. Yet if you stop this 'folk hero,' the populace, the electorate, will cast you in their minds as a villain." The governor relaxed, moved forward in his chair. "And you haven't the slightest idea what to do."

The mayor felt like a schoolboy being lectured. "No," he said.

"Mayor, it's all very simple. If the public stays home, have your police back the Teamsters and stop the man. On the other hand, if the multitudes do arrive, sit back, let the man through, then hire minorities to clean up the cow shit."

The governor let his advice sink in. "Now, how hard was that?"

*   *   *

Jolene wore her amazement with wide eyes. The way Chicago suddenly popped out, so tall and majestic, from the never-ending flatness of the great plains, held a wonder touched only by the natural majesty of her own Rocky Mountains. The two were similiar in the way they appeared so abruptly, and by the power they each held, the lure, the mysteries within both panoramas.

Once over her initial awe, Jolene pulled to the side of the highway and reacquainted herself with the map Brains gave her. She drove straight to the Chicago Auction Hall, keeping as level a head as she knew how.

The Auction Hall was a giant amphitheatre-like structure in which the cattle delivered to the stockyards were auctioned off to buyers from all parts of America. The parking lot was one of the largest Jolene had seen, except for the larger arenas on the rodeo circuit.

As she stood outside the door, she could hear the auctioneer singing his classic, incoherent song: "Ten thousand pounds corn-fed beef from Missouri . . . *bip be pa dee bop* . . . *bip be pa dee bop*, ninety-seven, ninety-seven, ninety-seven, do I hear ninety-eight? Do I hear ninety-eight? Ninety-eight! Do I hear a dollar? A dollar? One dollar? *Bip be pa dee bop!*" His voice sang, like those preachers on Sunday morning TV. It was fantastic. Jolene walked in. She felt bashful about entering the Auction Hall. There was so much she knew nothing about. She felt totally overwhelmed. How could she compete? These men had been doing this all their lives. It wasn't courage, but ignorance of her mission and baby-like innocence that pulled Jolene Cantrell inside.

She immediately felt people staring at her though she was sure no one was. But they were. They were looking at her. Ah, Jolene realized, it was because she was a woman. She made eye contact with one man. He turned away. She made eye contact with a second man. He too turned away. What was wrong with these men? Didn't they like females?

Jolene let her eyes wander. There were very few women around. The auctioneer had taken a break so momentarily the noise subsided. She began to walk. Like a newcomer to a big city, her legs wouldn't stop. She avoided eye contact as much as possible, stared instead at the lapels of the buyers, where they wore large badges with their pictures on them. Under their beefy faces were the names of the stores they represented. Jolene recognized Albertsons, Safeway, A&P, and many other famous market chains. They were all here, from the West, the Midwest, the East, bidding on cattle in this sweaty, insane, unique hall in Chicago, Illinois, America.

The auctioneer returned. *"Bip be pa dee bop!"* The noise came back. Everybody began yelling, pleading to be recognized by the auctioneer. There was action at the auction.

The auctioneer screamed louder than anyone else.

"Ninety-nine? Ninety-nine? Ninety-nine? I'm looking for ninety-nine."

"Ninety-nine!" yelled a man near Jolene.

The auctioneer recognized him. "A dollar five. Do I hear a dollar five? *Bip be pa dee bop!*"

"A dollar five!" The man near Jolene upped the price. He was nervously making chicken scratches in a notebook with a chewed-off golfer's pencil.

"A dollar five?" thought Jolene. "I can beat a dollar five." She watched and waited. She knew right then how she was going to compete. By price. She offered better beef at a better price. She wore her pride high again, like a Cantrell.

"How about a dollar seven?" the auctioneer sang.

It was too high a price. The man near Jolene cursed. "Shit!" Then he walked away from the bidding.

Jolene didn't move right away. Something, probably fear, kept her from pouncing on the frustrated buyer with a price better than the one he walked away from. Then she sprung after the man. *Oof!* Somebody's elbow jolted into Jolene's breastbone. She grabbed onto the man's coat to keep herself from blacking out. Her head got queasy, began spinning.

"Jesus, lady!"

The man tried to shake her off. She felt his corpulent arm underneath his coat sleeve. He didn't even know he had hit her. She got her feet underneath her again, put her weight back on them. Her legs held though her eyes were dizzy and glazed. The man continued on his way, also making chicken scratches in his notebook, cursing the lady, cursing the auctioneer.

Jolene spun her head, looking for the man who was outbid just a minute ago. Oh, it hurt so much where she got elbowed. She couldn't see clearly. Then all she saw were animals. All the men in this auction house were animals. There was no difference between them and the animals they bought and sold.

"A dollar fifteen," the auctioneer called.

Around her, men were closing their notebooks, cursing under their breaths. The prices were climbing way out of sight.

"Sir," Jolene said, trying to catch a man's attention. He looked at her, a twitchy sudden little look, then scurried away, deeper into the sweltering crowd of animals.

The noise was overpowering to Jolene. It came in waves, stayed high, then more waves came, louder waves of noise. Jolene felt the beginnings of a splitting headache. It hurt behind the temples on both sides, was creeping inward. Jolene held her head. Then came a tremendous fear that people were watching. They were watching. A deeper fear told her not to show weakness so she took her hands from her head, walked quickly away from where she was. She had to sell that beef. She had to make a sale. How would she do it? She walked, wouldn't stop looking and learning until she found a way.

Yes, this was where it all happened. One sweaty bidder raised his hand. His face, collar, tie, and shirt were all covered with sweat. Jolene thought his suit would rip under the arm, but it didn't. The bidder was overlooked, waited until the next round.

The bigger supermarket chains bought slaughtered beef in quarters, then had their own butchers cut the beef into more select cuts, like filet, or New York, or T-bone. Other, smaller operations bought their select cuts right from here, from the more specialized packing houses.

She tried to speak to another bidder. He wouldn't talk to her either. It was as if they all knew who she was. It felt spooky. She would come way below what they were bidding. What was it now?

"Bip be pa dee bop, a dollar twenty . . . "

It was all worth it to Jolene. From forty cents on the ranch, to a dollar twenty right here. Coyote was right. Trucking did triple the price of beef. It was robbery. Jolene began to feel righteous. It was worth all those hard miles, just to see the facts in front of her eyes.

Jolene tried to speak to another bidder. Instead, the bidder gave her a cold shoulder, yelled to the auctioneer.

Jolene went to another man yelling bids to the auctioneer. Like the others, he turned away, screamed even louder to the auctioneer, as if he thought that if he screamed, Jolene would go away.

He began walking. She followed. "Wait. Do you know who I am?"

The bidder stopped, turned back, showed his first touch of humanity. "Of course I know."

"Then let's talk. Please. I can beat any price I've heard in the last hour."

The bidder's eyes darted around the room, as if to see who was watching him. He spoke from the side of his mouth. "Lady, forget it. There's a squeeze on. Go home!" Then he walked away.

"Please! Why won't you talk to me?"

But Jolene was left ranting. The man never once looked back.

The rest of the afternoon was like that. She would size up one man, approach him, and he would walk away. It began to drive her crazy, like the silent treatment kids used to give each other at school.

The hall began thinning out. The men were heading for their homes or motels to drink themselves to sleep and wait for tomorrow's bidding.

Jolene was so intense in her pursuit, that when she stopped to collect herself, she saw the hall two-thirds empty. She tried to approach the auctioneer but by the time she reached the stand, he had already left.

She screamed, "What's the matter with you people?" She was a woman possessed by the knowledge that whatever she did, she was going to fail. "What's the matter with you?"

She cornered a bidder who was rolling up his notes. "We're selling over 1,000 head!" She had seen the bidder before, was trying to shock him into making a commitment.

He tried to leave. She thrust herself in his way. He pushed her aside. "Do we have to slaughter them ourselves?" Now everybody left was listening. "Right outside this hall?"

But nobody stopped. Everybody avoided her. She felt as though she were back in Walsenburg, in the market line with those two bitchy women from town. She stood alone, one island in an ocean of people. She waited and waited for someone to approach her, but no one did.

She waited until the last person left. Then she was alone. She had no idea what to do, where to go next. Her husband was a long way away. There was nothing left to do. She left the hall, walked to the battered white truck, the last car in the lot, got in, and sat there and stared.

While Jolene was gone, Stephanie was trying to spend as much time as possible near Coyote. This evening she was dressed to the hilt, looking really good in loose fitting clothes. As a conversation piece, she had drawn her own map of the different on-ramps leading into the stockyards. She had selected one that, in her opinion, was the best way in.

"We'll be here, this time tomorrow," she told Coyote, moving closer to his body as she spoke. Coyote made no response. "The January Street on-ramp, here, seems the easiest way onto the interstate. It's right off a ranch. I've spoken to the owner, we can cut through to the road, here, then go right to the on-ramp."

Coyote was sick of maps. He looked around for Brains, but didn't see him. He was sick of everything. Really, he was worried for Jolene. All he could think about was Jolene, if she sold the cattle or not, if she was all right. He didn't give a shit for Stephanie right now, or for her advances.

He simply replied, "You know the area best."

"Good." She stood, folded the map. "I'll make

sure my station has it for the morning." She smiled. "You're the biggest story in town."

Coyote didn't know how to reply.

He stood. She moved a step closer to him, then brushed against his chest with her arm. "Uh," she said. "I don't want to mess this up sexually."

Startled, Coyote made no move.

"I really admire your wife. And, well, if you're ever interested."

"Maybe sometime." Coyote didn't know what to do.

"O.K.," she nodded, then backed away and started walking. Soon she was gone from his sight.

Coyote's blood was boiling. He was hot inside, filled with flattery. He wished he had reacted soon enough to have done something with her.

Times had changed. He had never had a woman try to pick up on him before. He waited, decided not to pursue Stephanie. He couldn't feel much better after sex than he did right now. What the hell? He let it go.

Instead, he saw Fun Truckin' coming his way. The boy had passed Stephanie, was looking back, smiling.

Coyote showed Fun Truckin' the map. "Check this January Street on-ramp for me tomorrow morning. See if that broad knows what she's doing."

"Sure, no problem. I'll do it first thing." Fun Truckin' folded the map into his pocket, grinned at Coyote. "That woman. She hit on you, yet?"

Coyote shook his head. He could feel his ego deflating. Fun Truckin' smiled, folded his arms across his chest. "I'll say one thing 'bout drivin' cattle. Sure makes a man horny."

He left to find Stephanie. Inside, Coyote laughed at himself. Not every advance, he realized, was a compliment.

Jolene was uncomfortable lying awake in the front seat of the pickup truck. She tried to stretch but hit the gear shift. The seat was on a slant which kept her body bunched in the rear downhill section. The upholstery was torn in places. The springs were sharp and cold. The windows were shut tightly, but a cold wind blew through Chicago and nothing kept it from coming inside. She cuddled closer to the backrest part of the seat, but nothing kept her warm. She began to get very cold.

Jolene got down on herself for not coming prepared. She had brought no blanket, no pillow. She felt stupid, a woman dependent on dumb luck, like a person in the mountains on his first camping trip.

She prayed that tomorrow would be different. She knew she would somehow have to get the auctioneer to announce her presence, to announce her beef. But would he do it? Would he undercut the other sellers? She doubted it. Jolene felt a momentary satisfaction. She was learning the ropes. Of course he wouldn't undercut everybody else. But she could try.

She would have to try. Everything depended on her. She had to sell the cattle. Oh, how she wanted to sleep! She tried to toss, tried to find a comfortable position. But nothing was comfortable, nothing felt right. She felt a nervousness about tomorrow she couldn't compare with anything she had ever felt. She recognized these nerves as a man's feelings. She had seen Coyote toss and turn with them, lie awake many nights. Before, all she could do was try to calm him, never truly understanding. Now she knew his nervousness.

She waited out the night. The battered white truck was the only vehicle left in the immense parking lot. She had pulled way off to the far corner, away from the guard. All around were acres and acres of concrete with perfectly measured white lines. She put saliva on her face, rubbed it into her face. At least she could try to stay fresh for the coming day.

Coyote couldn't sleep either. He spent the whole night worrying about Jolene. Every hour or so, he would get out of his sleeping bag and walk a little way toward the road. He hoped to see those two out-of-line headlights coming his way. But the battered truck never came.

When he finally gave up on Jolene for the night, the sun was beginning to rise. It shone flat over the horizon, into Coyote's eyes. He was nervous. His blood churned. This was the last day. He felt an anger that he had come so far and his wife might have failed. Or that she might have sold the beef, but would not be here. Coyote already felt that he had lost. No victory could satiate the emptiness he was experiencing. He began to hate. He hated Gateways for hurrying his father's death. He hated the truckers for interfering with his natural right to make a living. He hated ranching for taking rodeo away, and he hated himself for not being able to cope with any of it.

Wrestler came over, interrupted the smouldering coals that were his temper this morning. "You're not going to believe this."

Coyote boiled. "What?"

"Look." Wrestler began walking. Coyote followed him to a rise. The ground was strange to him; they had arrived at this spot last evening, when it was partly dark. Wrestler pointed.

"My God," Coyote said.

"Isn't that something?"

They were witnessing the skyline of Chicago. The horizontal sun sparkled and glistened off the tallest window panes of the skyscrapers. It was spectacular.

As Jolene had before, Wrestler and Coyote were reminded of the great wall of the Rocky Mountains, out West. Urban and rural were unified. The experiences became the same.

Wrestler pointed out one particular skyscraper. "Looks like Pike's Peak from a distance."

"Or Mt. Evans," said Coyote. "If you were in Denver." Coyote looked affectionately at Wrestler. "I wouldn't know how to describe this to anybody else."

"Yeah." Wrestler understood. He felt the same way.

They walked down. The sightseeing temporarily relieved Coyote's seething. But as soon as they reached the bottom of the rise, his anger heated up.

"Well, old buddy," Wrestler said. "This is it. We're goin' in."

"I wish Jolene were here. I wish I knew she sold the beef."

"She'll be here," Wrestler assured him. "That lady never misses a finish."

"I can taste blood, Wrestler. That woman gets touched, anyone messes with her, it's their blood."

"Well, well, there's still some animal left in you."

"What?" Coyote asked.

"I thought you had turned one hundred percent diplomat."

"There's lots of animal left." Coyote looked mean, crazy, as he had before Frontier Days.

"Well, I'm gonna be watchin you, and you ain't gonna do nuthin' to nobody. We've come too far. Just get the cattle into that chute. Ain't nobody gonna remember the fight. Just who won. Use your mind, boy. Keep using your mind!"

As soon as it opened, Jolene charged into the Auction Hall. She found a ladies' room, washed up. She was surprised that there even was a ladies' room in this place. She searched her purse. Finally, there it was. Her toothbrush. It felt excellent to brush her teeth.

She began to experience cramps. Where was her calendar? She hoped it wasn't her time of the month. She had forgotten to bring her pocket calendar, truthfully had no idea what the date or even the day was. The cramping came and went. She would have to live with it.

By the time she was ready, teeth brushed, face washed, cream applied and rubbed in, then again washed off, the auctioneer was already barking like a maniac. By the time he made his first sale, Jolene was already standing under the podium, to his left.

"Hey! Over 1,000 head for sale. Down here!"

When the auctioneer saw Jolene, he made no pretense of ignoring her. He leaned down, said abruptly, "Lady, that's scab beef. I won't touch it."

She recoiled. "Scab beef?"

"That's right. I can't touch it!" He went back to selling of cattle from everywhere, everywhere but southern Colorado.

It hit her like a wall of ocean water. She was going down. She was in the wrong place. She would never sell the cattle. "Scab beef," they were calling it. Scab beef? That meant there was something wrong with it, meaning it wasn't brought in the proper way.

"Oh God," Jolene thought. With so little sleep for so many nights, she was ready to cave in. She saw it clearly. No matter how long she and Coyote stayed on the road, no matter what they did, the system was locked up. It began and finished with the money people, and the rancher couldn't buck it. The tragedy was that they had come so far to find this out. Suspicions were one thing, but to know that they were up against a stone wall was the singular most depressing moment Jolene had ever lived through.

It was over for her, over for Coyote.

With nothing left to do, she bought some black coffee from a machine. It began to perk her up. Her blood ran again. Her body woke up. She felt alive. She felt like trying. She would not lose. She would not lie down.

She squashed her cup, said to herself, "You'll never see the day." She was referring to quitting.

There was three bidders conferring away from the rat pack, near the front door. Jolene cornered them. "Please." She looked at their name plaques. "You represent markets from coast to coast. We have 1,000 head, and we will beat anybody's prices."

It was obvious that the bidders knew she was Coyote's wife. They ceased their discussion, talked with her. They decided to tell her the truth.

"Look, lady," one of them began. "I would love to buy your beef. I'll be honest. I can hardly afford not to."

She was listening.

The second bidder said, "Do you understand?"

Jolene's spirits were rising, but she had a fear of soaring too high. But this wasn't a shut down. They were talking with her.

The other bidder stepped in, spoke for his company.

"So would I. We're all in the same tempting position. But you must realize neither of us can possibly tie up our company's funds, not knowing if your husband's beef is going to get slaughtered, or whether it's going to rot out on the highway."

"What? What are you talking about? Of course it's going to get slaughtered!"

The first bidder replied firmly. "No, Mrs. Cantrell. Not in Chicago it won't!"

The auctioneer resumed. *"Bip be pa dee bop."* The sound deafened everybody. Jolene screamed.

"He's right outside the city. He's going to the stockyards. Tell me what you mean!"

The second bidder leaned into her ear. "Mrs. Cantrell, take your notoriety home with you. Cherish what you have done. But believe me, they'll never let your husband drive his cattle into this city."

The others saw total confusion on Jolene's face.

"Who won't?" She screamed even louder.

The auctioneer made a sale, toned down. The bidders spoke to each other. "I don't think she knows. You don't know what we're talking about. Do you?"

"She's the only one who doesn't," the third bidder cracked.

Jolene was shaking her head as he said this. The second bidder broke the news in a fatherly way. "You really haven't heard." He knew she hadn't. "The truckers, Mrs. Cantrell, have set up a blockade of your husband's cattle drive. The police are backing them. Mrs. Cantrell, there is no way. They won't let him in."

Almost melancholy, the three bidders moved away, back into the action. Jolene tried to move her lips, to call them back, but she couldn't make a sound. She looked around. Among thousands of people, Jolene was alone, ostracized. She didn't know which way to turn.

She noticed two men whom she had seen earlier. They seemed to be watching her. She got timid, didn't know who they were. They were talking with one another.

In fact, they had been following her. They were two small-time meat packers, who had recently purchased their own small slaughterhouse. By the quality of their meat, they hoped to compete with the majors.

The two were father and son. The father was Bela Beck, wearing a conservative, immaculate suit. He was fifty-seven, short, with traces of curly black hair over an otherwise bald head.

The son, Bruce Beck, was also short, around twenty-eight, dressed more casually. He was definitely in his father's mold, he was in his father's business, and he was also bald.

The son left the father to approach Jolene.

Meanwhile, Jolene forgot them, was looking toward the auctioneer, biding time. When she looked back down, there was Bruce Beck next to her, waiting politely to be recognized.

At first she recoiled. She had been approaching everybody, now she was approached. She didn't like Bruce so close to her; then, in an instant, she didn't mind. She realized he was waiting for her attention. She gave it to him.

He said only one thing.

"Mrs. Cantrell, we'll buy from you. We'll buy your cattle."

Jolene stared empty-headed into his face. Then a buckling sensation hit her in the middle of the thighs, weakened both her knees. She began to collapse, toppled. She fought it, righted herself.

Bela Beck, rushed over, though neither man

touched her. If she had fallen, even slightly, they would have stopped her.

"Are you all right, Mrs. Cantrell?"

Her eyes were closed. Why? She opened them. It was the same boy. His father was with him. She knew right away the man next to him was his father. She had memorized their faces.

She stiffened, recovered, looked at them. "I'm fine."

They made their arrangements. Jolene took a down payment and a note for the rest, on delivery. The price was what both parties considered more than fair. As the two meat packers walked Jolene out to the parking lot to her truck, she wanted to ask about the blockade. It was a point of tension for she wanted desperately to know, yet she was afraid to alert these men to it if indeed they hadn't heard of it.

Standing by the truck, the older Beck put his hand on Jolene's shoulder. "Nothing comes easy, does it?"

"No," she said, startled by this kind of philosophy at a time like this. She started to get in, remembered to put directions to the Becks' stockyards in her purse.

"Don't worry about that blockade," said the father. "There's too many people out there. They can't stop you."

The boy smiled. "We think you'll make it. Our money is on you."

So they did know. Jolene guessed she probably was the only one who didn't. She and Coyote. Oh my God, Coyote! He'd be riding right into it.

263

"You come to us next year," said Bruce Beck. "We'll buy from you then, too."

She nodded, smiled. "See you tomorrow, or later today."

"Yes, you will," said the older Beck.

Jolene waited until she left the parking lot, then tore like hell to get to the interstate.

The Blockade

Jolene found the interstate, drove down it like a maniac. She had to be with Jake. There was no one else in the world who could keep him from doing something crazy, no one left but her. She knew what would happen, how Jake would react in a confrontation. He would fight. It would get ugly, he would fight harder and someone might die.

Riding away from the skyline of Chicago, the road was wide open. She goosed the gas pedal even further. Then, suddenly, Jolene encountered tons of traffic on her side of the road, as if there had been an accident ahead on the other side of the freeway, and everybody on her side was slowing down to look across and gape.

Jolene speeded up, slowed down, changed a lane, changed right back. Nothing she did could keep her moving with any speed. Like so many others, her car crawled behind miles of traffic.

People thought she was crazy. When the bumper to bumper got really bad, she climbed out, got on the hood of the truck, then lifted herself up to the car's roof. For miles and miles all she saw were other vehicles.

Jolene had to reach Coyote. She angled for the shoulder of the road, punched up the speedometer, until she ran into other people doing the same thing. Again she was backed up.

Now Jolene was really stuck. She had that in common with half the world. She didn't know the January Street on-ramp had been on television last night along with the issues surrounding the whole cattle drive. Today, that was the place to be to see if over 1,000 head of cattle could successfully run a Teamster blockade. It seemed to Jolene as if all of Chicago had turned out to watch.

Above the January Street on-ramp, up on the interstate highway, the scene was a madhouse. Many people were gathering although it was still early in the day. It seemed that every car for miles had stalled. There was nothing anybody could do. Nobody tried to break things up. Certainly not the police. Drivers were leaving their vehicles, turning off the engines, then getting out to sightsee.

The crowd was well monitored from within. The people who seemed to be directing things were from consumer groups in Chicago. Intelligently they had seen to it that the two right lanes were left open for any emergency vehicles, and presumably for the cattle to climb the ramp and travel into the city. Any person having legitimate business, knew well ahead of time not to use this interstate. Stephanie had seen to that.

At this point, most of those people who were in the forefront on the highway were women.

They held signs saying that consumer groups supported the cattle drive, or demanding lower beef prices. One hippie female held a placard saying, VEGETARIANS FOR COYOTE.

Fortunately the crowd was not forceful enough to push anybody over the edge, for there was a movement, a surging forward, with everybody trying to get to the edge of the interstate for a look below.

Down below the blockade was forming, only the Teamsters hadn't come on as strong as their boss had planned. Four trucks were spread in an arc around the entrance to the on-ramp, but instead of thirty, only ten or so drivers waited by the entrance. Twelve or thirteen more trucks waited off to the side, hopefully, to make a symbolic first loading of the cattle and transport them to the stockyards.

The Teamster boss was furious. "Where's the rest of the men?"

"It's all I could get," the aide answered meekly. "It's all the guys who would show up."

The Teamster boss felt like strangling his assistant. Instead he turned back to the blockade. He hoped those men, hand picked, would at least hold their line.

There was one key driver, an angry looking truck driver, who stood in front of the central truck parked directly in front of the on-ramp. He wore a bulgy leather jacket, looked to be squeezing a pistol in his belt.

"Get out of my way," threatened the Teamster boss to his assistant. "Out of here." The aide disappeared. The Teamster boss was a frustrated man. Pounding his fist into his palm, he eyed the key driver. The driver was looking around, waiting for a sign of more support, more men. Finally the Teamster boss's hand became bruised and painful. He stopped his incessant pounding.

He knew the aide's assessment to be true. The majority of truckers sympathized with Coyote. They had no quarrel with him. They were big beef eaters. They admired his guts. Most of all, they admired his time spent on the road.

The mayor arrived in his limousine. A younger aide got out, opened the door. The mayor was very careful to arrive on the down side of the blockade, so as to be out of view from the interstate. He wanted no one to know he was even there, let alone in charge. The matter was to stay between the truckers, the police, and Coyote.

"Give me a count," the mayor told his young aide. Dispatched to the freeway, the aide quickly made an estimate of how big the crowd was, and what kind of people were in it. Were they voters? Troublemakers? What was this crowd?

The mayor stood on the driver's side of his limousine. He was short. His head barely came above the limousine's roof. Squinting, he could see the crowd growing past the blockade, up on the interstate.

Below the highway, blocking the on-ramp at the base, was the truck blockade, with the drivers guarding the entrance to the interstate. As the mayor had planned, their trucks kept him and the others down here hidden from the crowd assembling up above.

On the left of the mayor, farthest of all from the interstate, the thirty police officers assigned to be present were arriving in unmarked vehicles. The cops were wearing uniforms, as requested, but also by request their cars were unmarked.

The mayor reasoned that if his gamble on public opinion carried the day, and he decided to let the cattle drive through, he didn't want any newspapers or anybody at all remembering that he had the police there, especially not behind the truckers' lines.

Farther to the right, the Teamster boss saw the police arrive, waited for them to leave their vehicles. They never did. There was no show of force as he had been promised would happen.

The Teamster began searching for the police chief. He'd have to take matters into his own hands. When he looked behind, the railroad boss was standing there. "Where's the rest of your men?" the railroad boss asked.

"We got all we need," said the Teamster boss.

The railroad boss didn't answer. They presented such a contrast, the dignified railroad boss and the irate Teamster.

"He'll cave in in ten minutes," said the Teamster. "As soon as he sees the blockade, that cowboy'll load right into our trucks. Our trucks are as good as loaded."

"Keep dreaming."

"You don't give a shit whether we stop him

or not, do you?" The Teamster whirled on his counterpart.

"I care. But I'm not a lunatic."

"What?"

"I just want to keep the union clean."

"Whose union?"

"Your union. My union."

"You're gonna keep my union clean?" The Teamster boss started laughing weirdly. "You don't have enough Twenty Mule Team Borax."

The railroad boss found it hard to laugh. The Teamster got mad again. "All you care about is your public image. Well, I don't give a shit about mine. Nobody, understand, nobody breaks a Teamster contract. I give my life to this union."

"You are talking about a man on a lark. He'll make his cattle drive and you'll never see him again. Go after the man and you'll make him and his cause famous."

"You're awfully fucking smug. That's my men out there. He's trying to bust my union and I won't allow it."

"You're imagining it. You're creating problems that don't exist."

"This is not a one shot! Let him through and he'll be back. So will every goddamn rancher who wants to beat the price of a truck."

"At that time, I'll believe you."

"At that time it'll be too late!"

"What is it you want me to do?"

"Look at those cops, hiding. Get the police chief, your buddy, to put out a goddamn show of force!"

The railroad boss shook his head. "I've called

out enough favors already. Why don't you wait it out and see what happens?"

"That's what you're all doing! Waiting it out. You, the cops, the mayor . . . "

"What did you expect? You want the charge of the light brigade over a local union issue?"

"I want to keep what's mine. What we fought for."

The Teamster boss saw the police chief. He looked back at the railroad boss. "No more favors," said the railroad boss, who raised his hands.

The Teamster boss cursed under his breath. He moved to intercept the police chief. "Hey! Get your men into view!" The Teamster motioned to the thirty men still seated patiently in unmarked cars. "Who's going to see them down there?"

"Just remember something. You got no stroke with my department. Nothing!"

The police chief left the Teamster, not bothering to wait for a reply.

The Teamster boss felt the isolation pressing in on him from all sides. He saw through the mayor's strategy of playing it safe.

He knew there was only one person to count on to stop this drive. Himself, and his men. Only they could save the union from being busted. He couldn't depend on help from any of the others.

The Teamster looked around at the crowd mulling on the interstate. He saw the railroad boss doing nothing, the police chief returning to unmarked vehicles, shielded from the public eye by distance and the cover of his own trucks. The Teamster boss saw enemies all around. It made him crazy for revenge.

Although they were only a couple of hours out of Chicago, the Illinois countryside was still rural. In cattle time, Chicago was a few miles away, but only a few modern ranch houses and newer cars gave any indication that America's third largest city was this close.

Coyote chose to take the last miles over private ranch land, offered by a gracious gentleman farmer. Fun Truckin' was checking the January Street on-ramp for accessibility. He was also looking for Jolene. Coyote hoped Fun Truckin' might find her there.

The reporters and other followers had formed their own caravan, on a road several hundred yards to the left. The reason Coyote chose the private ranch was to avoid the chaos and general hubbub his arrival was creating among the reporters. For this morning at least, he chose the most familiar elements, the wind, the cattle, and the grass. Coyote rode silently, stoically, unaware of what lay ahead. The aloneness he felt reminded him of that first day out of jail. Then, like now, his mind was on Jolene. And the uncertainty was the same, not knowing how it would end, or even what was in front of him. Coyote remembered those feelings of walking head cocked, into the unknown. As always, he was ready. But this time the unknown frightened him. Deep inside where his confidence was supposed to lie, Coyote had a fear he hadn't known before. His throat was empty, his stomach felt sick, as if he had to throw up. Everything was uneven. There was no paying crowd to impress. His battle wasn't with a slippery calf.

That was it. He didn't know who his battle was with. All he could depend on was his preparation. If he had done everything correctly, he would win. This was a different kind of fight than Coyote had known. It was more like chess.

That was what he had become. A diplomat. Wrestler was right. Coyote was a manager of people. He remembered a tour of suburban Washington, D.C. that he had taken once between rodeos. He passed rows and rows of expensive houses. "Who lives there?" he remembered asking his driver. "That's where the diplomats live," Coyote was told.

Coyote's ducks were in a row. He hoped he knew how to shoot them down when the time came.

Then Coyote saw Fun Truckin's van scooping dust. The boy was driving as though trouble were on its way. Coyote knew the dust trouble made.

The boy left the road, broke through the caravan of reporters, then slowed down until he spotted Coyote. So as not to spook the cattle, Fun Truckin' parked ahead of the drive, ran back to tell the rebel rancher what waited ahead at the on-ramp. Stephanie lagged behind.

"They've set up a blockade! Across that on-ramp!"

Coyote got down from his horse. "Who? Who has?"

"Truckers."

Coyote started going crazy. "They suckered us this far. They ain't pushin' us. We're going through!" Then he turned on Stehpanie, saw her as a charlatan. "You knew. You knew! You set us up."

"How could I know?" Stephanie proclaimed her innocence.

Wrestler rode up, got off his horse. "What is it?"

"A blockade," Fun Truckin' told him.

"How many?" Wrestler asked.

"It doesn't matter how many 'cause we're gonna kick their asses!" Fun Truckin' was ready.

"You're gettin' crazy boy. Calm down." Wrestler knew it was no time to get crazy. He had to watch Coyote.

"Where's Jolene? Did you see Jolene?"

"I didn't see her."

Coyote whirled on Wrestler. "If they touched Jolene, you understand—"

Wrestler interrupted. "Now why would they hurt Jolene? C'mon, let's be realistic. Nobody is going to hurt Jolene."

Coyote turned to Fun Truckin'. "O.K., kid, don't be hotheaded. How many drivers?"

Like Coyote, Fun Truckin' returned to this world.

"I'd say ten, eleven, with trucks blocking the way. There's one truck across the ramp itself."

Coyote asked Stephanie, "Any other way into this town?"

"No," she said. "Not to the stockyards."

274

"Shit," Coyote muttered. "Everywhere we turn." Coyote slid further into a funk. "We came so far." Then he became optimistic. He was a chameleon. All his emotions were visible.

"People. Were there people there?" Coyote needed to know.

"People? Where?"

"Anywhere. Up on the interstate?"

"Oh, yeah, there was a big crowd growing up there. There seemed to be."

Wrestler asked, "Were there police?"

Stephanie shook her head. Fun Truckin' replied, "None that I could see. Maybe a few spread around." Fun Truckin' took Coyote by the shoulders, shook him. "We're gonna take 'em, man! Nobody's gonna stop us!"

"There were people there." Coyote turned to Wrestler. Crazily, he seemed overjoyed. This one fact changed his demeanor.

"Let's go, man." Fun Truckin' was fired up. "Let's stampede 'em right up the interstate!"

"Kid," Coyote said. "We're gonna take 'em, but no hot stuff. O.K.?"

Fun Truckin' nodded. "O.K."

"Just let me talk our way in. You got that?" The kid nodded.

"You got that good?" Coyote wanted to make sure.

"Yeah."

"O.K., then get up to the front of this cattle drive where you belong. And lead me in."

Fun Truckin' and Stephanie left, to get the van. Wrestler stared at Coyote. Coyote said to him. "I just didn't want the boy to do anything crazy. If there's any pushing to do, I'll be the one. It's my party."

"I'll be watchin' you, Coyote. I'll be watchin' you like a country schoolteacher."

"Thank you, Wrestler. We're going through!"

The Confrontation

The morning turned into noon.

For Jolene, the traffic got worse, until it was backed up in a hopeless standstill.

She felt sick, nauseous from breathing other people's exhaust fumes. "Move!" Jolene screamed from her window. "Move!"

She didn't know why she screamed. It was hopeless. She had run into the crowd from the blockade up ahead. Her lane was jammed. The whole side of the highway was stuck, like cement. The left side of the interstate, going into Chicago, was the same way.

Jolene honked and honked again. Certainly nobody was going to move, even if they could. Jolene looked at herself in the rearview mirror. She looked away, looked again at her face.

She didn't recognize her face. She looked crazed, her eyes were red and hollow, her face pale, greasy from no sleep and no soap.

Desperately, on instinct, Jolene veered her truck right, went the lane over, then another, until she climbed onto the raised cement curb that was the interstate shoulder.

She had to get to Coyote. She thought, "Fuck

it," then stopped caring about the truck. She could get it on the way back.

She parked the truck, locked it, and left it. She began running. Dodging cars, Jolene ran across her side, up and over the small fence center divider, then again across the interstate on the far sides. Once on the shoulder, she continued out of Chicago, in the direction of the blockade.

One highway sign passed, then another. The quarter mile markers became one mile, then two, then two more. Finally Jolene reached the outskirts of the blockade perimeter of human flesh. She began bumping into the maze of expanding spectators, all wandering toward the center on the interstate shoulder. All the people were moving in the same direction. Now Jolene was one of many. She felt like a cow in a herd of cattle.

For the first time, she began to comprehend the magnitude of the cattle drive and the effect it was having, the impact of Chicago's citizenry. It was as if the whole world were there, in that one traffic jam. She was too excited to think about how tired she was. Jolene pushed away her feeling of faintness, shoved and jostled her way through the thickening crowd. She only hoped she would get there in time.

The cattle drive was moving slowly toward Chicago. They had left the farm, now travelled over a definite road. The blockade waited less than two miles away. Word of it had filtered back, so everybody knew to some degree what was up ahead. Coyote tried to maintain an aura of confidence, keeping the cattle at a steady, even pace, staying unapproachably near the front of the drive. This place became his respite. For some reason nobody bothered Coyote when he rode at the front.

It was incredibly hard for Coyote to comprehend that this close to such a major city, there were rural roads such as these. The contrasts Chicago presented made an indelible impression on Coyote.

Coyote rode up farther, closed the ground between him and the van, until he was next to the boy on the driver's window side. He nodded confidently to Fun Truckin'. Coyote's rifle hung from its sheath, on the right side of his saddle.

Coyote caught the boy staring at the gun. Since they left Walsenburg, Coyote had all but forgotten the gun was there. It was one more thing he had to carry, banging against his leg, and it was one more thing he had gotten adjusted to and that was that. Coyote removed the rifle from its sheath, rested it across his lap.

Wrestler rode behind Coyote. He rode stoically, unafraid, ready, willing, and more than able to tangle. He rode calmly, as if he were wearing blinders, his eyes facing straight ahead. His eyes were on one thing, one man, Coyote. He would watch the boy for his pa. He had to make sure nothing happened to Coyote, or nothing happened to anybody else because of Coyote. Coyote had no idea what a loyal friend he had in Wrestler.

Food rode nervously, second from the rear.

The Cantrell herd was separated from the others. Coyote wanted it that way. If there was trouble, Coyote felt the other ranchers should suffer as little as possible, so he moved their herds back, away from his own. If they broke the blockade, Coyote could slow the pace, and the other cattle would catch up. Food was more than glad to switch back to horseback. By taking the same position near the rear that he had started riding in Walsenburg, he stayed that much farther from the front, where the trouble would be.

Brains was superstitious. Besides, he had never been in a fight. He started the drive in the rear. It had been successful this far. He wanted to end it in the rear. His part had been played. They didn't need maps any more. Everybody knew where to go and apparently everybody knew where they were going. Brains didn't want to meet the people who were waiting there. He had done his part. He was a thinker. Nobody needed thinkers now. They needed fighters. Brains wished he were a fighter, but now wasn't the time to play games as to who he was.

Somewhat apprehensively, Stephanie rode in her station's van. She chose to ride in the van driven by her cameraman instead of with Fun Truckin'. She rode well behind Coyote, waited out the conclusion of her story with a zealous curiosity.

Her loyalty had shifted. It was no longer so much with the drive as it was in presenting a good ending to her wonderful event, a story she had originated and followed for over two weeks. She hoped for a happy, successful ending to the cattle drive because her image depended on it. This story was making her career and if it ended in the right way, she would be, as a newswoman, forever identified with winners.

With each passing moment, the crowd at the blockade was growing larger and larger. The mayor's aide looked conspicuously formal in his coat and tie, as he observed the large flow of people trying to move toward the center, hoping to get a view of the cattle drive. He saw those who didn't care to be at the heart of the action fanning out along the guard rail. They were farther away but still able to see down below with a good view.

The aide was trying to pinpoint his observations, in order to present them to the mayor in a way he could easily understand. The young man was hoping to determine if the crowd represented a cross-section of people, or mainly pseudo-liberal groups and environmentalists.

As he scanned the crowd, he saw it had the earmarks of being organized. The aide found it was a consumer group that was doing the monitoring. A group of mostly women had formed a human chain, which kept the two right lanes free and clear. Most of the others in the forefront were also women, mostly middle class, dressed in nice slacks or comfortable jeans. Many signs and placards were present, held high in the air. The aide guessed many of these people were veterans of the protest movements of the '60s. He surmised they were certainly the right age.

But then there were so many others. There was an unruly element, like in all crowds, trying, pushing, doing anything to get through. There were kids, many young kids. The aide was actually impressed by the crowd's general good manners. The unruly persons might have been agitators, trying to start trouble, to give the crowd a bad name.

The aide got closer so he could read the signs. There was so much of what he labelled "general public" to wade through. Movement was almost impossible. The signs were all pro cattle drive. Some said MOTHER TRUCKERS, LOWER BEEF PRICES, and CONSUMERS FOR COYOTE. One obscure environmentalist confused the aide with a sign saying SAVE THE EAGLES, SHOOT A RANCHER. But the aide hadn't heard about any eagle shootings in Colorado, so he dismissed the sign.

The aide began to feel closed in. Mobility was nonexistent. He had to make a decision but couldn't come to one. What would he tell the mayor? Was this crowd spontaneous or was it planned? Were these people a cross-section of Chicago or were they those who showed up for every cause? And most important, what did the mayor want to hear? He knew that the public supplied the votes, not some local Teamster union boss. The aide made his way, as best he could, to the edge of the interstate. He snuck across the two empty lanes, climbed down the ivy, which lowered him to the level of the mayor, but far behind the blockade. He began running, to tell the mayor exactly what he saw.

Nervously, the mayor waited down below, by

his limousine, for his aide to return. He spent his time listening to reports over the police radio in his car about the whereabouts of the cattle drive, how fast it was moving, and approximately when it would reach the blockade.

He wished his aide would get back. The mayor tried to avoid the stare of the Teamster boss. But he couldn't look away forever. The Teamster boss nodded menacingly, motioned toward the police still sitting in their unmarked cars.

The mayor nodded back to the Teamster boss. The Teamster made a motion with his hand, like talking into a radio. The mayor knew what he meant, knew what he wanted. He had to make some sort of move to please the Teamster boss. He couldn't stand there and do nothing.

So he reached inside the car, gave his instructions over the radio to the police chief. "Have your men get out of their cars."

"Out of their cars?"

"Right!"

"Then what?" the police chief asked.

"For now, have them stand there."

"By their cars."

"Yes, by their cars. We'll play it by ear from there."

"O.K."

One by one, the uniformed policemen left their cars, stood next to them. The Teamster boss nodded his approval to the mayor. He also nodded to the railroad boss, showing he was still in control, when the railroad boss turned to see what had happened.

The mayor was sensitive to noise. He noticed

there was no additional crowd noise when the police left their cars. His strategy of holding his decision to the last minute was paying off. He was right. From the interstate, nobody could see where the police were except one pocket of people. And for now, most of these people's necks were craned, hoping to be the first to see Coyote and the cattle drive.

The key truck driver sensed something, turned, saw the police standing by their vehicles. The Teamster boss clenched his fist at the key driver, urging him on.

Jolene figured her truck had probably been towed away by now. She was in the thick of blockade congestion, though she didn't know how close she was to the actual trucks. She couldn't see over taller people's heads and shoulders. All she heard was a groundswell of unbearably loud crowd noise. Occasionally she heard cries ringing above the crowd noise, cries like "let him through." Then she heard vicious remarks like "stop him," and "kill the sonofabitch." Everybody was bulling their way to the same place she was.

Then came a rumbling noise. People began to point, literally climbing each other's backs to see.

Somebody yelled, "There he is!"

Jolene knew they were reacting to Coyote. Everyone was jumping up and down like pogo sticks. People were stretching their necks to look above the people in front of them, to see the long ribbon of cattle which now appeared behind a rise in the terrain, a quarter mile away.

The noise was so unyielding, that it brought Jolene's energy level up with it. Then she found her passage. She began to squeeze underneath, made her forward progress that way. Nobody tried to interfere because nobody noticed her.

Coyote heard the cheering, but as yet couldn't see a thing. Then he came up over the rise.

There it was!

Coyote couldn't believe the masses and masses of people. Overwhelmed, he continued to ride forward. His blood circulated fast, with high excitement. His hand trembled on the reins. His feet struggled to stay in the stirrups. They felt lighter than air, even inside his boots. He didn't even try to locate his familiar inner calm.

Coyote looked back to his men, trying to calm himself with familiarity. But nothing else could hold his interest. He turned ahead. Coyote rode into the absolute unknown, feeling singular, rare, almost outlandish. He tensed his back, found his courage still there. He flexed his shoulders, loosened his wings.

At this pace, he calculated, he'd have fifteen minutes before reaching the melee. He used the time to take it all in. It was once in a lifetime, so as he rode he stared at the people who were watching him. It wasn't an audience, it was a spectacle.

Ahead was the January Street on-ramp which rose into a gateway leading to the interstate and the mob on it. At the base of the on-ramp waited the trucks that were the great obstacle.

He studied the truck that blocked the on-ramp. He surveyed the arc of three other trucks that kept him from trying any kind of end run around the center truck.

Coyote panicked, wondered how, even if he got by the main truck, he could lead cattle onto the highway with all those people up there. Coyote feared his scheme to arouse the public with his cattle drive had backfired.

Then as he got closer, he saw space on the interstate, the created space, which was the two open lanes. His fortune had turned miraculous, he thought. He concentrated once again on the truck. There was no other way but straight through. That truck would have to be moved forcibly. There was no other way. Coyote prepared himself for one thing. To get through!

Further to the right, he saw the police standing by their cars. Their blue uniforms now became clearer. Coyote wondered why the cops were so far from the actual blockade. It didn't make sense. Or were they just spectators like the people on the highway? Coyote could not comprehend why the set-up was this way. His only guess was that the police were guarding the far flank against penetration by the cattle drive.

But the police, to a man, felt their own common fear. What if there was a stampede? It wasn't Coyote they were afraid of. They liked him, and like most of the rank and file truck drivers in Chicago, wanted him to succeed. But what became apparent to each cop at about the same time was the likelihood of a stampede right into their position. The fear remained, unstated, but each policeman privately turned his head, searching for his own shelter or possible route of escape. But for now, their orders were to stay put. So they waited, but back on their heels. The cattle drive moved closer.

The pace of the cattle drive had slowed. Coyote looked back. With an exaggerated sweep of his commanding arm, he brought the drive back up to its normal pace. With the wave of Coyote's arm, the screaming on the interstate intensified even more, soon became more thundering than 1,500 head of cattle charging down a cobblestone street.

Coyote decided to ride ahead even farther, until he was in front of the van. He directed the drive's path toward the one key truck blocking the interstate. The police relaxed slightly when the cattle altered their direction away from them.

The truck was now several hundred yards away. Coyote focused on the driver, saw his hand touching a bulge in his belt, which Coyote assumed was a gun.

In full view, Coyote cocked his rifle. Wrestler saw this, rode up even closer. He hated to think that he might have to be the one who stopped Coyote. The key driver looked back at the Teamster boss, who again urged him on. Coyote kept up his pace, in a macabre game of chicken, tons of beef against tons of steel truck, but nobody backed off. The cattle drive couldn't turn, and the truckers refused. Both sides were imbedded in their points of view.

Both sides had come too far.

From this vantage point, Coyote was now able to see the tops of Chicago's tallest buildings, not so far in the distance. Wrestler calmed the cattle as he slowly rode almost behind Coyote. Coyote's intensity riveted on the driver. He never noticed Wrestler's proximity. It was obvious Coyote would soon be stopped, but he kept leading the cattle until he was twenty yards from the key driver.

Then the other trucks, at the same time, blared their air horns, kept them exploding in a constant pandemonium of noise. The resonance deafened all the other noise in a frightening fanfare of threatened violence. The cows began to spook. Brains and Food veered closer to the livestock, calming them.

Coyote raised his arm, stopped the drive. Fun Truckin' stopped he van, put the gear in park, but left the motor running. Food and Brains, still well back, exhaled gladly, relieved to avoid the confrontation. Trying not to inflame tensions, Wrestler rode next to Fun Truckin', stayed there, behind Coyote.

Wrestler could see the anger building in Coyote. Angrily Coyote motioned the key driver to move his truck. At the sight of contact between the opposing forces, the crowd noise increased even more. The air horns stopped blowing.

People in the crowd started rooting. "Move the truck!" "Get the trucks out of the way!" "Let him through!" People were screaming from the crowd, but nobody heard. With the total noise so vociferous, Coyote could only continue with his threatening arm motions. His rifle lay still across his lap.

Coyote got a closer look at the driver. He looked more like a goon, like the "axe" for the union, than a trucker. The driver mouthed the words, "Fuck you." Again, Coyote motioned him away, but the driver refused to budge. With his lips he cut through the noise, cussing Coyote a second time.

Fun Truckin' jumped out of his van. "Fuck you yourself, you goddamn goon punk! C'mon!" Fun Truckin' landed on the ground next to Coyote and Wrestler. Coyote saw Wrestler for the first time. They formed a wall of three.

Now the other truckers began to move from the doors of their trucks, closer to the first driver. The standoff held. On the interstate, people were trying to hear what was being said. Many of the women monitors were using arm movements to quiet the crowd. Calls for silence could be heard rising above the chaotic noise. "*Sshhh! Sshhh!*" came from the crowd. The noise began subsiding and quiet took over.

The mayor was going out of his mind waiting for his assistant to return. He had to have additional information. Should he bring the police to the forefront? Should he dismiss them altogether?

Finally he came. Puffing, sweating, out of breath, the aide arrived with his summation. He leaned on the limousine, tried to get his breath back. He was gasping, out of wind.

"C'mon! C'mon!" The mayor moved closer, forcing the aide to speak.

He stated, "There's 2,000 people up there, most of them voters."

"Do they know I'm here?" the mayor asked. "Did they see the police?"

"No! No on both counts. But they're for the cattle drive getting through. Almost all of them. I think there's some Teamster agitators up there."

"We should let them through?" the mayor speculated.

"I would. I definitely would," concurred the aide.

The mayor nodded. His decision was made.

"What about the Teamster?" the aide asked.

"We'll let him hang himself." The aide and the mayor looked back to the interplay going on between the Teamster boss and the key driver.

The weight of indecision left the mayor. Now he knew what to do. He leaned into the limousine, spoke over the police radio. "Get your men back into their cars!"

"Back into their cars?" The police chief was caught by surprise. "Are you sure?"

Their conversation transcended car radios. Both saw each other over the tops of the police cars. The police chief saw that the mayor was certain. "Back your cars, men," he commanded. The cops didn't have to be told twice. To them, their vehicles were tanks, steel fortresses, shelters.

Doors slammed gladly.

The Teamster boss whirled around when he heard the doors closing. He turned to the mayor to threaten him. But the mayor had already gotten into his limousine, was backing out of the immediate area. The cops started their cars, began backing out, also. The Teamster boss looked back at the key driver. He and Coyote were locked into a stare. The Teamster boss knew he had been sold out. He would have to take matters into his own hands. He knew he should have listened to the non-support of his own rank and file, but now it was too late. He couldn't back off. He had to stop the cattle drive from crossing a Teamster line. Years from now, they would remember him for his victory.

Still, there was the railroad boss, trying to calm things down. "Will you let him through? By tomorrow, a week from now, nobody is going to remember."

"Fuck you, let him through. You want to compete with that?" He motioned to the cattle. "They're moving them for free!"

Then both union bosses noticed how quickly the quiet had settled. They forgot each other for the moment.

For Coyote, the quiet had a tranquilizing effect. He relaxed a bit, realized that the truck driver could probably hear him. "C'mon, buddy," Coyote said calmly. "Get out of the way."

The driver, unlike Coyote, hadn't seen the police leave. He was still smirking.

"C'mon, move your fuckin' truck!" Coyote now screamed. "Move it! Move it or we'll run right over you!"

The driver heard an argument rage to his left. The Teamster boss was screaming at the last two police officers. The driver saw that the police were gone. Two of the other truckers were also in the argument.

The driver realized he was on his own, alone,

with no backup. He was filled with distrust. What was going on?"

Now he thought of protecting his truck. He couldn't let his truck be damaged. He didn't like it. He was too close to the cattle as it was. Then the Teamster boss saw him.

"Kill him! Kill him!" the Teamster boss told him.

Ferociously, the railroad boss grabbed the Teamster boss by the shoulders. "Will you relax! Tomorrow will be business as usual!"

"For you, maybe."

"Forget it! You're beat!"

The Teamster boss elbowed the silver-haired railroad leader out of the way, moved behind the trucks, in the direction of the actual blockade.

Coyote didn't know what to do next. He tried to humor the truck driver. "C'mon, buddy. I'm just like you. You just ride a higher horse."

Nobody budged, nobody smiled. For Coyote that was the last straw. It was insane. Everybody was on his side. Everyone. The police had vanished, the people were screaming for him to annihilate, to power through the blockade. But then what? Coyote knew he couldn't stampede. Instant death would lie ahead. Death that those people watching from the highway never considered. All that was in his way were a few damn truckers, and probably a goon squad at that. Who were they? Who did these people think he was? He was Coyote. He'd never lie down.

Fun Truckin' was pacing, waiting for the kill like a blood-hungry doberman whose master is in danger. Wrestler waited on his horse, alongside Coyote. The crowd was stone silent.

"*You sonofabitch*!" Coyote erupted in uncontrolled fury. He dismounted, jumped off his horse before Wrestler could stop him. He was brandishing his rifle, waving it with arm gestures. "Who do you think you are?" Coyote was still screaming, but he stayed by his horse.

"Do you hear me?" he called to the trucker. Everybody heard Coyote. "Do you hear me? You're stepping on my rights! You're taking my freedom away!" He pointed at the driver with his rifle. "Don't do that to me!" Coyote took a step in front of his horse. "You can steal me blind, rob me until I can't make it anymore! But don't ever step on my rights! Are you listening to me?"

Coyote paused. There was Jolene. He saw Jolene running through no-man's land, from down the on-ramp where nobody dared to stand, through the open space, past the trucks, to her husband and the cattle drive.

"I sold them! They're all sold!"

She had been watching, knew Coyote's intensity right now. She put a hand on his waist, checked with Wrestler. The old man nodded. Everything was in control. He sensed that Coyote wouldn't lose his head, that he was playing out a bluff.

Jolene trusted Wrestler. She nodded back, hoped he was right.

Coyote paused. Now his anger built again. He resumed screaming like a fanatic. His face turned beet red, the veins in his neck bulged like the steel cable holding the tension wires high above. Coyote moved ahead of the others, two steps closer to the driver.

"I'll die before you take my freedom! You can't take that. You understand you are facing a man who'll die for his rights!"

Behind the truck on the passenger side, the Teamster boss moved closer to the driver. He was in that floating space where paranoia had conquered reality.

"C'mon!"

Coyote's voice was an echo. He motioned Fun Truckin' and Wrestler to come beside him. Both inched forward. They formed a wall of cowboy. "Now, driver! Move your truck!"

The driver didn't respond.

"You!" Coyote called. "You!"

Then Coyote levelled his rifle at the driver. Wrestler and Fun Truckin' stopped along with Coyote.

"No." Jolene's voice was heard from behind them. But she didn't move to stop Coyote. Fear paralyzed her.

The driver looked for the Teamster boss, but he had left his position. The driver opened his jacket, showed Coyote. No gun!

"Move it!" Coyote commanded. The driver didn't respond. "Now don't panic! I'm not gonna shoot anyone!" Coyote aimed.

Coyote pulled the trigger. *Blast!* went the rifle. Everyone waited. Coyote blew out the driver's left front tire, blasted it off the rim.

The truck sunk to the ground.

Jolene felt herself gagging, unable to breath. Then she realized her husband had killed nobody. Relieved, she exhaled. What a genius idea. He was going to shoot the tires off the truck until it toppled.

Wrestler realized it too. A grin came across his face.

"That's five hundred dollars, trucker." Coyote called to the key driver. The driver knew the price. He recovered, shaking, glad he was still alive.

"You want another?" Coyote called.

Coyote fired again, blasting a second tire, behind the first. The truck began to tilt. The driver looked up. The truck was leaning over him.

"Now move your truck!"

The driver moved toward the front of his truck. None of his cronies moved in. All moved away.

Frozen during the shooting, the Teamster boss now moved past the passenger door, to near the right front headlight of the driver's truck. He saw the driver pass the left front headlight as he moved away from his truck.

Not another sound was made anywhere. Only the ringing from the rifle blasts filled the air.

Coyote aimed, blew a third tire into oblivion. Then he stopped. There was no more opposition. Almost casually, Coyote turned to Wrestler. "Back that man's truck out of my way."

Coyote winked at Jolene. She cautiously raised her eyebrows. She wondered how he did it. How was he so resourceful under pressure?

Wrestler calmly stepped into no-man's land, that vacant space between Coyote's rifle and the step-up door to the driver's truck.

Backing it up would be tricky, thought Wrestler. Already the truck was sitting on three rims. Wrestler made a mental note to swing the wheel fully to the left, letting the rear wheels pick up the tilt, using a drag principle to back it up out of the way.

Wrestler was ten yards from the truck.

The driver had moved entirely past the front headlights, out of the way. Wrestler was left a free clear path up into the truck.

Now Wrestler was five yards from the step up.

The Teamster boss waited on the other side.

Coyote relaxed. They had made it. He exhaled. The drive was over. He turned back, smiled at Jolene.

Then he remembered Food and Brains. He wanted them ready to move right after Wrestler backed the truck. Turning around, Coyote called back. "Get ready to move 'em out!"

Brains waved, cheerfully acknowledging.

Wrestler stepped up to open the door.

The Teamster boss moved around the truck grille, grabbed Wrestler by the neck, slammed him face first into the truck door. The Teamster wrapped his forearm tighter around Wrestler's Adam's apple, held him in a death grip choke hold. He spun him around, facing Coyote. His forearm squeezed like a vice around the old man's neck.

At the same time, Fun Truckin' snatched Coyote's rifle, trained it on the Teamster boss. It happened fast, before Coyote could turn back around.

Coyote stood completely still. He froze, did nothing to antagonize the Teamster boss. Coyote could see Wrestler's legs going out from under him. He knew one snap, any tightening of the Teamster's forearm, and it was all over for the old man.

Fun Truckin' shuffled forward for a better angle. He was intense, completely locked in, the rifle squarely aimed into the Teamster boss's mid section.

They had another standoff.

"O.K., cowboy. You load your cattle onto our trucks, and that's the way it's gonna be!"

Full of new confidence, the other truckers moved closer, supporting the Teamster boss.

Wrestler gasped, trying to find an air passage. Fun Truckin' still held his rifle trained. The boy sweated profusely, frozen in his military position.

Coyote started walking toward the Teamster boss. Everybody was stunned. The Teamster boss tightened his leverage around Wrestler's neck.

"Stop, cowboy! Stop or I'll snap his neck."

Wrestler was losing his ruddy color. Coyote kept walking deliberately, making no sudden movements. As his boots closed ground, he turned back. "Fun Truckin'! If that man kills Wrestler, shoot him, and do it quick, in the belly." Coyote kept stalking. "Then I want you to hit the fuel tank and blow these motherfuckers away!"

The other truckers stopped moving forward.

Coyote was now five feet from the Teamster boss.

"Let him go!"

Fun Truckin' moved forward, into the flow, rifle levelled.

Coyote could see the Teamster's forearm loosen slightly around Wrestler's neck, but it wasn't enough.

"I said let him go!"

At two feet away, Coyote tensed his right bicep. He aimed, absolutely cratered the Teamster boss with a right hand blow crashing into his face. The man's nose shattered. The cartilage hung limply.

Wrestler dropped to the ground, catching his breath. The Teamster boss saw the blood gushing from the middle of his face, felt the delayed pain of a broken nose. He began to crumble to the ground.

Coyote felt a second punch coming, went to bash in the Teamster's ribs. Then he stopped. The damage was done.

Coyote looked around. None of the truckers was coming to stop him. Fun Truckin' was still aiming the gun. They might have to thaw the boy out of that pose.

Wrestler stood beside Coyote. He was regaining his natural color, the whiteness leaving his face with every new breath of air.

"You all right?" Coyote asked.

Wrestler nodded. Then it hit him. He smiled. He pushed Coyote's shoulder. "Hey! We did it! We made it! We're here!"

Coyote realized it, too.

"Well then," Coyote said with a sweep of his arm. "Move this man's truck."

Somebody *whooped* from the drive. Coyote turned, saw Brains up front, grinning.

Coyote felt his tension release. It became joy. Exhilaration set in. He had won. The drive was over. For sure!

Wrestler climbed into the truck cab, found the keys still in the ignition. The driver dragged away the Teamster boss, but no one paid any attention.

Jolene breathed out, pushed the fear from her system. Nobody really felt excited yet. Victory was too new.

"Ha!" Coyote had to laugh. Fun Truckin' still hadn't lowered the gun. He was covering Wrestler. Coyote came to him, lightly tapped the boy on his shoulder. Fun Truckin' came to his senses, gave in, lowered the gun to his knees.

Then it hit him. They had conquered. Ahead was the payoff, the celebration. Fun Truckin' let out a *whoop*.

A few people on the interstate *whooped*, too.

Coyote looked up, *whooped* back. He waved. He had completely forgotten these people were there. With his wave the noise picked up, but most of the people on the interstate were too wrapped up in the suspense to "get happy" as yet.

The boys from Colorado fell back into formation.

Brains led Wrestler's horse to Jolene, who already had mounted Coyote's pony. The map wizard handed her the reins.

Food rode to the rear. Nearing the back, he stuck two fingers in his mouth, whistled like a blue jay being pursued. He waved to the other ranchers to rejoin the Cantrell herd with their cattle. Food looked down. His belly wasn't hanging over the saddle horn anymore. He had lost thirty pounds on the drive, would be returning home not a bad-looking man.

Brains then rode back, alongside the cattle, taking a position second from the rear. When he saw Food, Brains clenched both arms, raised them into the air, started shaking them triumphantly. They shared a private victory of their own.

Up front, Coyote stood watching Wrestler as he carefully backed the truck, clearing the on-ramp entrance. The grizzled old cowboy was tasting success, yet if Coyote had seen Wrestler for the first time, he wouldn't be able to tell if he were happy, or if it was an ordinary day.

A hum intensified from the people above. Then someone *whooped*, cowboy-style. Someone else did, too. Soon there was a *whoop* from the interstate every few seconds.

Brains *whooped* from the back of the drive.

Coyote was nervously laughing. He *whooped* too, as Jolene led Wrestler's horse to him, held it as he stepped down from the cab. Coyote saw Jolene, the woman with the courage to back her man, to lead him when he was lost, to step out and fight when she had to. Jolene had all she wanted. She was wealthy by her standards, and she was secure, confident she could do anything. Not even your man could give you security.

"Hey!" She slapped Wrestler on the thigh once he mounted.

"Whoop!" Coyote yelled again. He put his foot in the stirrup, mounted in front of Jolene.

"Let's take 'em in!"

"Let's do it!" Wrestler said, rode back to the drive.

Coyote was grinning from ear to ear. He turned back to Jolene. "You know where to take 'em?"

"Little ways up that highway!"

Coyote screamed his last command. "Let's take these cattle home!"

Coyote rode double with Jolene back to the front of the drive. Fun Truckin' finally was convinced all was safe. He got back in the van, turned on his blinking lights.

Jolene smiled at the gorgeous boy. There was a Coyote "junior" if ever she saw one.

Fun Truckin' put the van in gear, began rolling forward. He fell back into second. Coyote led the way.

Motion resumed. For a few moments, all turned silent, everybody listening to tons and tons of beef starting to walk.

Coyote *whooped* when he passed through the empty space in the arc of trucks. Then yelps and Western calls started coming again from the rear members of the cattle drive.

Coyote was on the on-ramp, moving up onto the interstate. The *whoops* and *yahooos* were coming from more than one mile back. Everybody was *whooping*!

Soon the air was filled with the sounds of cattle hooves and cowboy calls. Jolene *yelped* as she rode onto the interstate. They could see the buildings of the Windy City in the background as they climbed onto the two open lanes of the highway.

Everybody was waving. Everybody knew Coyote. Coyote lifted off his hat, raised it high in the air.

"Hello, Chicago!" he called.

DIRTY LINEN

The following pages are edited excerpts from BENNETT #2: DIRTY LINEN,* by Elliott Lewis, which will be published in August 1980. Be sure to watch for this exciting new Pinnacle series featuring the most upbeat, offbeat detective ever!

Christine Walker lived up in the hills on the western edge of Brentwood, in a low ranch-style home that contradicted her image. America's premiere sex symbol, bedmate in every virile American man's dream, poster girl to young and old alike, should have lived in an ornate place of drapes and canopies, floor cushions and water beds and mirrored ceilings. Christine's house was functional and matter-of-fact. Bennett sensed trouble before he made the last curve, so the flashing emergency vehicle lights up ahead somehow didn't surprise him. The police cars, the fire department rescue truck, the paramedic ambulance, all simply confirmed what he'd known at the gallery when he'd first looked at his watch and noted that Christine was late.

He stopped a few houses away from Christine's, doused his lights, and slowly walked the rest of the way. Rufus Drang seemed to have been expecting him.

"Very lousy news, Fred," is how he greeted Bennett.

"Christine?"

"Christine." Drang drew himself even more erect. He tucked in his flat stomach, threw back his well-muscled shoulders, and sadly aimed his blue eyes at Bennett. "Dead."

Bennett's belly cramped. He nodded his head rapidly and licked his suddenly dry lips with his tongue. "How, uh . . ." He stopped because he wasn't sure he wanted to hear the answer to his question.

"Looks like she did it to herself."

"Suicide?" Bennett was so startled, his voice broke.

"Looks like it. She's alone. Radio still playing. Empty sleeping pill bottle on the bedtable."

As he spoke, Drang watched Bennett carefully. You never knew what the crazy son of a bitch would do, he thought. He could punch me out for being the bearer of bad news, or just start yelling here in the middle of the street, whatever. But Bennett stood stolidly in place and wearily blinked his eyes.

"Did you know her?" he asked Drang.

"No. Saw her pictures, of course. Never met her."

"I knew her. Real good. Worked for her for a while, that first year after you threw me off the force. She was the only one in town who believed in me."

"Well, not the only one . . ." Drang always felt ruffled when Bennett got onto the subject of being thrown off the force.

"The only one," Bennett repeated. Then, after a thoughtful silence, he added, "Chris didn't kill herself."

"I told you we don't know," Drang said stiffly. "I told you what it looked like, pill bottle empty and so on. And there's no doubt she's dead, so . . ." he gestured hopelessly.

"Shit!" Bennett was getting angry. He'd suspected something was wrong, and he hadn't acted. "God-damn it!" he muttered.

"Nothing you could have done," Drang said.

"I could have driven the hell up here and saved her, is what I could have done. Son of a bitch!"

"Not unless you were wandering around at three, four this morning."

"What?"

"She probably died early this morning."

"She's been lying in there all day?"

"Yeah. Housekeeper was away, got back about an hour ago and found her."

"Annie wasn't here? Where's she now?"

"Inside."

The front door of the house opened, and two paramedics walked out with an empty stretcher. They loaded it in the back of their ambulance, turned off the flashers, and silently drove away. The fire department truck quietly followed, flashers switched off. Respect for the dead, Bennett thought. As the red pumper passed him, the radio squawked on, the gibberish advising of a new emergency. The truck had just disappeared down the hill, when the coroner's station wagon arrived and took the space the paramedic ambulance had just vacated.

"System's working good," Bennett said dryly, try-ing not to think of what was happening.

"As far as we're concerned, there's no reason to believe anyone else was involved." Drang sounded embarrassed. "No criminal act, so I wouldn't have anything here for you to do."

"I don't want a damn assignment. She was a friend of mine."

"What's that supposed to mean?"

Bennett didn't bother to answer. He watched the coroner's men carry their gurney into the house. The front door had been left open, and lamps were lighted inside. A couple of uniformed officers were talking quietly. One of them said something funny, and his partner laughed, face breaking into a new shape, cheeks pushed up, eyes half closed, lips pulled back.

"I can't have you wandering around in there," Drang said. "You're not officially a member of the department . . ."

"Come on, Drang, knock it off. I know procedure." Bennett stopped talking and cleared his throat. The sound bounced through the quiet night like a flat pebble skimming across the lake.

"The papers hear about this? TV ladies and gentlemen?" Bennett's voice was more in control now, although a strange huskiness remained. "They'll have a ball, that group," he continued. "They love Christine Walker stories. And pictures. What's it worth to them, do you think? For a phone call that alerts them Chris is dead, a probable suicide. Fifty? A hundred? How was she found? In bed? In the crapper? Lot of pictures of her lying around the room? Nude centerfolds? What?"

He stopped for a breath, which gave Drang an opening. "Someone probably tipped a paper or a TV station, and I expect they'll be arriving. She was lying on the bed in her bedroom. And she . . ." He stopped.

"And she what?"

"She was reaching."

"How do you know?"

"Her right arm was stretched out."

Bennett swallowed the information, but made no comment.

A day later, in Artie's Century City office, while he waited for photocopies of Christine Walker's more recent phone bills, Bennett thumbed through the Hollywood trade papers, each of them perhaps a dozen pages long, containing rumor, gossip, inflated box office figures, items about important literary property purchases, and, on this particular day, front page stories about Chris's death. Bennett quick-read the articles, tributes from those who'd known her or worked with her, sly implications that anyone who'd been paying attention would have recognized that Chris was suicidal, vague suggestions that her present lover, the brand-new number one in her bed, that this new person was someone to be reckoned with, someone of power, someone she should perhaps not have become involved with, since whoever he was couldn't do anything about the relationship except deny it existed. Bennett went through both trade papers more carefully, looking for a more definite clue to the identity of the present lover. He found nothing.

"Here you are," Artie said, hurrying into the room with a handful of Xeroxed phone bills, which he stuffed into a manila envelope. "All but the most recent one, which isn't due for two weeks."

"The cops are at the phone company right now getting copies of that one." Bennett looked at Artie so directly that the little man turned away. "You think they might find a number she called frequently? Maybe even the night she died?" he asked.

Artie hedged. "Why ask me?" he said. "You knew Chris. You knew her better than I did." He faced

Bennett. "You knew her pretty damn good, so why ask me these questions? What the hell are you up to, anyway? Is there money in this for you, is that it? Whose payroll are you on?"

Bennett's jaw jumped as he took the envelope. "Listen, Artie, I know you loved Chris and you're very hurt about what's happened. But don't dump on me, damn it! Because if what it says here is true about a powerful secret lover . . ." He tapped the trade paper stories with his finger. "Then it would be to your advantage to suddenly be forgetful. Not mine. To yours." He glared, then strode out, feeling ashamed and embarrassed that he'd stuck pins into the little man.

But that was how Bennett worked. He'd stick pins in everyone connected with a case, anger and enrage them, until someone acted overtly to stop him and tried to shut him up. In the process things were inadvertently said, promises were broken, anger was encouraged, confidences destroyed, all to bring the bugs out of the woodwork, to watch creatures who only existed in the dark scramble in sudden bright light. Bennett had no reason to believe Christine Walker's death was anything but what it appeared to be, suicide, but he wasn't working on reason. His instincts yelled foul, and he'd poke and prod at everyone who'd ever known her, until he was satisfied he had the truth. Well, he thought, I'm doing it again. Good old smart ass Bennett is putting his neck in the noose in the cause of justice, mercy, and Christine Walker.